THE HAND OF ....

OLIVER ONIONS was born in Bradford in 1873. Although he legally changed his name to George Oliver in 1918, he always published under the name Oliver Onions. Onions originally worked as a commercial artist before turning to writing, and the dust jackets of his earliest works included illustrations painted by Onions himself.

Onions was a fairly prolific writer of short stories and novels and is best remembered today for his ghost stories, the most famous of which is probably 'The Beckoning Fair One', originally published in *Widdershins* (1911). Despite being known today chiefly for his supernatural short fiction, Onions also published more than a dozen novels in a variety of genres, including *In Accordance with the Evidence* (1912), *The Tower of Oblivion* (1921), *The Hand of Kornelius Voyt* (1939), *The Story of Ragged Robyn* (1945), and *Poor Man's Tapestry* (1946), which won the prestigious James Tait Black Memorial Prize as the best work of fiction published that year.

Onions was apparently a very private individual, and though admired and well respected in his time, he appears not to have moved in literary circles, and few personal memoirs of him survive. He spent most of his later life in Wales, where he lived with his wife, Berta Ruck (1878-1978), herself a prolific and popular novelist; they had two sons, Arthur (b. 1912) and William (b. 1913). Oliver Onions died in 1961.

MARK VALENTINE is the author of several collections of short fiction and has published biographies of Arthur Machen and Sarban. He is the editor of *Wormwood*, a journal of the literature of the fantastic, supernatural, and decadent, and has written the introductions to Valancourt's editions of volumes by John Davidson, Forrest Reid, Michael Arlen, R. C. Ashby, Claude Houghton, and Russell Thorndike.

OLIVER ONIONS

THE HAND OF KORNELIUS VOYT

With a new introduction by

MARK VALENTINE

VALANCOURT BOOKS

The Hand of Kornelius Voyt by Oliver Onions
First published London: Hamish Hamilton, 1939
First Valancourt Books edition 2013

Published by Valancourt Books, Kansas City, Missouri
Publisher & Editor: James D. Jenkins
20th Century Series Editor: Simon Stern, University of Toronto
http://www.valancourtbooks.com

Library of Congress Cataloging-in-Publication Data

Onions, Oliver, 1873-1961
  The Hand of Kornelius Voyt / by Oliver Onions ; with a new
introduction by Mark Valentine. – First Valancourt Books edition.
    pages cm
  ISBN 978-1-939140-04-3 *(acid free paper)*
  1. Orphans–Fiction. 2. Telepathy–Fiction. 3. Gothic fiction. 4. Occult
fiction. I. Title.
  PR6029.N54H3 2013
  823'.912–dc23
                    2013001665

All Valancourt Books publications are printed on acid free paper
that meets all ANSI standards for archival quality paper.

Also available as an electronic book.

Set in Dante MT 11/14

INTRODUCTION

OLIVER ONIONS (1873-1961) is best known today as the author of some distinctive, subtle ghost stories, most notably 'The Beckoning Fair One' and the collection *Widdershins* (1911). There are also enthusiasts of his historical novels, particularly the brooding, fateful *The Story of Ragged Robyn* (1945), set around the desolate East Yorkshire coastal terrain of Holderness. But Onions also wrote a few novels with a supernatural element and, of these, *The Hand of Kornelius Voyt* (1939) is one of the most compelling. It certainly deserves a new readership for its eerie, remorseless qualities and the under-stated craft of its prose.

Onions was a professional writer for most of his life, though he had started as a commercial artist. His first novel, *The Compleat Bachelor* (1900), was in a vein of light humour that he soon abandoned. Indeed, in his forty or so books he did not stay in one field, and this may have made his work less likely to get full attention, and harder to assess. There are examples in his books of crime fiction, fantasy, science fiction, historical fiction, society fiction and contemporary satire. This versatility puzzled people. A critic for the *New Statesman* called him 'the greatest enigma among English writers of fiction', with, of his novels, 'at least half a dozen, any of which taken separately is big enough to establish a reputation'.

Probably his biggest seller was the account of a murder, *In Accordance With the Evidence* (1912), though it was no ordinary crime story, and Onions later extended it to a trilogy, *Whom God Hath Sundered* (1925), telling the story from differing perspectives. This was regarded at the time as having enduring worth as a bleak character study, and John Cowper Powys was sufficiently impressed to include one of its volumes, *The Story of Louie* (1913) in his survey of the world's *One Hundred Best Books* (1916). But around this time Onions was also seen as part of a new, modern school of realist writing, influenced by Arnold Bennett and the later work of H.G.

Wells. Frank Swinnerton treated him in this way in his study *The Georgian Literary Scene, A Panorama* (1935). Onions' books in this vein, said Swinnerton, somewhat tepidly, 'skim the lives of young men who, with artistic impulses, have their misadventures in business', such as the semi-autobiographical studies of ambitious young men caught up in the advertising trade, *Little Devil Doubt* (1909) and *Good Boy Seldom* (1911). His books had 'a joyless jocularity', were 'harsh': we might read them 'with respect for their veracity' but 'the author is not a natural creator of illusion. He has no magic'.

Onions had a brief vogue in the aftermath of the First World War with his novel *Peace in Our Time* (1923), where he was seen to characterise the new spirit of a generation that wanted to forget about the war and start anew. And his later books abandon contemporary realism for some of the rich imagination and original vision that Swinnerton said he earlier lacked. He won critical acclaim for his historical fiction: *Poor Man's Tapestry* (1946) was awarded the James Tait Black Prize for the best novel of the year, then one of the most esteemed accolades. But he still remained a respected rather than a bestselling author, and never quite in either the literary or commercial mainstream. Onions had married in 1909, Berta Ruck, a popular author of romantic fiction whose work did sell well, but whereas she was a prolific writer, he only worked with great difficulty, 'even with anguish', according to the *Times* obituary.

Though he was admired, Onions does not seem to have mingled socially in literary circles, and there are few personal memoirs of him. He was evidently a very private man. In 1933, the youthful and enthusiastic poet and bibliophile John Gawsworth compiled a second volume of bibliographies of authors he admired, *Ten Contemporaries* II. He asked each author to provide a short note about their work to preface his listing of their books. Most, including H.E. Bates, Thomas Burke, and Dorothy Richardson, either dutifully or cheerfully obliged. But Onions, instead of writing about himself, supplied an appreciation of an earlier, American, bibliographer of his books, the late Randolph Edgar. From this, as to Onions himself, we learn only that he did not keep manuscripts: 'mine are destroyed page by page as they are written' and that he thought Edgar showed 'a more continuous interest in me than I often did in myself', a somewhat rueful note. Again when Gawsworth asked him for some autobiographical recollections for a journal he was editing, Onions obliged only with a reprint of a light, wry account of his days in advertising, which gives little away.

The impression we gain is that he was a reserved, taciturn individual. Swinnerton clearly did not warm to him, noting that he had 'a grimness of demeanour which throws out a suggestion of force and resentment', and it is true that the few public photographs tend to show him frowning and serious. Onions seems to have had an intense inner life, and to have given much thought to both the problems of his day and the personal concerns of individuals. After his very early work, he can never be said to provide comfortable, complacent reading. His imagination was clearly restless, and he ranged widely, but wherever he gave his attention it was with concentration and a profound respect for his characters and their situations. Readers often find his books have a brooding power that is hard to define: it isn't due to incident, vivid colouring, or surface allure, but derives from a certain fierce remorselessness in the narration. We are drawn in and held by Onions' integrity and the sense of the depth of his engagement with his story.

In his later work, the *Times Literary Supplement* saw in him 'a divination of beauty and a linked apprehension of the sources of tragedy . . . an uncommonly sensitive and original imagination'. His style was of 'pellucid and gleaming beauty . . . a wonderful justness of word and clarity of tone and accent'. John Betjeman was more succinct: 'Mr. Onions is an inspired writer . . . A poet of prose'. Several reviewers had to fall back on such terms as 'enchanting' and 'spellbinding' and 'wizardry', freely admitting they could not think of any other way to describe the effect of his work.

The Hand of Kornelius Voyt appeared after an unusual five year break in Onions' publishing history (1934-9), the longest he had been without issuing a new book since his career began. There were, however, reprints, and it may be significant that this period saw his supernatural stories come to the fore, with an omnibus edition of his *Collected Ghost Stories* in 1935 and a Penguin paperback edition of *Widdershins* in 1939. These may have led Onions to consider resuming the fantastical in his work. But his new book can also be seen as the first in the late flowering of Onions' imagination, leading up to the praised historical novels.

It concerns a young orphan boy, Peter Byles, who is sent to the house of his new guardian, the German Dr. Voyt, an old friend and chess partner of his father. The story is set in a large, prosperous town which we can reasonably assume is based on Bradford, Yorkshire, where Onions was born: like that city, then, its main trade is in wool products. Bradford had a community of German expatriate traders and indeed part of the city even today is known by the historic name of Little Germany. Across the Pennines, Friedrich Engels had earlier been one such merchant in Manchester, also a mill city.

Doktor Voyt is no longer in trade, but his house is 'black with the smoke that had made [his] family rich': he therefore fits into that late Victorian era when Onions was growing up among the local cotton and textile factories, where young women in clogs and shawls (as noticed in the story) laboured long hours. We know very little of Onions' childhood: his father was a bank cashier, and his home was in a back-to-back terraced house (now demolished) among the 'respectable' working class, in the same area as the vast Victorian Undercliff cemetery, and the green spaces of Peel Park, the city's first recreation ground, probably the model for the Park with a bandstand in the novel. But some other resonances from his childhood may perhaps be seen in the book—the boy's solitariness, his sense of being different, his secrecy and a certain wilfulness.

Dr. Voyt, who is deaf and mute, is at first kept mostly off stage, and we see Peter's deftly-drawn relationship with his kindly German tutor. There is no sentimentality in the depiction of Peter, who is shown to be adaptable, curious, questioning and self-reliant, though also beset with some apprehensions. Nor is his guardian a cut-out brutal villain, as such figures often are in fiction. Onions' work is stealthy and subtle, and gradually he enables us to see that the Herr Doktor's influence pervades the lonely house. Deprived of two senses, Voyt has developed other faculties, and it begins to seem that he can exercise his will on the tutor, and on Peter. A form of hypnotism at a distance is in play. But it begins to emerge that it is not just his will in small matters that Voyt wishes to impose on his ward: it is also his philosophy, one based in contempt for humanity, and scepticism about any shared values. He believes that most men do not know their true self and are ignorant of certain vital essences they possess. They are deceived by the superficial apparatus of words, and act only in line with a banal veneer of common wisdom. But they could be much more, as only he sees: and this greater power he proposes to work on through his ward.

Insidiously, he begins to inculcate his beliefs in the previously open-hearted boy. We see that Peter's fate is in the balance: will the domination of his wealthy, haughty, disdainful guardian twist his soul, or will the friendship of his few, frailer but more fully human allies (his troubled tutor, and an amorous maid) prevail and help him preserve his personal qualities? Will he be able to resist the allure of developing the powers that Dr. Voyt has? The resolution of the book is not what we might expect, and fully demonstrates Onions' artistic honesty and wide sympathies.

As noted above, Onions' choice of a German industrialist for the character of Voyt is consistent with the Bradford of his childhood: but given the timing of the book's publication in 1939, it must also be supposed that Onions intended some reference to the sinister spectacles in contemporary Germany of figures in power obsessed with the idea of 'higher' men, exercising a seemingly magnetic power over minds, and aiming to become masters of the world. If so, it is a mark of his care as a writer that he also presents a 'good German', Peter's conscientious and gentle tutor, a man marked of deep humanity. Even so, the sombre theme and the book's refusal to contrive any cheap victory might have contributed to its overshadowing during wartime, and subsequent neglect.

The city of Bradford, evoked so gloomily in the book ('with chimneys for pens and smoke curls for ink'), now celebrates its more famous literary son, J. B. Priestley, but largely overlooks Onions, despite some gallant attempts to make him better known there. Onions himself, it is true, did not return to the city of his youth: he and Bertha made their home in North Wales, in the coastal resort of Aberdovey, and he died in the hospital at the nearby university city of Aberystwyth in 1961. His historical novels and the crime fiction were reprinted in the 1960s and 1970s, as was *The Hand of Kornelius Voyt*; and his ghost stories continued to have anthology appearances; but otherwise there was a forty year period after his death when his work was distinctly under-appreciated.

That is now beginning to change. There are signs of a gradual new appreciation of Onions' work, beginning with several recent collections of his ghost stories, which continue to have a discerning readership: his work here is increasingly seen as comparable to the elusive, nuanced stories of Walter de la Mare, and also as a forerunner to the enigmatic, psychological 'strange stories' of Robert Aickman. But interest in him should not stop there, and his masterly work in the ghost story ought to lead us to a fresh appreciation of his longer fiction in the fantastic.

The Hand of Kornelius Voyt is a formidable achievement in sustaining an atmosphere of uncanny dread. Its enigmatic recluse and his young ward are finely observed character studies which will leave a lasting impression on the reader. The black Victorian Gothic mansion, with its many echoing chambers, 'some of them dead rooms, it seemed to me', is also memorable. Most of all, the sense of tragedy, of a fate that cannot be evaded, holds us hard throughout the book, stark and insistent. We know we are in the presence of a profound and disturbing mystery.

MARK VALENTINE

January 10, 2013

THE HAND OF KORNELIUS VOYT

To

BERTA RUCK

TO-DAY

TO-DAY

Y ou would hardly believe there could be such a place as this within a few minutes of a great London terminus. The wide suburban High Street with its motors and trams, its cinemas and public-houses, its Home and Colonial and its United Dairies, runs not three hundred yards away. Nearer still, pressing on three sides of it, are the neat semi-detached houses, each with its name on its gate, and the high embankment of the main-line closes it in on the fourth. The door in the high brick wall has a little iron grill in it and is the only way in. You ring a bell and wait to be admitted. The door closes behind you again and the sounds of the world die away. You have entered a place of peace.

It has nine or ten acres in all, with many old trees and a plaster-fronted hundred-year-old house to which extensions have been made. The Brothers wear brown habits as they wheel their barrows along the paths or walk with their eyes on their breviaries, but you are asked no questions. You believe what you please, and need pay no attention to the chapel bell that rings four times a day. If you are not of the Faith you wear your ordinary clothes, and there is a place for you at the refectory table just the same. You are given no key, but there is always a Brother at the door to let you in, though no woman may accompany you.

You choose your own task. It may be you have a gift for carpentry or building a wall, know the ways of fruit-trees or are able to milk, for our pasture supports four cows and we have even surplus vegetables to sell. I am in charge of the chickens, and in my cubicle I write.

It is at the back, looking out over the kitchen-gardens to the wire-netted enclosure where my chickens run. Its walls are plain white, and there is no clock on them. I make my own bed and do the other necessary things, and sometimes Brother John comes in to sit with me for an hour. He knows what I am writing, and the grave brown eyes I sometimes find fixed on me as I read to him are full of understanding. His beard reminds me a little of the Herr Doktor's, except that it is of a rich chestnut brown instead of grizzled black. Downstairs in the refectory Brother John and Brother Nicholas occasionally play chess together, but if they see me coming they always pretend their game is just finished and put the board away.

It is my own story that I am writing, many years afterwards. I was forty-one when the war broke out, but I had been forty-one for a long time before that. Brother John is not forty-one yet in spite of his beard, and is as unlike the Herr Doktor in everything else as he could well be, but even when I came to this difficult matter of the Sentient Image (surely enough to stagger any man) he merely nodded as if he knew all about it. So though I profess no Faith I suppose that when I read to Brother John I am in a sense confessing to him. Perhaps in that way the ghost of the Herr Doktor and his Image may be laid.

The trains that pass along the embankment come in from the North, but I know nothing of the North nowadays. It is farther off in years than it is in miles, and I don't suppose even the station at the other end is the same one as in my time. But I have heard that the Herr Doktor's house still stands on its height, though no longer on the fringe of the town. As for this unimaginable city of London that lies about me, I hardly know it, for I seldom go beyond these walls.

And I should not like to say of any man that he never had a soul to lose, for to be godless is not therefore to be wicked, and I prefer to say of the Herr Doktor Kornelius Voyt that he thought that by searching he could find out God. But it was at my cost that he did so. In my tender years, my rosy years, when the bloom should have lain as delicately on my cheek as the dust lies on an insect's wing, he vivisected me and pinned me down like one of the dead butter-flies in his big drawing-room. He crammed me as a pegged-down goose is crammed for its liver's sake. He forced me as an unnatural flower or vegetable is forced, till gazing at the prodigy men forget what it started from. He distended my growing body with factitious health till my very pores seemed an inch apart. He raced my faculties as an engine is raced when the brakes and governors are taken off, and by the brakes and governors I mean mankind's collective ignorance and stupidity and cowardice and fear, that drive them to stone the prophet for making the way through the desert too straight, but at the same time restrain them from rushing too violently down the slope to destruction. With the path in which wayfaring men though fools cannot err he would have nothing to do. And in the closing years of my life his Hand is on me still. I am not sorry, I am not glad. I only wish to tell how it came about.

THEN

CHAPTER I

A LL my father's other friends, such of them I mean as came to
the house, I knew by face, name and voice. They pulled my
ears, rumpled my hair, said 'Well, young man,' and in a general
way I looked on them as a sort of circle of goodnatured occasional
uncles. But whenever I saw the Herr Doktor Voyt it was as part
of the stuffily-comfortable background of my father's den at the
end of the passage, the heavy curtains that always smelt of cigar-
smoke, the kettle and sugar and lemon from the kitchen, and the
reflection in the glass front of the bookcase of the green-shaded
double-wicked lamp that in the evenings always made the chessboard the bright spot of the room. I never saw the Herr Doktor
come, I never saw him go. He always occupied the same chair, just
behind the lamp from where I sat, very rarely played, and never
spoke. Except when he held a paper spill over the lamp to light his
large porcelain pipe I often did not know he was there. But occasionally a situation arose on the board and he would be appealed
to. Then from round the lamp a long white knuckly hand would
come forward into the light. With the deftness of a conjurer it
would sweep up the pieces, half a dozen of them in the hand at
the same time, and re-set the position, all with bewildering speed,
while the others watched, for the Herr Doktor was a Master. And
from my place by the fire, following the hand to its body of origin,
I could distinguish past the lamp the dimly-outlined semi-circle of
a bald forehead, a pair of round silver spectacles, and below that
nothing, for like the moon on some nights the forehead seemed to
rise out of a heavy bank of greying black beard. Then hand, moon
and spectacles would sink back into the shadows again and the
board would be set for a new game.

My only concern with chess at that time was that it frequently
so engrossed the players that I and my bedtime were forgotten,

and many a time I have brought the game to a standstill by sliding from my stool into the fender, overcome with sleep. When this happened my father would rise and draw the door-curtain, put his head outside, and call for Margaret, for I had no mother, and Margaret looked after my eight-year-old sister and myself. Up to the suddenly chill air of the attic at the top of the house I would stumble, half awake again by this time, perhaps to see outside the dormer, like the Herr Doktor's bald head, the top edge of the moon, and almost to expect it to put out a long knuckly hand, chockfull of black and white chessmen, and to set up a game on the counterpane. Nora slept in the other bed. She was not allowed these late sittings-up, and if my arrival happened to wake her she would drowsily ask what everybody was doing downstairs. In fact I am tempted to begin my story at that point—Nora in her short tight pigtails, sitting up on the pillow where the ceiling sloped down over her head, yawning as she said it, and asking what they were all doing downstairs.

For in telling her I sometimes gave my fancy play, making it up as I went along. We had, I say, no mother. My father went out each morning at a little after nine o'clock and did not return till half-past six or later at night. At my day-school I was in the Upper Fourth, Nora went to a small private school that was also a kindergarten. And while she was doing her needlework text or cutting out her strings of paper dolls my father's friends pulled me by the ear and called me 'Young man'. You see the difference. When my father was not there I looked on myself as the head of the house. But Margaret, who was pious, called me a limb, by which she meant a limb of Satan.

'What time is it?' Nora asked sleepily one night as I was kicking off my slippers and feeling under the pillow for my nightshirt. Margaret always took the light away when she had seen Nora into bed, but that night the sky was a marbling of moving cloud and moonlight, enough to see by.

'Ten o'clock,' I answered. 'Shut up till I say my prayers.'

'What are they doing?' Nora asked when I had said them.

'Just talking.'

'What are they talking about?'

'About somebody called Morphy. I shall get father to teach me chess. Morphy was only as old as me and he whacked all the grown-ups in the town. Then I'll play the Herr Doktor, and you see if I don't whack him,' I boasted.

'Which one's the Herr Doktor?' she said, but could hardly get it out for drowsiness.

'The Herr Doktor? He just sits smoking a big china pipe with roses on it. He just watches. Then they get stuck, and you can hardly see him there behind the lamp, but—you can see me now?'

'Only just.'

'Well, you're Mr. Tenison, and I'm father, and this is the chess-board, and I'm playing you——', and in that attic at the top of the house, with the batswings of cloud coming and going before the moon, I showed her. 'He's got large clean nails, and knuckles as white as these bedclothes, and his hand's so big it can hold all the chessmen in the box, and it comes out and jiggers up and down like this——', and I worked my own hand about till she began to whimper.

'I want Margaret to come,' she said.

'It's her night out. She's gone to her Gospel Hall. And he's a black beard that's beginning to get grey, and his spectacles shine behind the lamp when his head moves—you see only his spectacles sometimes——'

'Stop telling me, I don't want to hear,' she said, and made herself a lump under the bedclothes; so as she couldn't hear me I stopped and was soon asleep.

But some time later I awoke. She was tossing about in bed, and I asked her what was the matter.

'I can't go to sleep,' she said.

'Rot. You were asleep.'

'I wasn't, and I want to go into Margaret's bed. It's that name.'

'What name?'

'The one who beat the grown-ups.'

'Morphy?'

'Oh, I want Margaret!' she wailed.

I don't suppose you were very different yourself, and perhaps too yours was not a motherless home. At Nora's desolate cry I felt my skin give a little shiver, but for all that I sat up in bed, went through my pantomime of the hand again, and repeated the ill-sounding, ill-omened name.

'Morphy——'

She had shrieked before the syllables were out of my mouth. She was out of bed. Snatching the bedclothes about her, dragging them after her along the floor, she ran to the head of the stairs. '*Margaret!*' I heard her terrified cry, and from the floor below there came the sound of an opening door. '*Mar*——,' but the cry this time was stifled against Margaret's bosom. The door below shut again and there was silence.

But what had I done, not to Nora, but to myself? In her flight she had left the attic door open, and I expected every moment to hear Margaret's voice again, promising me the dressing-down I should receive in the morning, but the silence continued, till presently I would have welcomed any voice, however angry. What were they doing downstairs? I felt as if I was the only living person in the house, and yet I was not alone. I had frightened myself too, and now had my invention to keep me company. To me too the name of Morphy seemed a terrifying name, the Herr Doktor a sinister figure. The whiteness of his hand was the whiteness of my mother's hand when they had taken me to see her where she lay. For half the night the lamp downstairs haunted me, the Herr Doktor's silver spectacles peering behind it like something in eclipse. I had forgotten all about it the next day. In their nature such things quickly go. But it is also in their nature that they return.

CHAPTER II

WHEN I was told that I was to go away for a holiday it did not occur to me that they wanted to get me out of the house, and this in spite of the fact that my father no longer went out at nine o'clock each morning, that trays stood outside his bedroom

door, that there was no more chess of an evening, and that sometimes in the street some half-remembered person would stop me
and ask me how my father was to-day. The schools had broken up,
it was the holiday season, and to a large farmhouse many miles
away in the country Nora and I were taken by Margaret. Margaret
sobbed so long on leaving us that she set Nora off too, and I don't
know which of them made the greater hullaballoo. Then trap and
train took her off, and among fields and hay-stacks and cattle that
seemed quite twice as big as any I had ever seen before, my sister
and I were left with the long days to ourselves.

You have probably guessed the next. In the middle of that
summer my father died, and a red-eyed Margaret in black kid
gloves came to fetch us away again. But we were not returning to
our former home. Nora was going, for the present at any rate, to
Margaret's own relatives, who lived many miles away. I myself, I
learned to my astonishment and dismay, was to be handed over to
the Herr Doktor Voyt.

My poor father's reasons are clear enough to me now. Men who
spend much time over a chessboard are seldom rich, and he was no
exception. All his friends had families quite as large as they could
support, and Mr. Tenison in particular, the 'uncle' I was fondest of,
was least of all able to do anything for me. But the Herr Doktor
was unmarried and a wealthy man. Apart from that my father's
admiration for the brain behind that bald dome knew no bounds,
and his heart must have been so set on my having chances that had
been denied to himself that it blinded him to the rest. I suppose
he had got used to it and counted on my doing the same. So from
my giant haystacks and cattle straight to the Herr Doktor's house
I was taken.

It stood in its own grounds on a height a couple of miles out
from the centre of the town, and its stones were black with the
smoke that had made the Herr Doktor's family rich. Perhaps
the word mansion would describe it better than house. A rockery with sparse heath and London-pride rose to a stone terrace
that was flanked by shrubberies and backed by a steep plantation.
From this terrace a further short flight of steps led to a doorway

of overdone domestic Gothic, and the roof of a pretentious front-
age in the same ornate style had a square four-windowed turret at
either end. It was all very intimidating to me, and with so grand a
residence of his own I wondered that the Herr Doktor should ever
have deigned to spend so many of his evenings watching the chess
in my father's unventilated little den.

He was not there to receive me. A blue-eyed, blond young man,
who seemed to me to be built on the same scale as the cattle and
haystacks I had just left, was waiting for me at the top of the steps
that ended at the Gothic porch. He clicked his heels together,
jerked himself forward in a stiff bow from the hips, and then shot
out a hand at me as if he was going to fence me. Down the length
of his left cheek there ran in fact two healed fencing-scars.

'I am Heinrich Opfer,' he said. 'It is the Herr Doktor's wish that
you should be under my tuition. You are Peter Byles, and I shall
call you Peter. You will call me Heinrich, not Herr Opfer. We shall
have supper together one hour from now. You will rise at eight in
the morning, and we shall have breakfast at half-past. At half-past
nine the lesson will begin. But to-night there will be no lesson. We
amuse ourselves instead. You play Word-making?'

'Yes.'

'You will please to speak distinctly, and look at me when you
speak. Then to-night it shall be Word-making, or if you prefer it
some game to steady the hand, such as Fishponds. You play Fishponds?'

'Yes.'

'Good. The play also is to be directed to an end. Now if you
please, follow me,' and without further words he led the way
across a large and bare and lofty hall and up a staircase to a series
of rooms on the first floor that apparently were to be our quarters.

But it will hasten matters if, instead of going through all the
incidents of that first evening in the Herr Doktor's house, I try to
sort out the jumble of impressions that danced in my head when at
half-past nine I at last placed it on the pillow. Naturally the uppermost of these, the Word-making, came first. The little squares of
cardboard jumped about before my eyes, each with a letter of the

alphabet on it, shaken up like dice in the blond Heinrich's great hands and thrown down on the table for me to make the word. Then came the Fishponds game, with the bent pin at the end of its thread dangling and bobbing against the noses of the tiny fish before it caught them—all this in a sort of schoolroom or study, with myself at one end of the table and Heinrich at the other, telling me that when I had written seated for a certain time there was a second desk for me to stand up at, the change of position being also directed to an end. Then there rose to the surface that hour earlier still, in which, left to myself, I had ventured to move about the house, peeping into rooms, ready to fly if I found anybody in one of them, but meeting nobody. A bewildering number of rooms there seemed to me to be, some of them dead rooms like mortuaries, with newspapers spread over table-surfaces and the chairs like sitting mummies in holland dustsheets. Never had I dreamed of such a wealth of plush, valances with handpainted flowers on them, trophies of dead butterflies, lustres, glass domes over stuffed birds, white marble pillars in corners, each with a bust or an ornate oil-lamp on it. At the end of a long passage I pushed at a door and found myself in a great dim room with a covered-up billiard-table in it and green shades and cue-racks on the walls. But the passage had several other doors too, red baize doors, and I had nearly jumped out of my skin when a harsh voice had suddenly asked me what I was doing there. But the next moment I had realised it was the voice of a parrot, for it croaked 'Wipe your boots, Alice,' but all the same I crept on tiptoe away. So back on my pillow I came to the Word-making and the Fishponds again, and at last to sleep.

Breakfast was laid for two next morning, in my tutor's sitting-room, which was next to the schoolroom. Breakfast too was directed to an end, for Heinrich, who seemed to keep every subject in a watertight compartment of its own, first asked me how I had slept, and then, taking our porridge as a text, went on to speak of the nutritive properties of oatmeal, eggs, and the rest of what was on the table. Then at half-past nine sharp he looked at his watch. We left the breakfast-room and entered the schoolroom.

He pointed to my chair of last night and himself took the one opposite. First he told me to look at him, and as I fixed my eyes on his face he proceeded to address me.

'So. We begin. How old are you, Peter?'

'Nearly thirteen, Herr Opfer,' but at the Herr Opfer he put up his hand.

'*Bitte*—Heinrich. And do not forget to look at me when you talk, and you must speak very distinctly. At the same time it will not do to speak distinctly as a ventriloquist speaks, who must make it appear that another is speaking, a puppet or a doll perhaps. The Herr Doktor came often to your home?'

'Pretty often.'

'Then you saw him frequently?'

I am afraid I forgot to look at Heinrich as I suddenly wondered on how many occasions I had in fact seen the Herr Doktor. As I told you, I never saw him arrive, never saw him leave. He had always sat in the same place, in the penumbra of my father's lamp, and it was his hand that I had seen most frequently, coming forward into the light to set the chessmen. Then, as I realised that never once had I heard him speak, a queer feeling began to come over me. If I had been sent to Mr. Tenison's house Mr. Tenison would have been there with a jovial 'Well, young man,' or some such greeting. But here I was turned over to this young German, who talked to me about clear articulation and looking at him when I spoke, and was now saying that it was no good my talking as a ventriloquist talks, moving the puppet's jaw up and down instead of his own. And all at once I noticed something on the wall behind Heinrich's cropped and bristly head that had not been there the night before. It seemed to be a map or chart, rolled up and the roll secured by a loop of string to its nail. The time to display this thing had evidently come, for Heinrich rose. He unfastened the loop and down it dropped. It was covered with rows of hands, sprinkled with letters of the alphabet like the Word-making game. I was looking at the alphabet for the deaf-and-dumb. I told you that my father's heart must have been so set on my having my chance in the world that it had blinded him to the rest. Here the rest was. The Herr Doktor was a deaf-mute.

Why had I not been told? Why had I never guessed? I hardly know. I had no mother. My father had not been a talkative man, chess is not a talkative game, and often the Herr Doktor had been no more silent than the rest of them. Margaret had had her hands full with Nora, and it had been nobody's business to tell a boy who ought to have been in bed of the infirmities of his elders. This however it was now Heinrich's duty to do.

'You will quickly become accustomed to it,' he said. 'To the afflicted more consideration is due, not less, and you must understand that in many ways it is more pitiful to be deaf and dumb than to be blind. Everybody helps the blind. You or I will take a blind man across the street or warn him of some small danger. It is not so with the deaf. Because it is troublesome to talk to them they are avoided. When you do talk to them you must raise your voice so that others hear, and so you do not talk about the things you do not wish others to hear. You cannot whisper to them. Only the things that everybody knows can be spoken of. Therefore the deaf man is left to himself, and he is very lonely. You see this?'

Of course I saw it, but it did very little to cheer me.

'So,' he went on, 'other ways of communication have had to be invented. To begin with you will learn this alphabet. But only to begin with. Very soon you will put it away again, for with practice many words are not necessary. You say you have seen the Herr Doktor play chess?'

'He hardly ever played. He just watched,' I answered sullenly, for I would have given anything to get away that very moment, back to the house I had left, where Margaret had a tongue to scold with and ears to hear Nora when she cried at night.

'Still, you have seen how little need there is for words. With a chessboard between you you can understand a man from Lapland, or from India, or from Germany, and not a word is used. And so with other things. You know what an angle is?'

'Yes.'

'Angles are three, the right-angle, the acute and the obtuse. Which one is this?' and he drew it on a piece of paper.

'A right-angle.'

'And this? And this?' and I named the other two also. 'Good. But without the names every man can see the difference and with the names he cannot see more. So you will find it with the Herr Doktor. These hands that I am now pointing at are the signs that people have agreed on, and at first you will spell every word a letter at a time. But there are also abbreviated words. Presently the beginning of a word will be enough, and then less and less, till by the time you have become proficient you will sit with your *Zwischenredner*, the person you are talking to, hardly moving, but a complete conversation will be going on between you. However this morning we begin at the beginning. The language we use will be English. Later you are to learn German, but the words this morning will be English words. We now place our chairs before the chart, so, and begin with the English letter "a".'

So that dreadful morning began. Letter by letter he took me through the alphabet, the two-handed one first, but the single-handed one was to follow later. Methodical in everything, he glanced from time to time at his watch, not to weary my attention by keeping it too long on any one thing, but already there was rebellion in my breast. 'No,' Heinrich was saying, 'just as you must not mumble with your lips, so you must be clean and precise in each movement of the fingers,' but my eyes kept straying to the window and to the pale grey town spread out a couple of miles away. If I had been among my late schoolfellows, learning some caggermagger language as boys will learn such things, for the fun of it, I might have kept my mind on my lesson, but who was going to spend months and months at this? Vic Tenison was my great chum. His bedroom window was at the back of the house. If I threw a stone up at it one night he would open it and see me down in the yard with my father's gladstone bag, and I'd tell him I wanted to sleep on their sofa, and he'd come down and let me in.

'For the present,' Heinrich's voice broke in on me, 'it will not be necessary for you to see the Herr Doktor. He has his own rooms, and he wishes you to have first made a little progress. Now for this morning the lesson will be enough. We will take a walk in the garden. I do not know botany, so for a change you shall tell me the names of the trees and plants and question me as I have questioned you about the lesson. Come.'

But, except that it was out in the air, I found the relaxation almost as tiresome as the lesson. Along the blackened rockery to the shrubbery we passed, thence to the plantation that sheltered the house from the north, I naming holly and rhododendron and birch and mountain-ash to him as we came to them and he repeating the names after me with heavy patience. But on the way back, at the foot of the plantation, he stopped to look at me again.

'You say you are nearly thirteen?' he asked.

'In November,' I said.

'You are not very tall, but you are slender and of a good proportion. It is perhaps your fair hair, which you must have cut, that makes you look young. What is your height?'

'I don't know.'

'I will measure you. Remember if you ever require a measure that an English ha'penny is one inch. For a yard you need not measure it thirty-six times. Measure three, then double it into four, and you have a foot, *undsoweiter*. I will measure you. The growth of the body should march with the growth of the mind. Would you, presently, like me to teach you to fence?'

'Oh, yes!' I said eagerly. It seemed to me the first interesting thing he had said. It would be grand, I thought, to swagger through the world with scars like those on his left cheek.

'We will see. The studies the Herr Doktor requires of you must come first. We will now go into the house again.'

But the prospect of fencing later on brightened the outlook very considerably, and the more diligently I applied myself to my lessons the sooner that hateful part of it would be over.

CHAPTER III

IT had only taken one hand, my own, creeping and crawling over the counterpane in our moonlit attic at home, to scare my little sister half out of her wits. Now hands began to fill my world to the exclusion of everything else. Hands were my daily study, they accompanied me to my bed at night. They floated before my eyes in the darkness, not in the shadow-rabbits and butterflies I had made on the wall at home, but living, talking hands, hands in pairs, one finger, two, three, a fist, an outstuck thumb, hands that were really tongues, asking questions and requiring answers. Heinrich's hands were his living too. They were big and mobile, with a little powdering of golden bristles down the backs of them, and he kept them with the greatest care. He made me do the same with my own, and to this day a man's hands are the first things I look at after I have seen his face. At the same time it was all a little frightening to me, and I begged him to let me have a nightlight and a box of matches by my bed, so that I could watch the little flame till I grew sufficiently sleepy to blow it out, but always with the matches ready for if the hands began their dance again. But gradually this strangeness wore off. The chart remained on the wall, but I no longer had any need of it, and Heinrich drew up a set of general rules. They were few and simple. If for any reason I wished to go beyond the grounds I must first ask his permission. The time between tea and supper was to be my own, but this would be modified as the days shortened and the lamps were lighted earlier. And I was to keep away from the servants' quarters. Those were the chief ones.

I naturally wondered what the 'end' was to which all this was directed, but that did not seem very difficult to guess. The staple trade of the town was wool, and one of its oldest-established businesses, Voyt, Sons & Successors, bore the Herr Doktor's name, though he himself had no part in it. Into this I supposed I should presently go. No doubt I should begin at the bottom, but with the comfortable prospect that if I behaved myself I should end up somewhere near the top. In that case it seemed a little odd that I was not already being prepared for it, say by lessons in book-keeping or some such subject, whereas I was only to learn German. But there was plenty of time, for I was not yet thirteen.

But the house got little more home-like as I began to learn my way about it. Had all its rooms been opened up it would have taken half a dozen servants to run it; as it was I gathered that these were no more than three, a housekeeper and two maids, with a man who took his orders direct from the Herr Doktor himself. And what high, draughty waiting-rooms for furniture those sheeted rooms seemed to be, chill, crowded and forbidding! The chill began in the hall, where nowadays would be the warmth and welcome of central heating. It had a doormat in the Gothic porch, but no rugs or anything to sit down on, only an echoing floor patterned like a chessboard in large squares of black and white. There were a couple of grotesquely human-armed branching racks to hang hats and coats on, and a polished brass tray for the cards of callers, though I never saw a card on it. Facing the porch was a double staircase, the right-hand one leading to our first-floor quarters, but when I went up the other branch and walked a little way along it a locked door barred my way. Beneath the stairs a passage ran the whole length of the house, with the kitchens and what not at the back and the billiard-room at the farther end of it, and it was in this billiard-room that the first of my mishaps in the Herr Doktor's house befell me.

I had finished my tea one afternoon and had left Heinrich in his room writing a letter. Wandering down to the ground floor I had suddenly bethought me of this billiard-room. I had only peeped into it once, on the day of my arrival, and though it lay beyond the servants' quarters, I had not been forbidden to enter it. I had nothing to do, and grew bold. Tip-toeing past the red baize doors I opened the door at the end and stood looking in.

The room was in that portion of the house just beyond the yard, and as the plantation rose steeply at the back, its windows were of coloured greenish glass to prevent anybody from looking in. Glass and trees gave it a light rather like that of an aquarium. A leather-seated couch ran along that end of it just inside the door. At the other end was the marking-board. Along one side wall stood the cues in their racks, several of them in locked tin cases. And in the middle, with the green-shaded oil-lamps hanging over it, stood the great table covered with a sheet.

I had a guilty feeling that I ought not to have been there, but anyway there I was. Closing the door softly behind me I first began to caress with my fingers the beautiful shiny length of the cues. Then I lifted a corner of the sheet to have a peep at the surface underneath. As I did so something clicked. There in one of the corner pockets lay the balls. Glancing over my shoulder towards the door I began to remove the cloth. It fell in heavy drifts to the floor, and I began to roll the balls gently along the smooth green surface. There were lovely soft shocks as they rebounded from the cushions, and I next got a cue from the rack. I began to knock ball against ball. I had not been so happy since I had entered the Herr Doktor's house as I was in that room that afternoon, all by myself, playing my solitary game while the light failed outside.

And suddenly came disaster. Trying to hit two balls at once I had placed my own ball in position. The cue was poised over my cocked-up thumb. And at that moment a harsh voice spoke:

'What are you doing there?'

I was in the very act of the stroke. That voice seemed to plunge the cue suddenly forward. With an involuntary gulp I spun round, but nobody stood behind me. It was in front of me that the damage lay. The tip of the cue had ploughed through the green cloth, showing the raw slate beneath.

Terrified I stood looking at it. The Herr Doktor's quarters must be somewhere overhead, but how could the Herr Doktor have asked me what I was doing there? Only then did I remember the parrot I had heard on the day of my arrival. The housekeeper's room was the first of the red baize doors, and the door must have happened to open at that precise moment. Perhaps she had heard the clicking of the balls and opened it. But—there the ripped cloth was, gaping as Heinrich's scars must have gaped before they healed.

Miserably I stole to the rack, replaced the cue, and stooped to the sheet on the floor.

But at home I had never been able to make my own bed as Margaret made it, and that sheet was as vast and unwieldy as the mainsail of a ship. I had been walking on it, it had got tangled and twisted on itself, and the more I struggled with it the worse it got. I did not dare to ask for help, and by the time I had got it on the table again it seemed to be crying aloud to the whole world to come and see what lay beneath it. Then with crime and concealment on my soul I stole guiltily away.

For I dared not confess. I could only cower and wait for some-body to go into the room, see the sprawl I had left the cloth in, lift it, and raise the hue-and-cry. Then I thought of Margaret at home and hardened my heart. She would have gone about the house praying for me, but if I was a limb of Satan I couldn't help it. They ought to have kept the door locked. It was that beastly parrot's fault. How was I to know that accidents happened all in a moment like that? Anyway they couldn't hang me for it, and I actually began to feel a strange impulse to revisit the scene of my crime. A dozen times I was on the point of stealing along the pas-sage to see whether the cloth was still as I had left it, but a dozen times my courage failed me. Talking hands at night were not my spectre now. A gashed billiard-table was the horror, and I could only wait for discovery and punishment.

But two days passed, three, four, and not a word was said. Heinrich had started me in German, but I had already learned my declensions at school and was making fair progress, while at the finger-speech too I was becoming fairly expert. He kept me to simple things, and as I got used to his habits and turns of thought I could sometimes exchange meanings with him by the merest ges-ture, hint or glance at an object.

'*Gut. Ganz gut,*' he said to me briefly on the fourth day after the accident. 'It is now time for something a little more difficult. You are accustomed to my ways. I am the Heinrich you know. Soon you will stop and get no further. It is now necessary,' and his whole manner changed as abruptly as if some alarm-clock had been set to strike the hour beforehand, 'to take the next step. Suppose I were to speak to you in a language you did not understand, on a subject of which you knew nothing? What would you do?'

I could only shake my head, wondering what was coming. He nodded.

'*Natürlich.* It would be stupid of me. But suppose the subject was one that spoke for itself? Told its own story? Would it not be foolish to say one thing when the subject itself said another?'

'I don't know what you mean, Heinrich,' I faltered.

'Then we will see. Please to follow me,' and I followed his erect military figure out of the room.

Down the stairs he led me and across the chessboard hall. He preceded me along the housekeeper's passage and at the end of it held the billiard-room door open for me to go in first. The dust-sheet lay smooth and flat over the table. He turned back a quarter of it. Like his scars the rent in the cloth had been repaired and ironed evenly over. Then he stood, towering over me, looking from the green cloth to my face.

Young as I was I saw the mean imposture of it. Of course one of the maids had made the discovery and the housekeeper had told him. He had told the Herr Doktor, who had given orders that it should be repaired. Now, playing with me as a cat plays with a mouse, he was talking about 'letting the subject speak for itself!' It was meaner than Margaret. He was just a spying, dull-witted German who thought he was doing something clever. Suddenly I cared not a rap either for him or the table. I looked him in his bullying face.

'Sneak!' I said.

But even as I said it I noticed the troubled look on his face. Placing one hand on my shoulder, while I shrank from his touch, he led me to the leather couch on its raised step. Slowly he shook his head.

'It is of course what you would think,' he said. 'It is the simple explanation. But if I tell you it is *not* so? If I tell you on my honour it is not so? You think that Mrs. Pitt told me or one of the servants. You think I—*wie sagt Man?*—laid a trap for you. But—Struwwel-peter—' and he looked earnestly at me as he gave me the nick-name, '—I say it is not so. *No* servant told me. I do not go about the house asking questions of the servants who am a servant myself. It was the Herr Doktor himself who told me, and it is why I am presently leaving you.'

At this sudden turn of events, so little to have been expected, I could only look at him in bewilderment. 'Leaving!' I echoed.

'Listen, for I have not finished. Nor does the Herr Doktor go about his house questioning his own servants. How is he able to do so? Except Fearnley who drives the brougham they do not see him. It is not by questioning, even of Fearnley, that the Herr Doktor knows. This is very difficult for me. If I were rich I should not be here, but I take his money and therefore have a duty to him. I have also a duty to you, and a duty to myself. I am not a cheat and a sneak, Struwwelpeter. I did not lay a trap for you. It has been coming for some little time. At first I was not sure, but now I am sure. I think that as if he had been in this room the Herr Doktor knew when you did that to the table. I think that upstairs, without eyes to see you with or ears to hear you with, he knew. And I will be truthful. It is because I begin to be afraid of such knowledge that I go.'

But at that I could only seize him by the arm in sudden panic. 'Oh, don't go, Heinrich—don't go!' I implored, but he went heavily on.

'You have shown courage. You stood up to me. You said I was a sneak. But there are occasions when even courage is out of place. It is better to fly from them, and I did not bring you down here to reproach you for hiding something from me. I brought you because it seemed to me better that you should see for yourself. If I were anything but a poor tutor——'

But as suddenly as I had seized his arm he now seized mine. He gave a soft 'Sssh!' The door of the billiard-room had been left partly open, and now I saw his blue eyes fixed on it. Slowly it was opening inwards. Round the edge of it four fingers came into view, fingers that I should have known anywhere by their knuckles and their large flat clean nails. They were the fingers that had swept up my father's chessmen, the fingers of the Herr Doktor Voyt.

CHAPTER IV

I WILL now try to describe the Herr Doktor as I saw him for the first time, full length, in his own house, and in the light of day.

Standing motionless in the doorway, with his hand still on the door's edge, was a tall, high-shouldered figure in a black alpaca jacket such as was then commonly worn by clerks in offices. This he seemed to have outgrown, for it had shrunk some way up his wrists, which were slender but sinewy. His greying beard covered the opening of his waistcoat like a long flowing cravat, and a pair of black-and-white check trousers ended at a pair of foreign-looking house-slippers. His large porcelain pipe with the roses on it was in his hand. His round silver spectacles lay across the bridge of his nose, and no semi-circular dome of forehead reminded you of the face in the moon now, for in the house he wore a round smoking-cap, coloured like his slippers, with a red tassel dangling down one side of it.

Slowly he closed the door behind him, and stood looking round the room as if it had been empty.

Quakingly I was on my feet, not daring to lift my eyes above the middle button of his waistcoat. Then he seemed to become aware of me. Apparently I was to be welcomed to his house whatever I did to its billiard-tables, for he slowly put out a hand, which I nerved myself to take. After I had let it go again it remained hesitatingly in the air, and then I saw it move in a small sign. The sign was for Heinrich, who had risen too. Without looking at the Herr Doktor he moved to the table and began to turn back the holland cover longitudinally, first one edge, then the other, so that the edges met together down the middle of the table. He then doubled it into squares the other way, drawing it towards himself a yard at a time. Tremblingly I watched him carry it away and waited for the Herr Doktor's pointing finger to show me the damage I had done. But he had turned his back. With a little key he was unlocking one of the long tin sheaths and taking a cue from it. Heinrich, touching me on the shoulder, signed to me that I too was to take a cue. Then he marched down the room and took up his station at the marking-board, with the short rest ready in his hand. For all the notice the Herr Doktor took of the mended scar on the table it might not have been there. He placed the red ball in position and motioned me forward. He showed me his hands, first one, then the other. The bridge was made so; the butt was held loosely and easily, so; the cue must travel in a mathematically straight line, so. For perhaps five minutes he did this, while I tried to copy his movements. Then he brushed me and my cue aside and took possession of the table.

And take a man from Lapland or a man from Germany, Heinrich had said, and place a chessboard between them, and they need no further language, and I have sometimes wondered what John Roberts would have thought if he had been present in the Herr Doktor's billiard-room that afternoon. For this was his language, or one of them. Not his tongue, but a polished piece of wood was doing his talking for him, and what was it saying? I am not trying to read into this afterwards something that was not there at the time. I know how difficult these early things are to recall, and how we are sometimes so certain of them that out of our very certainty a doubt is born. But that was my first revelation of the inherent properties of inanimate things and man's control and mastery of them, and I had it from Kornelius Voyt. At me he did not again look. Once he had struck them he hardly deigned to look at the balls. But if I had had a hundred eyes they would have been dropping out of my head with the wonder of it. I will tell you what he did, and you may believe this or not as you please. From the bowl of his pipe he took a small pinch of ash. He dropped this on some random spot on the table. Then, taking the cue and splaying out his hand till it looked like a white spider straddling over the green cloth, he struck the ball, with what force I leave you to judge. For thudding round the cushions it careered as I watched. Four, five, six cushions it rebounded from, ever slowing down, and on the speck of ash it at last rested motionless. Not once, but thrice he did this that afternoon, choosing a different spot of the table each time, and the third time he did it with the other hand, for both hands came alike to him. And this in its completeness may indeed be a later thought, namely, that after a thousand years of motion the billiard-ball once struck has its appointed resting-place and no other, but even then, on the mere threshold of these things, I knew once and for the rest of my days that strike the ball as he had struck it and then leave it to itself and the powers of light and darkness combined could not have brought it to rest on any other spot.

But what was the matter with Heinrich? He was standing by the marking-board as rigid as a grenadier, holding the rest like a grounded musket, moving only when the Herr Doktor made some sign. He showed neither amazement nor admiration of what was happening on the table. And he had just told me that he was leaving the Herr Doktor's service because he was afraid. Afraid of what? Of a man who could use his left hand as easily and naturally as he used his right? We are not afraid of a blind man because he cannot see or of a lame man because he cannot run. I saw nothing to be afraid of. True, the Herr Doktor had not once smiled. There had been neither warmth nor pressure in the hand he had held out for me to take. But only a kindly man could have ignored that mended patch on the table and played with the youngster who had caused it as if nothing had happened. What was passing between those two? Could Heinrich truly believe that the Herr Doktor, stone-deaf and in another room, had known about that accident?

Suddenly I thought I saw the reason. Heinrich was not leaving of his own accord. He was leaving because for some reason or other he had been dismissed, and now thought he had a grudge. But the Herr Doktor was at his stroke-play again, as much a part of what he was doing as if there had been nobody else in the room, in the house, in the whole world. Astounding things he was doing, and watching fascinated, I forgot Heinrich. The Herr Doktor, too, evidently forgot me, for as he drew back his cue for a stroke I happened to be behind him and the butt of it caught me on the face. He half turned for a moment and paused, but his expression was blank. He prepared for the stroke again, played it, and of course I ought to have kept out of the way of a man who could not know when people were behind him.

But as if my clumsiness had put him off his game, the display came abruptly to an end. He attempted another stroke or two, but listlessly, irresolutely, changing from one angle to another, and leaving the ball unstruck. Then, with as little announcement as when he had entered, he moved to the rack and replaced the cue in its tin sheath, locked it, put the key in his pocket, and turned towards the door, his heels lifting in and out of the foreign-looking slippers. The door closed behind him, but the oppression of his deafness seemed to remain with us, for it was in silence that Heinrich put the rest back in its corner and came forward from the marking-board. From the couch where he had placed it he lifted the folded sheet. Between us we covered the table again, he at one end and I at the other. Then he showed me the way with his eyes, and out of the back of the house we passed into the air.

We had reached the foot of the plantation before he spoke.

'What have you done to your face, Struwwelpeter?' he asked. Now that he had given me that name he seemed to have taken a fancy to it. I felt my nose.

'It's nothing,' I said. 'He didn't know I was behind him and touched it with his cue. But—— I say! Weren't you watching? You just stood there like a piece of wood!'

'I was watching,' he said.

'Why, it's just like magic the way he knows exactly where the balls are going to stop! And then doing it left-hand too! Gosh!'

'You found that amusing, Struwwelpeter?'

'Why, didn't you? And he never said a word about my tearing the cloth!'

We were ascending the plantation. And of course if the Herr Doktor had sacked him he wouldn't feel much like talking, but where the plantation began to thin out towards the top he stopped.

'You say he did not know you were behind him, and hit your face with the cue, whereas when you tore the cloth he was in another part of the house, yet he told me about it, and directed me to get it mended?'

'Pooh! I expect he went in, and saw it, and he knew it wouldn't be you or the servants, so there was only me left.'

'You think so? Very well. And this tree with the red berries—*wie heisst es?*'

'That? It's a mountain-ash. But you don't really think——?'

'A mountain-ash. I remember you told me before. I must try not to forget again. And this one?'

'You're trying to talk about something else. I say—Heinrich—about your going. I don't want you to go. He isn't sending you away, is he?'

He looked at me in surprise. 'Sending me away? No. Why do you ask that?'

'Only because you said that about leaving.'

'Perhaps I have changed my mind. You say that I stood like a piece of wood in the billiard-room. I was thinking. You are still only at the beginning. I am a good teacher, as the Herr Doktor knows, and he has no wish to lose my services. But I see now that it would not be right if I were to leave at once. There are other things I wish to teach you.'

'Fencing?' I asked eagerly.

'I wish to teach you also happy and amusing things, not directed to an end. No, not Word-making. Not Fishponds. Fencing perhaps, presently. When is your birthday?'

'The ninth of November.'

'And you have been here five weeks. During that time you have not once seen your friends and schoolfellows. You have not asked them to tea. It is not right that you should not see those of your own age. Would you like me to suggest to the Herr Doktor that you should have a birthday-party?'

'Oh, rather!' I exclaimed gleefully, not noticing how completely he had changed the subject.

'Then tell me who you would like to ask.'

That set me off. There was Vic Tenison and Tommy Summerscales, and Wilf and Horace, and I had a thousand things to tell them. I could talk a strange language on my fingers and bet them I could tell what they were saying by just watching their lips. I had had my first lesson in billiards and was going to be taught to fence. I could boast of a tutor who was a duellist and show them the scars on his face. And as Heinrich had *not* got the sack, and was *not* now leaving on his own account, my tongue ran on wheels as we descended the plantation again and approached the back of the house. It was there that the delivery carts from the town drew up, and as we came to the door of the yard I saw that one with the name of a railway company on it had just arrived. It was in charge of a couple of draymen, and they were lifting two wooden cases from it, a large one and a smaller. I asked Heinrich what they were, but he did not know, and we advanced to have a look at them. They were from London, and they had 'With Care' labels on them, and the smaller one 'With Great Care: Instruments'.

'They are addressed to the Herr Doktor,' Heinrich said. 'I had better tell Fearnley,' and he went off to find him.

That evening after supper Heinrich left me to my own devices. I did not see him till he came in to tell me it was time I went to bed, and I asked him what he had been doing.

'Helping Fearnley,' he said.

'With those boxes? What was in them?' I asked him.

'Only a pendulum,' he replied. 'And I have spoken to the Herr Doktor about your party. I do not think he was very pleased, for he wishes you to get on with your studies, but you may have your friends. I should have thought of it sooner. It is not right that you should not see young people of your own age.'

CHAPTER V

M Y birthday was still more than a fortnight off, but Heinrich made as much fuss about it as if there hadn't been a minute to waste. He rubbed his big hands together and said we must be setting about things at once. There were the invitations; my friends must be given plenty of notice in case they arranged something else for that day. I said I didn't suppose Vic and Wilf had as many parties to go to as all that, but he said you never knew, and the invitations were written and sent off. I had supposed at first that the party would be held in our own first-floor portion of the house, but Heinrich said no, it would be my first birthday to have a 'teen at the end of it, which made it an important event. So the rule about my having nothing to do with the servants was relaxed. One day after lessons Mrs. Pitt came up into our room. Addressing Heinrich she said that if Master Peter was ready she was, and the three of us went downstairs together. I had heard her voice raised to one or other of the maids now and then, and had pictured her as a big, masterful sort of woman. Actually she was short and thick-set, with a gritty sort of complexion, but I dare say it was partly her name that made me think of coal-dust. She was always dressed as if for Sunday, in a black satin bodice even in the morning and cloth-topped buttoned boots, and the jet brooch she wore at her neck was no blacker than her hair.

'This would be my idea,' she said, opening the door of the drawing-room which adjoined one side of the hall. 'This for them to have their tea in, and this other'—and she threw open a door on the other side of the hall—'this other that used to be the morning-room for them to play their games in afterwards. That would give Alice and Minna time to clear away.'

'Aren't we to be allowed to go into the billiard-room?' I asked.

'Ja,' said Heinrich in an aside, and Mrs. Pitt continued:

'And upstairs you can do the same as you always do. There's to be, how many of you, did you say?'

'Six, and me and Heinrich.'

'That's eight. The little drawing-room will be big enough. I'll move the lustres and the birds, and the upstairs cushions will be good enough for pillow-fighting. I'll take this away now in case some of you sets light to it,' and she picked up the ornate bustle of tinsel and paper flowers that hid the emptiness of the grate and carried it in front of her like an apron as she continued to make her plans.

But all this was so long before my birthday that it seemed to me that half the things would be to do again before the time came. It looked like making work for work's sake, all this cleaning and opening windows, stripping the covers from the chairs and sofas, carrying things away to places of safety, putting sofas across corners wherever a pedestal with a bust or a basket of wax fruits on it looked as if it might get upset, and as for pillow-fighting, did Mrs. Pitt think the fellows were a lot of kids? Some of them were in their last term at school. My own cake was going to have thirteen candles on it. In fact Heinrich overdid it to such a ridiculous extent

that I turned sulky. He fetched me out of the billiard-room one day
when all I wanted was to be left alone to practise shots.

'I don't think I want a birthday if there's got to be all this fuss
about it,' I said. 'First Mrs. Pitt talking about how *she* never had
money spent on her like that, and then you going about locking
doors and saying we're not to go here and we're not to go there.
Pillow-fighting! Vic and Wilf aren't kids——'

He laughed and patted me on the shoulder, but even that
seemed over-done too.

'Of course they are not, and Mrs. Pitt is a very foolish woman,
and I am a very foolish fellow. The time seems long? You think the
birthday will never come? Perhaps we can shorten the time a little.
You will not think so small a thing is a birthday-present, so as it is
not a birthday-present perhaps you can have it now.'

He went into his bedroom. He was back again in a couple of
minutes, and the thing he carried seemed an absurd little gift in his
great sandy-backed hands. It was just a cup and saucer, with flowers on them like there were on the Herr Doktor's pipe, and round
the saucer ran the motto: '*Als Frauenlieb und Kindermund Nichts
Schönres auf dem Erdenrund.*'

'It is *handgemahlt*, hand-painted,' he said, turning it round for
me to read it. 'As for Kindermund, of course you are right, and you
are all young men now, and that reminds me that I have not yet
measured you. But the time is not long, Struwwelpeter, it is short.
In a few years you will look back and wonder where they have
gone. But then comes the Frauenlieb, which is the most beautiful
of all. Shall we now forget about the party for a short while and
take a little walk?'

I know now what was troubling him. He was standing between
me and something, hoping I would not notice something, ready to
bear it on his own broad shoulders for the two of us. And a few evenings before my birthday a small thing happened that while it lasted
seemed to set me back a whole year, before I had heard of deaf-and-
dumb alphabets and the phenomena of billiard-balls. It was just getting dark. In our study the lamp was lighted, but I had gone into the
next room for something. I stood at the window, looking out over

the lights of the town, here a dust of gold, there broken spangles, the lights of a train just entering the station, the lonely lamp-dotted lines that led away through the darkness to other towns. And suddenly I heard a faint muffled crackling, followed by another, and remembered what night it was. It was Plot night.

Only a year ago! There had been no need to tell me what was in the large brown-paper parcel my father had brought home with him. They were fireworks, and my birthday seemed to be approaching by leaps and bounds compared with the interminable time he had taken that evening over his tea. But down into our strip of back garden he had come at last, and I could see our lighted faces again as Nora had held the walking-stick with the pin-wheel on the end of it, and Margaret had made loops of golden rain and blue starlight, and so to the roman-candles and the jack-in-the-box that had wound up the display. But I had let off squibs and rip-raps in my smoke-blackened fingers, and had gone on afterwards with Vic and Wilf and Horace to the big bonfire we had mounted guard over for a week past because of thieves from other fires, and a grand and gunpowdery time of it we had had.

And now, looking out of the window, I could almost hear the fiery crackle and rush of sparks as a greasy skep was hoisted on, and smell the glowing millband, and hear the single big bang of the maroons. And I felt lonely and shut out from it all. I didn't want a grand party like the pictures of the young squire coming of age. I wanted to be running loose with the other fellows instead of being tied down in this unhomely house with a private tutor of my own. Sullenly I turned away, and though Heinrich did his best to cheer me up I moped for the rest of the evening.

But the morning of my birthday dawned at last. There were to be no lessons that day, and if Heinrich told me once to go round and see if anything had been forgotten he did so a dozen times. In the smaller drawing-room everything was ready, the great bronze tea-urn standing among the cups and saucers on a side-table, the chairs drawn up, my cake with its thirteen candles ready for lighting. And I had had some idea of standing on the terrace in state to receive my guests, but when, at a little after four, they arrived in a body, I dashed down the steps to meet them, all my grandeur forgotten. 'My tutor, Herr Heinrich Opfer' I had intended to say, but instead I found myself shouting 'This is Heinrich, chaps,' and as I named each of them Heinrich clicked his heels together, and did his hip-jerk and lunged. Into the house we trooped straight into the smaller drawing-room, where Mrs. Pitt herself stood at the urn, with Alice and Minna standing with their backs to the wall in their caps and aprons, ready to wait on us.

What fun it was seeing them again! Down we sat, all talking at once. Vic Tenison on my right had a new stand-up collar on. Tommy Summerscales on my left was letting me have a peep at a cherrywood pipe he had in his pocket almost before he placed himself on his chair. Heinrich was at the other end of the table, between Horace and Wilf, and already I was wondering what I should show them first the moment tea was over, my study, or the deaf-and-dumb alphabet, or the billiard-room, or brag about the fencing-lessons I was going to have. I had managed to light my thirteenth candle before the first one had burned more than half-way down, and the big iced cake shone before me like a shrine. Heigho! Who with all this going on—Mrs. Pitt pouring more hot water into the urn, the girls coming and going with the cups and saucers, Heinrich talking to Wilf and Horace as if he'd known them all his life, every mouth full and every tongue loosened—who would have expected all this to come to a sudden dead stop, a silence without a moment's warning, as if like the palace in the fairy-story a spell had been laid on the whole enchanted place? Let me tell you.

It was half-way through tea. Wilf was calling down the table to me that I ought to have been with them at the bonfire. I, not to be outdone, was shouting back that I had been playing billiards instead. Everybody was full of himself and his doings, I loudest of them all. And then there fell upon our whole party this that I am speaking of. We all know these moments, and how in a few moments more we have forgotten them again. Everybody is silent at once, everybody begins again at once. So it was now. The hush was absolute. It lasted for perhaps seven or eight seconds. It ended, and Vic Tenison got in first.

'Bet you it's twenty past!' he challenged the table.

'You mean twenty to,' Wilf retorted. (They say it is always at one or other of these intervals that these hushes come.)

'It can be either . . . sometimes it's one and sometimes it's the other. . . .'

'It means an angel's passing over——'

'A lot you know about angels——!'

'I know as much as you do——'

'But which was it? *I* say twenty to,' and out came Wilf's Waterbury, and I looked at my father's silver Waltham, and everybody else who had a watch lugged it out too.

But no two watches said the same. Vic swore his was right, for he had set it by the Town Hall that very afternoon, and in less time than it has taken you to read about it that strange moment was a thing of the past.

'Heinrich'll know—which was it, Heinrich?'

But Heinrich had risen from his place. Muttering something about being back in a minute he walked quickly out of the room, shutting the door behind him. And of course no sooner was it closed than the talk was all about him.

'He says he got them in a duel——'

'Well, he did, in Heidelberg, and he's going to teach me to fence too——'

'Rot, those aren't proper duels. There's all about them in Mark Twain. They're a sort of gym, and they keep the wounds open by putting things in——'

'You mean *Turnhalle*. Gym's *Gymnasium*, and in German it means a school——'

'Got a German teacher all to himself now——'

'Well, I'll bet none of you know what *this* means,' and I began to talk rapidly on my fingers.

But they all broke into mocking imitation of me, as if I had been just making it up. The whole table became something like the chart upstairs, everybody 'M-mming' with his mouth and doing something nonsensical with his fingers.

But the silence this time was a very different sort of silence from that that means an angel is passing over your head.

When Heinrich came in again he did not return to his place at the other end of the table. He looked for Mrs. Pitt, but she had gone out, so he said something to Alice instead. Then he came up and bent over me.

'*Alles so gemütlich, Junge?* You are enjoying your party?' he said, giving me a little hug.

'Where have you been?'

'Where have I been? To my room, to mend the fire.'

'Jumping up all in a hurry like that?'

'And why not do a thing at once while one thinks of it instead of perhaps forgetting it again, Mister Peter Pry?'

'What were you saying to Alice just now?'

'I was asking her if the billiard-room was ready. What, you do not want to play billiards?' but he could see as plainly as I could that the fellows were getting impatient to do something.

'But you're coming with us, aren't you?' If he didn't come they wouldn't believe me when I told them of the marvellous things the Herr Doktor could do.

'I will join you presently. It will be cooler in there, and they can open these windows.'

But first he seemed to be cold, and then hot, and I too had a queer sort of feeling that something, I didn't know what, was missing from my party. But he had gone out, and the fellows had gathered about me.

'What was that you said about billiards? Does he say we mustn't?'

'No, he doesn't,' I said. 'Come on,' and off we trooped.

But that feeling that there was something I had forgotten would not let me alone, for it was on the very tip of my tongue. And there would be a fearful row too if the cloth got cut again, which looked like happening, for no sooner had the fellows seen the uncovered table than there had been a stampede for the cues, and there were the whole six of them, with a cue apiece, letting fly at the balls whenever they came near. Then suddenly, like a flash going off in my head, I knew what was wrong with my party. It wasn't that I hadn't asked my sister Nora, for Heinrich and I had talked about that, and he had said that she was too far away, and would have been the only girl among us boys. It was far worse than that. *I had forgotten to ask the Herr Doktor himself!*

It was, I say, like something going pop in my head, some cell bursting and scattering all the other cells about it, so that they didn't fit back again in the same places afterwards. Not to have asked him! It was no good telling myself that he wouldn't have come. I wasn't even sure that I particularly wanted him, but that made it all the worse that he hadn't been asked. He had given me everything, the run of the house, my cake with the thirteen candles on it, his servants to wait on us, a tutor, the very bed I slept in, and I had left him out! In the whole of my thirteen years nothing had ever seized me as this seized me now. The fellows would have to look after themselves for a bit. Out of the billiard-room I ran, past the red baize doors, across the hall, up into Heinrich's room. I burst in. Downstairs he had said he was hot, but here with the firelight glinting on the bristles of his hair he was huddled forward, gazing into the flames.

'Heinrich!' I broke out. 'An awful thing has happened!'

If I had told him the house was on fire he couldn't have started more violently. He stiffened as he sat, and his blue eyes came round to mine.

'I didn't ask the Herr Doktor to my party!'

'You—what do you say?'

'I was *going* to ask him—no, I wasn't—I mean it came on me all at once—no, I don't mean that either, I think it was there all the time we were having tea——'

He passed his hand over his brow, but his attitude relaxed a little.

'So. But the Herr Doktor does not go to the parties of young people. It is nothing.'

'It *isn't* nothing! I mean my not *thinking* of it till—till—till all at once it came——'

'Go and join them, Junge. I will come to you presently. And I will explain to the Herr Doktor. He will understand.'

'But it'll be no good when the party's over!' I cried in agitation. 'I want him to know now! Go and tell him, Heinrich—he'll be wondering—I *know* he's wondering. . . .'

'He did not expect to be asked. He has no wish to come. He wishes to be alone. I will tell him what you say to-morrow.'

But I cried out in greater agitation still: 'But you don't understand! It's a very important thing! If you don't go to him I shall——'

But he seized my arm and shook it.

'You are not going!'

'I am if you don't—it's—it matters an *awful* lot——'

'I tell you you are not going! Rather than that you should go I will lock you in this room—I will send them all away this minute——'

But suddenly his mouth gave a twitch of pain. He was in the act of jumping out of his chair, and his knee must have been cramped or in the wrong position, for he clapped his hand to it as if something had given way. There was a look of fright in his eyes. But he worked the knee backwards and forwards a few times to loosen it, and then spoke in a quieter voice:

'It is not polite to leave your friends by themselves. I will take you to them. They are nice boys. It is a touch of synovitis, of water on the knee. I strained it in fencing. I think it is a sign the weather is going to change. It is better now. Let us go downstairs.'

But he still limped as he moved towards the door, and the look of fright still lingered in his eyes.

CHAPTER VI

I NOW began to spend a good deal of time in the billiard-room, not idly knocking the balls about now, but working out angles, positions, speed and problems of side. But it was as if something had happened to me. I seemed to get worse the more I practised. I knew the strokes I wished to make, but my hands refused to execute them, and sometimes even shook a little when they ought to have been steady, as if I had been running quickly and my heart was beating too fast. This sudden slip back disheartened me, for I had thought I was getting on quite well, and presently I thought I would give billiards a rest, and cast about for something else to occupy my spare time. So I hit on chess. Let me tell you how this came about.

Heinrich had taken the chart of the hands down from the wall, but with its disappearance his own energies seemed to have slowed down almost to a standstill. In our room of an evening he would sometimes sit for an hour without speaking, and as the only books I had were schoolbooks the time often hung heavily. My drink before going to bed was cocoa; I drank it out of his cup and saucer with the motto; and *'Kindermund'*, I sometimes heard him say softly to himself, glancing at me when he thought I wasn't looking, *'Kindermund, Kindermund'*. And sometimes he didn't answer when I asked him things, but walked out of the room instead.

But one night, as I was drinking my cocoa he suddenly began to talk.

'I think the time has come to tell you, Struwwelpeter,' he said, 'that in some ways I am really a very stupid fellow. And—*gegen Dummheit*—you have passed from letters to words, and from words to meanings, and soon there will be nothing for me to do. Even in trying I shall offend. But you are not stupid. To you, only just thirteen, I can tell things I could not tell to others of seventeen or eighteen perhaps. That was Mr. Tenison's son who sat next to you at your birthday party?'

'Yes. Vic,' I said, wondering what was coming.

'So. And the Herr Doktor knows Mr. Tenison. He admits that he plays chess very well. But that is not to say that in the Herr Doktor's opinion Mr. Tenison is not a very stupid man.'

'Mr. Tenison stupid!' I exclaimed. 'But next to the Herr Doktor my father always said he was cleverer than anybody!'

'But your father,' Heinrich went on as if I had not spoken, 'though perhaps he played chess less well than Mr. Tenison, was not a stupid man. In the Herr Doktor's opinion he might easily have been a very important man. It is why you are here.'

My father an important man! But he had been nothing but a clerk, and poor! 'Is that what Herr Doktor says?' I asked.

'It is what the Herr Doktor means,' he corrected me. 'Shall I tell you a little story, which is also a true one?'

'Yes, please.'

'More than fifty years ago there was born a little girl who had a very grave early illness. This illness left her not only deaf and dumb, as the Herr Doktor is, but blind also. Yet she was taught to read and write and do sums, also geography and astronomy and many other things. It was my thesis before I myself became a teacher.'

'I know blind people can read with their fingers,' I said.

'So. There are also vibrations, so that they know a person by his tread, as he approaches. There is also smell, and the dumb can even be taught to speak as you or I do.'

'How?' I asked.

'If I were teaching you I should place your finger lightly on my lips and make a certain sound. You would feel in what position my lips were to produce that sound. I should then make a different sound, but your finger this time would be inside my mouth to feel the position of my tongue. So by copying these movements you would presently begin to produce the same sounds as I. I am not a stupid fellow at my business, Struwwelpeter.'

'Then why didn't the Herr Doktor learn to talk like that?'

'It is what I am coming to. With the Herr Doktor there is no need.'

'I should have thought that if anybody needed it he did.'

'I say there was no need. He has his own way, which is a different way. You know that the blood is always returning to the heart. When a person loses a limb what happens to the blood that used to flow that way?'

'It finds another one, I suppose.'

'So the Herr Doktor has found another way.'

'Well, what's the matter with that?'

'The matter, Junge, is this. If the Herr Doktor were a pupil, who had to be taught the thoughts of others, it would not matter. But the Herr Doktor is *not* a pupil. When I go, which may yet be soon, he will be in charge of you. *You* will be the pupil, not he. You will not be teaching him your thoughts. He will be teaching you his. The one who lacks two faculties, but has found another way, will be teaching the one who has all his faculties, and thinks they are everything,' and with that he looked at his watch. 'But it is after nine o'clock. Drink your cocoa. You have finished it? Then I will take your cup. To bed with you, Struwwelpeter, and sleep well,' and I left him standing there, with the cup and saucer in his hand, reading the motto to himself—'*Kindermund—Frauenlieb—Nichts Schönres. . . .*'

But—Mr. Tenison stupid and my father an important man! It turned all my ideas upside down. If Mr. Tenison was stupid who was not? I saw his pink, self-confident face again in the light of my father's lamp, looking anything but stupid as he made his move and then sat back, as much as to say he thought *that* settled it, while my father looked anything but important as he pushed his king away or turned the board round for a new game. The one important, the other stupid! I pondered it as I undressed and got into bed that night. I had spent my childhood in an atmosphere of chess without knowing anything about it except that I had once frightened my sister with the name of Morphy and had boasted that one day I would learn chess and beat the Herr Doktor Voyt. But things must have been very active in my mind that night, for suddenly I remembered something that until that moment I had completely forgotten. Among the few small possessions I had brought with me to the Herr Doktor's house was my father's red-backed Staunton, which Margaret must have come upon in my attic at home and packed with the rest. From the bottom of my father's gladstone bag I got it out. I began to read it that very night, but when Heinrich put his head in at my door to see whether I had turned my light out I hid it under the bedclothes, for for some reason I couldn't have explained I didn't want him to know I had it.

So, though I had neither board nor men, but only the book, I began to study chess in secret.

Staunton is still as good an introduction to the game as I know, and suddenly I remembered that there was in the house a chess-board already made. It was the floor of the hall downstairs. I shouldn't need more than a portion of it, for there was enough of it for half a dozen boards, but it would be a simple matter to mark off the portion I required by placing some object at each corner, and later I no longer had to do even this, for with practice I found I could do it 'in my eye' whatever part of the hall I happened to be standing in.

But the men to occupy these nine-inch squares of black and white? That was a difficulty, but my ingenuity found a way. This was to put the idea of scale and proportion out of my head altogether. Anything would do for a token as long as I knew what it represented, and I took the little cardboard squares of the Word-making game. Laboriously, with Staunton for my copy, and all the time concealing what I was doing from Heinrich, I drew on the back of them my rooks and knights and pawns. It took me days, and I nearly threw the whole idea aside when I came to put it into operation, but as it turned out there could have been no better preparation for presently dispensing with men altogether.

And it had the further advantage that a few shuffles with my feet would reduce everything to a meaningless heap if I should happen to be interrupted.

And why was I so careful to keep all this from Heinrich? He had not forbidden me chess. I was doing no wrong. And as the answer seems obscure I will simply say that *I wanted to play chess*. I should have wanted it no less if Heinrich had forbidden it, and should still have played it. Therefore it seemed best to say nothing about it. He couldn't forbid something he didn't know about. But I had also another reason.

For when he had told me that apart from his job he was really a rather stupid man he had told me nothing I was not beginning to find out for myself. He might well talk to me as if I was seventeen or eighteen; if he wanted to talk to me at all there was no other way. He was loyal and patient and becoming fonder of me with every day that passed, but the plain truth was that all the Hein-riches in the world could never have given birth to an idea among them. It was not that I was cleverer than he, though this was the way he always put it. Our minds no more met than oil and water meet. I cannot say I have ever given birth to a new idea myself. But I have been chosen for the demonstration of an ancient and better forgotten one, and had no means of knowing how far along that road I had already travelled. How then was Heinrich to know, as I sat with him of an evening, apparently doing nothing, that a black and white pattern of sixty-four squares was before my eyes, with my home-made tokens for men and a battle in progress? He did not know. From me he was not going to know. Men only tell things when there is a reason for telling them. When there is no reason they keep them to themselves. And from the very beginning I had had not the least intention of telling him.

For all that he came within an ace of finding out one afternoon. This was shortly before I discovered that I could do without my bits of cardboard altogether, and he came upon me at my game, red-handed if he had only known it. He had been into the town. I heard the door of the Gothic porch open, and there was just time for me to take a couple of slides along the hall floor and to give a shuffle with my feet. Then as he crossed to the hat-rack he saw me.

'What are you doing here all by yourself, Struwwelpeter?' he said. 'It is nearly dark.'

'Nothing,' I mumbled, and added, 'there isn't anything to do in this house.'

'And what is all this on the floor?'

'I've been tearing something up.'

'Here, in the hall? Is there not a basket upstairs? You should not make unnecessary work for the servants. Pick them up and take them upstairs. They will be bringing tea up in a few minutes.'

So, smiling to myself at having outwitted him, I put the cardboard men into my pocket and followed him upstairs.

But the next time he came upon me at my game there were no men to pick up, and it is to this turning-point of my life that I now come.

Perhaps it seems an astonishing thing that in a few weeks, with no instruction but that of an elementary textbook, I had been able to make as clean a sweep of the impedimenta of pawns and pieces as Heinrich had done when he had rolled up the chart of the talking hands. Read on: you will have plenty of time to disbelieve me before you come to the end. Again it took place in the hall. Again the afternoon had fallen almost completely dark. The lamp halfway up the stairs had been newly lighted but not yet fully turned up, but light and dark were the same to me now, and I, a slender, rumple-haired lad of thirteen, was deep in a game with an imaginary opponent, playing his side as well as my own. The flame of the lamp on the stairs barely reached the panes of the Gothic porch, the branching hat-racks were a mere knuckle or knob here and there in the gloom, the chequers of the floor stretched glimmeringly away and lost themselves. Once one of the baize doors along the passage had opened and I had heard the cackle of the parrot, but it had hardly broken my concentration, and everything was portentously still. It was black's move. In my head I saw the move I had decided to make for him as plainly as if I had been playing under my father's lamp at home. And in my head I made it.

Or rather, I should say I tried to make it, for the move remained unmade. It was more than a hesitation and thinking twice; quite simply, the move would not let itself be made. It was a pawn-move. As pawns do not move backwards all it had to do was to step to the compartment ahead. But as if it knew better than I did it stuck.

I opened my eyes, for I had been playing with them tightly shut. I was new to this concentration of playing without anything visible to play with, and it was possible that I had made a slip or false move somewhere. If so I had the squares on the floor to check it by. With my eyes open I pegged out my sixty-four squares again. Move by move I carefully played the game over again up to that point. I had made no slip. There the recalcitrant pawn stood, imaginary on its square, bidding me forget my own insignificant will and think again. Then, half impatiently, I took a step forward as if to push the thing on with my foot.

The next I must explain as best I can. I know that I stood on the nine-inch square, with no more than another nine inches to move if I had been a pawn myself. But a sort of numbness stole over me.

Some medium denser than the surrounding air seemed to come between me and everything about me. If fifty parrots had called, 'What are you doing there?' I should not have heard them. But, though I neither saw nor heard, the inner eyes I was using opened slowly on another world. *I saw that move and the reason why I could not make it.* Instead I saw *the true move*, rising as splendidly before me as the sun lifts himself out of the east. In its brightness it challenged me to put it to the test. 'Try!' it seemed to say. 'It is only a step—you are groping—come out of the shadows and see what knowledge will surround you then. . . .'

And I tried to take that step forward, but was no more able to do so than a tree is able to step forward from its own roots.

And all I remember feeling was wonder that so evident a thing should have been so long on the way. What had I been wasting my time over? Thirteen years old and my eyes only this moment opened! I felt that I had been growing to this from before my birth. I think it was, in fact, my birth, and now all life lay before me, shining and endless. And I told you at the beginning that I no longer play chess. Chess is no longer even played in my presence. All has gone except the memory that these things were so, and even that I have tried to shut out. But as I stood rooted there, for long enough for a youth to grow into manhood, never to be the same again, the spell was broken. That invisible medium about me lifted. There emerged again the shadowy arms of the hat-racks, the light behind me up the stairs, my own faint shadow on the floor. And suddenly I gave a tremendous yawn.

But the yawn almost ended in lockjaw, for gazing at me from the Gothic porch, with his hands clasped over his breast and his brows gathered into a knot, stood the massive figure of Heinrich. He gave a groan.

'*Lieber Gott, lieber Gott!*' I heard him choke. 'And he says that in this house he can find nothing to do!'

CHAPTER VII

THEY say it is England's dawns and twilights that have made of her artists the most sensitive landscape-painters in the world. I do not know whether such gentle transitions can make the English character beautiful too, for from that afternoon on my life divides itself into two portions as abruptly as in southerly countries the night descends on the day with hardly a moment between. Simply and in a word, I had no adolescence.

Consider for a moment even my personal appearance. My height as Heinrich had measured it on the edge of the schoolroom door was a fraction under five-foot-three. I was still wearing the knickerbocker suit in which I had come to the Herr Doktor's house, and my complexion was that of a young girl. When I pulled my cap off (if I had remembered to put one on) it usually left my hair sticking up all over the place, and I was treated as a schoolboy is treated, made to pick bits of paper up from the floor, told when to sit down to my lessons, when it was time I went to bed. That was one side of the picture.

And this tutor who was set over me? He had himself confessed that he was really a stupid fellow and that I was far cleverer than he was. In contrast to my cap and knickerbocker suit he always wore a narrow-brimmed comedian-looking hat many sizes too small for his face, a belted brown jacket with the narrowest possible V at the neck, and trousers that showed the shape of his muscular calves. These details of him emerged from the mists that afternoon as I finished that tremendous brain-clearing yawn. '*Lieber Gott!* And he says that in this house he can find nothing to do!' The next moment he was past me. I heard him stumbling up the stairs. He stopped halfway up them to turn up the lamp, but even the slow filling of the hall with light did not bring me at once to myself. Again and again I softly stamped the feet that had been so strangely held fast, and by the time they felt as if they belonged to me again my brain

49

was occupied with another task. This was the careful storing away
in my memory of that marvellous move for future use. I could
not say on which square *of the floor* the astounding thing had happened, but of its position *on the board* I was vividly sure. This done
I followed Heinrich upstairs. He had got out his writing-wallet and
was covering sheet after sheet of thin foreign paper with German
schrift, and did not look up. I wondered what they put in love-
letters, for I knew by this time what sort of letters he was so con-
stantly writing. Then I returned to that glamorous move again.

It continued to occupy me for the remainder of the evening.
When Heinrich got up to make my cocoa he handed me the cup
without a word and then sat down to his writing again. At nine
o'clock I didn't see why I should wait to be told to go to bed, and I
too got up.

'*Gute nacht*,' I said.

'*Gute nacht*,' and I left him.

But my moodiness had worked itself out the next morning.
Why, we might have quarrelled, in such a huff had I been all about
nothing! But when I went in to breakfast I found him standing, not
with his back to the fire as he usually did, but gazing into it with
his back turned to me. I said good morning, but he didn't seem
to hear. Anyway if he wasn't hungry I was, and down I sat. It was
then that he turned, and I saw that his blue eyes were red round
the rims.

'I did say good morning,' I said.

'Good morning.'

'Aren't you going to have any breakfast?'

'I will drink a cup of coffee. I had biscuits during the night. I did
not sleep. But perhaps you would rather not hear why I did not
sleep.'

'What's the matter?'

'Have you always been truthful with me, Struwwelpeter?'

'What do you mean?'

'You have not told me lies?'

'I don't know what you mean,' I said doggedly.

'Then I will tell you. You have told me a lie,' and from the pocket of the belted jacket he took out and laid on the table my home-made chessmen. 'I asked you one day what the bits of paper on the hall floor were. You told me you had been tearing something up. It was not the truth. Last night after you had gone to bed I found these. I say it was not the truth.'

It was so obviously not the truth that it wasn't worth while replying, and he went on.

'If you had told me you wished to play chess I should have said it would be better to wait a little. You are growing remarkably quickly and your brain must not be overworked. I do not say I should have forbidden you chess, but at present it is too much. But you did not ask me.'

'Everybody plays it,' I said surlily.

'Everybody does not tell lies. And now I wish to ask you something else. Yesterday when I came in why were you standing there in the hall staring at nothing?'

'I wasn't staring at nothing.'

'At what then were you staring?'

'At a chess move.'

'But you had not these,' and he pointed to the Word-making squares.

'I don't want them.'

He frowned—'You tell me you can play *without the men?*'

'I can do without the board too if I try.'

He shivered as if he had felt a sudden chill. '*Schlimm, schlimm!*' he muttered.

'Anyway my father played it, and everybody at home, the Herr Doktor too, and please when am I to see the Herr Doktor again? It's funny being in the same house with a person and never seeing him.'

'You will see the Herr Doktor when he sends for you.'

'That's another put-off,' I said, for I was finding that even when I answered him rudely nothing very much happened. 'I wanted to go to him on my birthday and you wouldn't let me. Anybody'd think there was something funny about him, all that rot about knowing when I'm in the billiard-room. You told me yourself blind people could tell who was coming by the vibrations, and perhaps he has a machine of some kind. What—' for a flash of enlightenment came to me, '—what's that pendulum you say he has?'

'Pendulum?'

'That came in those two cases that afternoon. You said it was a pendulum. What sort of a pendulum?'

'The accident in the billiard-room happened before the two cases came.'

'But what's he want a pendulum for, and why did it say "Instruments"? Is it a pendulum like a clock?'

'Yes, but also no. It is a compound pendulum, and it writes patterns as it swings.'

'Why is it compound?'

But his manner changed. 'Why the pendulum is compound has nothing to do with the subject we were speaking of. We were speaking of what happened in the hall yesterday. I wish to know if you were in any pain.'

'Pain? What should I be in pain for?' I asked in surprise.

'What did you feel?'

'I don't think I felt anything. I was looking at that move.'

'You say you can play chess without either men or board. Can you see that move now?'

'Of course,' I began, but suddenly stopped dead. To my unbounded astonishment that move, that had seemed fixed in my memory for ever, had completely gone from me.

'You say you can still see it?'

'No.'

'Yesterday you remembered it and to-day you have forgotten it?'

'That's with talking. I shall remember it presently. You can't play chess and talk.'

'Has this thing ever happened to you before?'

'What thing?' for it might have been something monstrous from the way he spoke of it. 'Everybody forgets things sometimes.'

'And you felt—nothing?'

'Well, I felt a bit muzzy when it was over, like pins-and-needles

running up and down me, and my feet were a bit stiff, if that's
what you mean.'

Then something seemed to give way in Heinrich. His hand had
been at his forehead; he let it fall like a dead weight on the table, so
that the breakfast things jumped.

'*Schrecklich, schrecklich!*' he groaned. 'I was waiting for it to
happen—and while I was waiting it happened! *Schrecklich!*'

But I was still thunderstruck about that vanished move and
hardly heard what he said. Minna came in to clear the table.
Heinrich was standing looking out of the window with his hands
clasped behind his back. As the door closed on Minna again he
turned with the air of a man whose mind is made up. He began
to walk up and down, talking as he walked, with many pauses for
thought.

'A little while ago I spoke to you of Laura Bridgman.'

I thought he had gone daft. I had never heard the name before,
and said so.

'Perhaps I forgot to mention her name. She was the little girl
who was deaf and dumb and blind and yet learned such difficult
subjects as astronomy.'

'Oh!'

'I was trying to tell you how these afflicted people were taught.
Now I should like to tell you how I first came to be here, in this
house.'

I waited, and he began.

'I was in Germany when I read in a scholastic paper that an English gentleman, of German origin but living in England, required
a tutor in the deaf-and-dumb language for a boy then twelve years
old. I answered this advertisement, but several weeks passed and
nothing happened and I supposed the place to have been filled.
This disappointed me, for I wanted the money because of a certain
person who is very, very dear to me.'

('That's the girl you're always writing long letters in German
to,' I commented to myself.)

'Then one day a telegram came. If I would come to England for
an interview my expenses would be paid. I came to England, and

found, not as I had expected, that my pupil was deaf-and-dumb, but that this German gentleman was. I also found that the reason for the delay was that two other persons had already presented themselves, but either they did not please this Herr Doktor or the Herr Doktor did not please them. You are following me?'

'Yes,' I said, for indeed I was, and closely.

'The circumstances were explained to me, but what struck me at first was that they were neither quite usual nor quite natural. For example, having taught you the deaf-and-dumb alphabet I must be careful to teach you *nothing* else, nor try to lead your mind in any direction whatever. You will agree that for the education of a boy of twelve these were somewhat unusual instructions.'

'Is that why you only taught me German?'

'Listen, and do not talk. I did not very much like the man who gave these instructions. For one thing he attempted to dominate me in a certain way that I neither understand nor approve of. I also asked myself why two other persons had excused themselves from going any further with this business, and whether he had tried to dominate them in this same way. But the time was running short and the matter pressed. There was also this reason in Germany of which I spoke.'

'But why didn't you like him? You keep on saying dominate, but what did he *do*?'

But he avoided my question and went on.

'You were not to go to school. You were not to be prepared for a University. You were not to be put into a business. You were to be trained to an end, and I will tell you, Struwwelpeter, that I did not find it easy to persuade the Herr Doktor even to allow you to have a simple birthday-party. In short it seemed to me that I was to assist in an experiment of which I did not know the nature.'

'Anyway I've learned billiards and chess,' I said offhandedly, for I did not see what all this rigmarole was about, and the Herr Doktor had been decent enough about my cutting the table.

'Both of which are extremely difficult things to learn, yet he begins with them.'

'*He* begins?'

'So. Have you not forgotten that move already?'

'That's nothing. It will come back.'

'Do you remember that on your birthday, when we were all sitting at tea, a sudden silence came, that even your friends noticed?'

'Yes,' I said. 'And they were betting it was twenty-past or twenty-to. What *is* it when it does that, Heinrich?'

'And that suddenly you remembered—*very* suddenly you remembered—that you had not asked the Herr Doktor to your party?'

'Yes.'

'And you came running to me, talking wildly—for you *were* talking wildly, Struwwelpeter—and saying that I must go to him at once. And I would not go, for though I dare not oppose him openly I oppose him none the less. Do you remember what happened then?'

'You jumped up to stop me.'

'I jumped up. I said it was synovitis, water on the knee. I said I had got it fencing. But I have never had water on the knee. It was a swift and violent pain. You think I am inventing this?' he asked sharply, for he must have seen my face. His knee! What had his knee to do with it?

'No—I mean of course not——' I said.

'I have been silent for a long time, for I did not wish to speak of things that perhaps would pass of themselves. Nobody was hurt but me, and I only that once. But after last night I can be silent no longer. I have done my military service and have seen men die, but I cannot see you again like that—a young boy in knickerbockers, as stiff as if you stood in a trance, with your eyes fixed on something many, many times your age. In learning chess without telling me you thought you were doing as you wished. For many weeks you have thought you were doing as you wished. But I will not allow myself to believe in these moves that are remembered one moment and forgotten the next. It would have been better if you had felt the pain, as I did, for pain is a consequence——'

But I could keep my face straight no longer. Rather a stupid fellow! Did he think chess was some sort of a miracle? Had I no brains of my own? I *could* play chess without the board, as I could have shown him if he had known anything about the game, and as for that move, did he think the Herr Doktor had posted it to me in some way, like a letter posted in a box and received by me at the other end?

And did he *really* think that the Herr Doktor, the whole length of the house away, could fetch him a whack over the knee like that? It was too much. I burst out laughing.

'Do tell me what he did to you that other time when those other tutors came—you said he tried to dominate you or something——'

But he had drawn himself austerely up. 'I shall tell you nothing more,' he said.

'Sorry,' I said, a little ashamed of myself. 'I didn't mean to laugh. But talk about *me* last night! If you'd only seen yourself, with your hands together like this, saying "And he says there's nothing to do in this house!"'

He reached for Otto's German Grammar. It had exercises in it as well as rules, and opened of itself at 'Aufgabe 12'. He dabbed his large clean forefinger on the page.

'Take this to your place and translate into German,' he ordered me. 'I will teach you German if I may teach you nothing else. Go.'

So I, none too sure of my Kings of England, took as my exercise some dull anecdote of Casimir II of Poland, the father of Casimir the Great, but as you may imagine my thoughts were elsewhere. What fun it would be (I was thinking) if the Herr Doktor really *could* do queer things and would show me the way he went about it!

CHAPTER VIII

ONE day in the early spring—you will notice I seem to be skipping a good many months, but in speaking of this extraordinary physical growth of mine it is convenient to do so, and anything that had happened in between can be picked up presently—one day in the early spring I had come down from the plantation and

was passing the gate of the yard where Minna and Alice were peg-
ging the clothes out on the line. I saw Minna's eyes peeping round
one of Fearnley's shirts at me and heard what she said, namely,
that they would have to be calling me Mr. Peter instead of Master
Peter soon. And I had blushed on occasions before, when I had lied
or been caught red-handed in something, but never quite that kind
of blush. My schoolboy suit was now barely decent on me. Even
Minna had giggled. In the house I went straight to Heinrich. He
made me stand by the study door again. I could now look down on
the mark he had made only a few weeks before.

'It is what I have been thinking,' he said, 'but at this rate you
will grow out of one suit while they are making another. Was your
father a very tall man?'

'No. He was just everybody's size.'

'We shall have to look for a tailor who makes clothes for giants,'
he jested, for he never remembered an injury for long. 'There is
also your appetite. You will be eating the joint off the meat-jack
soon and there will be nothing left for anybody else in the house.
First I shall have to find a tailor who has enough cloth.'

And when a day or two later a tailor came in specially from
the town to display his patterns and run over me with his tape-
measure it was no schoolboy outfit I was going to show to the
world now. Long trousers were going to encase my legs and a hat
such as my father had worn was going to cover my untidy head.
And when in due time these things arrived and I looked at myself
in the glass I felt almost on a footing with Heinrich himself.

My outside now corresponded a little more nearly with the
bursting growth I felt within myself. I am not thinking of chess and
billiards now, but of the enlarged significance to me of everything
about me, and as these things were few in number it was on Heinrich himself that my criticism settled. He, poor fellow, was only
too ready to meet me half-way, for this girl of his in Germany, who
up to then had always been 'a certain person' or 'somebody who is
very dear to me', suddenly acquired a name. It was Anna, and from
his description of her she was a half-angelic creature, of his own
fair and blue-eyed breed and in nature goodness itself descended

upon the earth. I suppose you can't tell from photographs, and the one he showed me didn't strike me as being anything out of the way, but I said nothing, and naturally I had no such confidence to give him in return.

'But her father is the Herr Hofrath,' he sighed, 'and though I have saved money while I have been here it is not yet enough. Would it not be splendid if the Herr Doktor would send us both to Germany, to a family where no English is spoken, so that presently you would speak German as you speak your own tongue!'

And by and by, as the spring went on, it became quite a usual thing for him to look up from one of his interminable letters, and say 'Do you send your greetings to Anna, Struwwelpeter?' to which I would reply 'Yes, please,' and perhaps invent some little message to put him in a good humour.

But he remained good and dull, and I could not forget this bee in his bonnet that he had about the Herr Doktor, of whom he now spoke as little as possible. What reports he made to him of my progress I did not know, but I remembered that he was saving up for his Anna, and guessed that he framed them in such a way as to praise my industry without bringing his job too suddenly to an end. During that time I think I saw the Herr Doktor perhaps twice, each time only for a moment. His end of the house had its own side door. Here of an evening his brougham sometimes waited to take him to the German club in the town. Fearnley drove him, and I had a half-formed idea of trying to use Fearnley as a sort of bridge to the Herr Doktor, but he was big and bearded and taciturn and not at all the sort bridges are made of, and I thought better of it. It would be better to wait and see what turned up.

As I got more and more independent of Heinrich I wanted less and less of his company and more time to think out the new things that were happening in myself. Rapidly as I was growing my strength more than kept pace with my inches, and once you left the plantation behind you you were clear of the smoke of the town too. Only a mile or two farther on the moors began, high and heathery and clean. Heinrich was conscientious, but if I wanted a day to myself I could always invent an excuse that satisfied him.

So to the moors I began to take myself off. I was flushing and tingling with health, twenty miles was little more than an afternoon's walk to me, if I took the day to it I could easily do thirty or thirty-five. Several times I was on the point of setting out for the place, nearly forty miles away, where my nine-year-old sister had gone to live with Margaret's relations, staying there the night, and returning the next day, but something always turned up to prevent me, and I never went. But I had what I wanted most, time to sort out my thoughts, and to make the acquaintance of a Peter Byles who began to loom up inside me as a complete stranger to myself.

I think I told you how at first that chart of the talking hands had haunted me at night, so that I had begged for a night-light to go to sleep by. All this had now gone. Assume for a moment there *was* something out of the ordinary about the Herr Doktor. The chessboard does not cease to be a single thing because one half of it is black and the other white. If a thing is truly extraordinary it is extraordinary by day and night alike, in equal distribution. It was only for the general convenience that at seven o'clock every morning the Herr Doktor's household woke up, the daily round began, and by eleven or so at night everything was still again. In reality there was no such dividing-line. It was after all a long way to the moors. I wanted somewhere in the house itself where I could spend frequent hours alone. I found it. One day Heinrich came on me on the stairs, not that portion of them that descended to the hall, but the flight that led to the parts above. I was carrying a chair.

'What are you doing?' he asked.

'Getting this chair up,' I answered. 'I've found a room nobody seems to use and I don't see why I shouldn't have it.'

'Let me take one end,' he said, and though I could have managed perfectly well without him he gave me a hand with the chair.

The place I had found was one of the two squat turrets that stood one at either end of the house. It was partly furnished, as a box or lumber-room may be said to be furnished. Four windows looked out to the four points of the compass, the southerly one overlooking the town, the one facing it showing only the plantation, and the westerly one looking along the roof itself. On a cheap chest of bedroom drawers stood the two arms that had once supported a looking-glass, there was a packing-case or two, and a rickety table, and I should not have Heinrich always at my elbow. He was walking round, looking out of the windows.

'And what would you do here?' he asked.

'I just want somewhere. At home I always had my attic.'

'There is no fireplace, no light.'

'I can have a lamp.'

But here he was firm—'No, no. There must be no carrying lamps about. A light up here would not be safe, and these last stairs are no more than a ladder.'

'Without a lamp then. It wouldn't interfere with my lessons. It's only for the time I have to myself.'

But presently he turned to me—'I would much rather you did not come up here,' he said.

'Why?' I asked defiantly. 'You do nothing but grumble at me nowadays. Anyway I shall be able to do what I like when you go.'

'What you do when I have gone will be no business of mine, Struwwelpeter.'

'Well, I'm coming up here, and I do wish you'd stop calling me that.'

'Calling you what?'

'Struwwelpeter, as if I was a kid.'

He lowered his head. 'I am sorry. I did not know you disliked the name.'

'It isn't even true now that I've got my hair cut.'

'I say I am sorry.'

'And I'm dashed if I see anything to cry about either,' for I noticed that two tears were keeping the sword-cuts on his cheek company. He flicked them away with his finger.

'We will talk about something else, if you please.'

But the devil was in me that day; it must have been the devil, for I had really no intention of saying what I did. I knew by this time that I could hurt him far worse than he could hurt me, but people shouldn't be as sensitive as all that, and I broke out.

THEN   61

'You tried to stop me playing chess, and you won't talk to me
about the Herr Doktor nor tell me any of the things I want to
know. There's only one thing you will talk about, and that's your
Anna——'

He froze, at least his blue eyes did. He was of course still inches
taller than I was, and he drew himself up. He walked to the door,
and at the top of the flimsy stairs turned.

'It appears that I have talked tiresomely to you. It was my fault.
I should have known better. You too will know one day, and that
some things are too beautiful to be talked about. You will forget
what I said. I will not mention my private affairs to you any more.
I say nothing of the other time, when I was more serious than I
have ever been, and you laughed in my face. You will now have
your lessons as usual, but I will not call you Struwwelpeter any
more. You are not to bring a lamp up here,' and with this last order
he descended the creaking stairs, leaving me alone in my newly-
found chamber. I knew why he didn't want me to come up there
but was afraid to say so. The house, as I say, had two of these
turrets, and by looking out of the western window I could see,
beyond the two big chimney-stacks that crowned the roof-ridge, a
corner of the other one. It was the one immediately over the Herr
Doktor's quarters.

I knew that I had gone a bit too far, and it was not a very comfortable thought that he would never call me Struwwelpeter again,
but I wasn't going to be the first to make it up this time. Anyway I should now have my eyrie to myself, and I looked round it
with an air of possession and privacy. Attics and the upper parts
of houses have always had for me a fascination of their own. Even
to-day I think that when Ugolino and his sons died in a lofty tower,
surrounded by light and space, with people able to look up and
see them from below, it was far more horrible than if they had
been thrown into the deepest dungeon. And all in a moment I felt
myself singularly free in spirit. Up there I was my own master,
could do as I liked. And—this was all in a moment, I say, the very
moment when Heinrich turned his back on me—I knew what it
was I intended to do. One night very soon I intended to steal up

quietly, climb out of the western window, creep along by the parapet to the other turret, and see for myself what there was to be
seen in the Herr Doktor's part of the house.

No sooner had I conceived the idea than it fastened itself upon
me. I could not sleep for thinking of it that night, it followed me
about the next day, came between me and my Otto, peeped at
me round corners of the shrubbery (for the thought of the moors
repelled me, there now seemed so much to do in that house),
and floated before my eyes again when I got to bed. And let me
explain what I mean by 'floated'. There had never been anything
the matter with my eyes. Show me an object and it is as plain to
me as it is to anybody else. But take it away again and I have never
been able to recall it with anything like the same clearness. It is
not even the same size or in the same position, but always a little
smaller and a little higher up to the left. So it was when I tried to
recall the image of the Herr Doktor. The reflection of my own
hands and face in the blackness of my turret-pane at night (for
you may be sure I wasn't up there very long without a light) was
more substantial than anything I was able to conjure up of him.
It seemed a year since I had seen him. I must see him again, face
to face, or if I couldn't see him at least find out a great deal more
about him. My mind was made up almost before Heinrich could
have got as far as his own room. And so let me come to my first
tentative roof-adventure.

It was on a mild night without moon and only a faint dust of
light over the distant town. It would not have done to risk my new
clothes, so in my shirt and outgrown knickers only I climbed over
the sill of the window and slid down the slope to the gutter, which
was guarded by the low parapet and choked with pine-needles and
dead leaves. On the ridge above me towered the two chimney-
stacks, and I made my way past them, but stopped, wondering
whether anybody below had heard me, as a loose slate slipped
and clattered down under the hand I steadied myself with. I came
abreast of the second turret, scrambled up to its eastern window,
and looked in. There was nothing at all to be seen. The interior
was the counterpart of my own, and apparently used for the same

purpose, the dumping of broken or unrequired objects. I could make out what I took to be a couple of newish wooden packing-cases, probably the same I had seen on the railway-company's cart, but even of this I could not be sure. I made my way round the outside. All four windows were securely fastened, and there was nothing for me to do but to make my way back to my own end of the house again.

But descending to my bedroom, where I had left the lamp turned low, I caught sight of myself in the glass. With a busy smoky town only a couple of miles away you may imagine the state the roof was in, and I was grimed to the eyes as black as a collier. I did the best I could over my basin before getting into bed, but I should have to manage better than that, and the first thing I should need would be a light.

On the following afternoon, having first watched Mrs. Pitt out of the way, I tiptoed through her parlour to the pantry where the stores and provisions were kept, in search of candles. Heinrich had forbidden me a lamp, but he had forgotten about candles. I opened cupboard after cupboard, and my head was deep in one of them when a voice suddenly cried, 'What are you doing there?' I started, and then remembered the parrot; but a 'Well I never!' followed in a voice that was not in the least like the parrot's, and I swung round. Minna was standing there watching me.

'*Mister* Peter!' she said in a shocked voice.

But as it was only Minna, and not Mrs. Pitt, I made sure of my candles, and giving her a look to say nothing closed the cupboard again. But she was still looking at me as if she wouldn't have believed such a thing of me. She was small and dark-haired and mischievous-looking, and once when I had seen her dressed for going into the town I had thought for the moment she was some visitor.

'You with your fingers in the store-cupboard, Mr. Peter!' she said.

'They're for Herr Opfer,' I told her.

'*I* should think so!'

'Well, shut up about it and I'll give you something on your

birthday,' I said, and she flattened herself against the door-jamb to make room for me to pass, though there was no reason why she shouldn't have just stepped back. And I was turning along the passage when she called after me as loudly as she dared.

'Mr. Peter!'

'Well?' I said, stopping, and as she didn't answer, 'Well?' I said again.

But she only laughed, and retorted 'How many wells make a river—as many as you could count for ever!' and skipped off the other way.

But I had my candles, and from an unused bedroom I borrowed a small looking-glass, a jug and a basin. I had stuffed the shirt and knickers of my first expedition into the chest of drawers in the turret, and was now ready. Except for my German lessons I had passed completely out of Heinrich's charge. It was not likely that he would go to the Herr Doktor and tell him there was nothing more he could teach me. The Herr Doktor himself made no sign. Very well. The next step was coming from me.

CHAPTER IX

T HE roof was much the easiest way. Downstairs was always in darkness after the household had gone to bed, there would be doors to open, matches to strike, and for all I knew the parrot might hear me and twang on his cage and ask me what I was doing. But outside on the slates would be perfectly simple. A second trip had shown me where the tricky places were, and there would be all the light I wanted in the sky, for the night I finally chose for my prowl was just such a one as I had always associated with the Herr Doktor's bald head at home—ragged silver-edged clouds southward over the town, with the moon swimming in and out among them. I had discovered that one of the windows could be opened from the outside with a penknife blade, and once inside I thought I should be able to find my way. The uppermost stairs would descend to the top floor of the house. The next flight would end on the same floor as that occupied by Heinrich and myself. And somewhere on that floor the Herr Doktor would be, for there was nothing below but the billiard-room and the domestic quarters.

I moved quietly because of the servants just underneath. The two chimney-stacks on the ridge had a very grim and fortress-like look above me, but I got past them and reached the window of the second turret. I opened it with my penknife and climbed noiselessly in. Inside was not in the least dark; past the lumber stacked against the walls the door at the head of the stairs glimmered a dingy white, and I tiptoed to it. If I heard sounds below I should know whether they were waking or sleeping ones. If everything was quiet I supposed I should have to return by the way I had come. Anyway here I was.

What it was on the stairs that I tripped over I did not know. I only know that half-way down them my foot stumbled against something, I shot out my hand to the flimsy rail but missed it, and finished my descent in a headlong neck-and-crop tumble to the bottom. There, half stunned, on the bare boards of a narrow whitewashed passage, I lay with my eyes closed, thinking of nothing.

But after some time, I do not know how long, my eyes opened of themselves. Somewhere below a light was moving. It grew brighter, and from the way in which the magnified shadow of a portion of the handrail spread and passed across the whitewashed wall it was a lamp or candle carried in the hand. Then I blinked, for the light itself appeared, the bright reflector of a lamp, level with the floor on which I lay, shining full on my face. There rose as if out of the ground the Herr Doktor's tasselled smoking-cap, followed by the two blank lozenges of his round silver spectacles. These things I watched with detached interest, as if they were no particular business of mine but might be amusing to tell somebody about afterwards. The lenses were turned on me. Lastly into this little trap-door-and-candlebox drama a finger rose. It beckoned me down. Finger, spectacles and smoking-cap dropped below the level of my sight again, and the light died away somewhere below.

Presently I was able to prop myself up on one numbed elbow and to run my hand over other portions of my body. But I didn't get up all at once. It was half seated that I shuffled down the next flight, and then, shakily upright again, found myself at the end of a passage half-way along which was the light from a partly-opened door. As I approached this I became conscious of a familiar and forgotten smell. It was the smell of my father's den, the smell of tobacco and toddy and cosy stuffiness. I stood in the doorway, looking into the room.

I learned well enough later how that room was furnished. It was very much my own study turned the other way round, and it had chairs and tables and objects on the mantelpiece and curtains at the windows like other rooms. Also it seemed to me it had an unusual number of clocks, for in my swimming head was a confused crepitation and tick-tocking. But all these surroundings seemed to fall back to make room for one piece of furniture only. It was the pendulum Heinrich had told me about, and as I am not shaken and dazed now I will try to describe it.

A strong hook had been fixed into the middle of the ceiling, and from this a rope descended that ended in a heavy iron weight a few inches from the floor. But the rope did not descend from ceiling to floor without interruption. A light wooden frame perhaps a couple of feet square broke the continuity of it. Free to swing in this square was a smaller weight, of a pound or two only, and through the square's opening, but clear of it and with its feet firmly on the floor, ran a narrow table with a card on it and a thin glass pen filled with ink. The whole apparatus was gently in motion, smoothly and complicatedly swinging a few inches either way as weight acted against weight, and with his eyes fixed on the pen the Herr Doktor was leaning forward from a deep lug-chair, his empty porcelain pipe clawed in his left hand.

It is because he seemed already to have forgotten my arrival that I wish to call your attention to just a few of the things he took not the slightest notice of. He had just found me, not much more than half conscious, lying at the foot of a breakneck flight of wooden stairs. In his slippers and smoking-cap, with a reflector lamp in his hand, he had come up to see what was the matter, had seen who it was, and had beckoned me down. Now, with the back of my head humming and unnaturally warm, so that I put my hand to it to see if there was any blood, I was standing before him, a grotesque, hobbledehoy figure neither boy nor man, in a grimed shirt and a pair of outgrown knickerbockers that only reached half-way down my thighs, showing my great bony blackened knees. With a hand also as black as a chimney-sweep's I was trying to keep my balance by holding on to the back of a chair. Yet he did not even lift his eyes. They were rigidly fixed on that rhythmically-moving apparatus, that wrote as it went, for ever changing its mind and then returning to the same orbit as before. It began to slow down. He put out a hand. He lifted the slender glass pen as nowadays one lifts a needle from a gramophone-disc. He stopped the weight, and with his slippered feet checked the heavy one under the table. Then, with his empty pipe nestling in his greying beard, he removed the card and sat looking at it.

'Please Herr Doktor,' I said faintly, clean forgetting all my lessons and that he couldn't hear a word I said, 'can I have a glass of water?'

Still there might have been nobody but himself in the room. His wrist crept forward out of its sleeve as he picked up another card from the floor, where half a dozen of them lay scattered. He compared the two. And anyone who has ever seen a compound pendulum knows that while time shall last no two of those patterns can ever be alike. They can no more be alike than the billiard-ball, after a thousand years of motion, can come to rest in any spot but the one appointed for it. You have seen the engine-turned weavings on the back of a watch, the watering of banknotes. These had the same cold and implacable finality. Five-pointed and six-pointed they were, strangely flower-like, but flowers from a garden tended by no human hand. They were the flowers of gravity and weight and law, and human accident could not touch them.

But human accident *had* touched one of them. Still without looking at me, but showing awareness of my presence for the first time, the Herr Doktor held out for my taking the two cards he had been comparing. And dizzy as I was I could see that while one of them was perfect the other had a flaw. It was such a flaw as Heinrich's left cheek carried, a scratch on a gramophone-disc, marring the music for ever. Then only did he look at me. From my rubber-soled sandshoes up the whole of my half-dressed figure his gaze passed, and then up again past the corner of the ceiling in the direction of the floor above.

And as his finger pointed I remembered what Heinrich had said about vibrations. *I*, he was telling me, had caused that flaw. I had caused it by my fall, and the unerring apparatus had paused for a moment to write down my accusation before moving on its way again.

Now I do not know what manner of man may read this tale of mine. He may be one who will say, 'Come, come, let us look at the facts. Here we have a lout of a lad, none too amiable in disposition, who falls foul of his tutor and prowls about roofs when he is supposed to be in bed. He has a fall, and this Herr Doktor has a pendulum, about which there is nothing more mysterious than there is about the whipping-tops and marbles the boy was playing with this time last year. The pendulum records the fall, for what else can it do? If he had not fallen it would have told the Herr Doktor nothing, and look at the size of him! He comes like a sack of coals down a ladder, enough to bring the ceiling down, so what is he standing there for with a colourless face? Let him go to the house-keeper and get something for that bump on his head. If this tutor is the credulous fool he says he is the sooner he goes the better. And let the lad join the army or run away to sea if he can find nothing better to do.' It may be, I say, that I shall have such a reader as this.

But as the Herr Doktor pointed upwards with his finger, and then, getting up out of his chair, looked me steadily in the face for the first time during all the months I had been in his house, I took an involuntary step back. For what was this? *This* had nothing to do with pendulums, this that he was doing now. His face drew a little nearer, so that the tassel of his smoking-cap fell a little forward. The lamp beside the pendulum seemed to be playing tricks with his silver spectacles. In the eyes behind them two tiny points seemed to come alive, like the lights of approaching carriage-candles a mile away in the night. They drew nearer, and for a moment I seemed to hear Heinrich's voice again, also a very long way off, saying that the Herr Doktor had tried to do something—something—to dominate—to dom—— Did he always sit up as late as this, or was this a special occasion? (His finger-tips were moving before my eyes.) Did his pendulum always hang in the middle of the room like that? If so, I thought, it must be very much in the way. (The carriage-lamps were now so near that they became one, lamps that squinted, and I had a queer feeling that I was squinting myself.) And even supposing that he had been expecting me, why should he want me in the middle of the night?

Then the lights ceased to dazzle. They became soft, smooth, faintly-hued rings, as the bits of coloured paper blend on a whipped top. He pointed to my lips. I might talk though he could not, and from the movements of my lips he would understand.

But not in a thousand years would you guess the words that broke from me.

'Yes, I know he's a fool, Herr Doktor, but you did punish him,' I heard my own voice saying.

Then this 'end' to which Heinrich's teaching had been directed became as plain as day. He was questioning me, as Heinrich had said he would question me, not in words, but by some medium of understanding that spoke for itself. True, *I* must speak in words. I must speak not only my own words, but his also, repeating them after him that he might be satisfied that I had received his thought. 'You have understood?' he was asking me. 'Then say it after me, for I must be sure.'

'Yes, Herr Doktor, I have understood.'

And so began as strange a conversation as a man could wish to be present at or to run away from, I taking both parts as if I had been an interpreter. To make it plainer I will put my version of what the Herr Doktor said in italics.

'*You say he is a fool?*'

'Yes, Herr Doktor, but he knows he's a fool, and that's something.'

'*But there must be fools. It is the fools who do the work of the world and therefore think they ought to govern it.*'

'Yes, Herr Doktor.'

'*Then why should he be punished?*'

'For being a fool, Herr Doktor.'

He nodded. '*Fool as he is I see he has taught you quite well.*'

'Oh, he isn't a fool at his job, but I don't think I need him now.'

'*Then there is no reason why he should stay?*'

'No, Herr Doktor—I mean yes,' for as the whipped top began to wobble a little my mind was desperately struggling. 'I—I don't know it all yet—he thinks it would be a good thing if I went to Germany and lived with a German family for a bit—and for a fool he isn't a bad sort——'

'*You mean you would like him to stay a little longer?*'

'Yes, Herr Doktor,' and there was a pause.

Then, with hardly a movement, he indicated the sleeping town two miles away. Somehow too his eyes seemed at the same time to be bent on a chessboard.

'*You remember me at your father's house?*'

'Yes, Herr Doktor. You watched them play from behind the lamp.'

'*You play?*'

The question surprised me a little. 'Why, you know I do. You saw me playing downstairs in the hall.'

'*What was the move, not a pawn-move, you should have played?*'

'Knight to Queen's square and mate in three,' I answered promptly.

'*You are sure?*'

'Positive.'

'*And you wish him to stay?*' He meant Heinrich.

'I think so.'

'*Then he shall stay a little longer. But he must behave himself. Why did you come by the roof?*'

'I don't know—just fun——'

'*That thing,*' he nodded to the pendulum, '*told me.*'

'No, Herr Doktor,' I said quickly. 'It only told you I fell. You knew I was coming without that.'

'*You have grown. You are twice the size. You feel well?*'

'Rather. I walked thirty-two miles the other day.'

'*You eat well? Sleep well? You feel no ache? No pain?*'

'Ache? Pain? No. But please, Herr Doktor, can I have a drink of water?'

He looked at me approvingly. '*Good. For a beginning it is very good. It is better even than I expected. Go and get it,*' and he pointed across the passage to his bedroom.

The window of his bedroom was heavily curtained, but by the light from his door across the passage I found his washstand and gulped down a glass of water. I was filling the glass again when the light began to fail. The next moment I was standing in total darkness, for he had closed his door. Evidently it was his good night. But out in the passage I knew my way to the stairs, and with my hand on the wall I felt my way to them. I mounted them; the white-washed wall glimmered in front of me, I was on the spot where the Herr Doktor had found me. Up to the turret again I climbed. Soft moonlight filled it, the window by which I had entered stood open. Putting my leg over the sill I was out on the roof again.

Then reaction came. It came as my head began to throb again while the rest of my body shivered. What had happened? What was I doing on a roof, in clothing that barely covered me, in the small hours of the morning? Nay, who was I? For some fellow I had known all my life, a fellow called Peter Byles, who had always been close to my side, seemed to have left me. It didn't matter what sort of a fellow he had been; I had got used to his company, and the place where he had been seemed horribly, horribly draughty and empty without him. '*I am* Peter Byles!' I wanted to cry, but I knew that I wasn't. I was a stranger to myself, a Peter Byles who called people fools, and said that because they were fools they ought to be punished. Fools, I had agreed with the Herr Doktor, must not think that because they did the work of the world they were therefore fit to govern it. I had remembered that chess-move again, nay, had remembered more than I had previously known, for I had added that it was mate in three. I had even corrected the Herr Doktor himself, for when he had said that the pendulum had told him of my arrival I had said that he had known I was there without that. Where had these things come from, and what was it that the Herr Doktor had done to me with his eyes? I was still outside the turret window, my feet on the sloping roof, my arm along the sill. I saw him rising slowly from his chair. I saw those eyes again, like carriage-candles in the distance, coming nearer, squinting together into one, while I squinted too. I saw his fingers making swift little passes, then pausing, to judge of my condition. Mesmerism they called it, domination, and it was what he had done to Heinrich and perhaps to those other tutors too.

And, without even a Peter Byles I could call myself, a panic, a dementia of loneliness took me. I slid down to the leaf-choked gutter and began to stumble blindly forward. The moon had moved westwards over the town, but it was not lonelier among its clouds than I, my body shivering on that swaying roof while a vast and timeless cold seemed to have frozen my self away. I thought of the pendulum. It did not even tell the time; it made nothing of time; yet I could not fall down a few stairs but it had its tale to tell about me. It was unendurable. In my terror I wanted to hide myself, and I have no recollection of how I regained my own turret. Careless of whether I made a noise or not I scrambled in and shut the window fast behind me.

But half-way down the turret stairs I nearly had my second fall that evening, for at the bottom of them stood something dimly, greyly white. My heart gave another jump as I saw that it moved and was alive. It also had a nightgown, and bare feet, and a pair of arms into which, big as I was, I flung myself sobbing.

'Mr. Peter! Quiet! Don't make that noise—ssh—they'll hear you——'

'Oh—I don't want to be alone——' I cried, as my terrified sister had cried.

But she held me against her with her hand over my mouth. A yard or two along the passage was a closed door. 'Alice!' her lips shaped as my own had talked to the Herr Doktor. But there was another door, partly open just beyond.

'Sssssh now! You shan't be alone!'

She pushed me through the second door and tiptoed in after me. At any other time I could have broken that softly-yielding body in two, but in its warmth and welcome all my strength now lay. She put her finger to her lips again and fastened the door. I was safe.

And what did it matter that my own bed had brass knobs at its corners while hers was only a cheap truckle of cast-iron? She put me into it. Presently her mouth was on mine, and gradually I ceased to shiver.

'Are you frightened now?'

'N—no—'

The light was creeping in at her window when she sat up, her hair about her face and shoulders. She shook me gently.

'Mr. Peter!' she whispered in my ear. 'Mr. Peter! Wake up— they'll be stirring presently—whatever you do don't make a sound—you'd better go down to your own bed now——'

CHAPTER X

I⊤ was midday when I awoke, to find Heinrich standing by my bedside, looking down on me with an expressionless face.

'Are you not feeling well?' he asked.

'Not very,' I said.

'I have been in three times but you did not hear me. Would you like me to send for a doctor?'

'No, I'll get up,' I said, and out he went.

But you see what it was that I had again forgotten. The moment he had gone I shot the bolt of my door and went to the glass. I won't try to describe the face that looked back at me. I glanced at my pillow. Heaven knows what Minna's bed was like, but the state of my own would not have to be seen by Mrs. Pitt. And Heinrich had been in three times, to watch me at his leisure while I slept, and had gone out without a word. Now what?

One thought only filled my head. That haggard, haunted night with its stark termination was a thing to be at all costs kept at arm's length for the present. But here it was, back already, and my very first thought made me quail. For that night would not allow itself to be divided into two portions as conveniently as that. The halves of it were interlocked so inextricably that it became a single thing, with two faces, the one white and ghostly with fear, the other red and burning with the experience in which the ghost had been laid. And he had been in three times without waking me. What now?

My first almost overmastering impulse was to run to him, just as I stood, and to tell him everything, everything. He would understand, for could there now be any doubt that *he* had seen those carriage-lights too, first glimmering half a mile away, then advancing, mingling, stupefying, mesmerising? Did he not know all about it without my telling him, and knowing more than I, had been able to save himself? There was no fear of these things that I did not now share with him. He had been right when he had said that it is better to see men die than to see me as he had come upon me in the hall that afternoon, struck stiff by some power at a distance and staring at nothing. This was my first impulse.

But the rest? How much of that *could* I tell him? What about Minna? Must I think of her as a nauseating delight, as a delight at all? Had she not rather come between me and the terror that walks by night, and for that must she be told to pack her box and take herself off? And what about Heinrich himself? Even though I had recalled my words the very next moment I had called him a fool, and that surely meant that his departure was now only a matter of weeks, perhaps of days. Was I to tell him that? Even if I avoided it would he not question me, give me no rest till he had got it out of me, all? Would it not be a thousand times better to tell him nothing?

And as I stood there irresolute, racking my wretched brains, even the quandary began to provide its glimmer of a solution. To tell him all was out of the question; the alternative was to tell him nothing; but to gain even a little time might be something. With time I should be able to conciliate him, show myself obedient and humble and submissive, win his affection back again. It was damnable to think that because of me he might not be able to marry his Anna. Behind my locked door I washed myself thoroughly and poured the black water into the bucket. I wondered which of them would come in to make my bed. Alice probably, because if Minna felt as I did she wouldn't want to see me ever again. No, Minna would make it, for her own was the same and she wouldn't want everybody to know. But as I put on my grown-up clothes again it was of neither Minna nor Alice that I was thinking, but of Anna—Anna and his long letters to her. No doubt they were full of things about me, for he couldn't find many things to write about in the Herr Doktor's house. My thoughts began to clear. I must win his confidence again, and in some way or other must make Anna my olive-branch. In the meantime I wanted nothing but to get out of the house with all speed.

When I got downstairs he was nowhere to be seen. So much the better. I wanted to be alone, for the time had not come yet when not to be alone for a single hour of the day became the most urgent need of my life.

How long this state of things would have lasted I do not know, for it was at eight o'clock that very same evening, as he sat at his table writing, that he unconsciously played straight into my hands. He must have heard me come into the room but he had not looked up. Wishing to be noticed I none the less sat as obstinately silent. But suddenly he did look up, and it was an unexpected question that he put to me.

'Do you often write to your little sister?' he said.

'Not very often,' I confessed, wondering what had put Nora into his head.

'When did you last write to her?'

Here was my chance for propitiation, and I took it. 'I haven't written to her since before my birthday,' I said. 'You know we talked about whether she was to come to the party, and you said it was a long way and they were all boys and she would be the only girl. I know I ought to have written again.'

'She has nobody but you.'

'I know I've been a beast. I will write to her, Heinrich, I truly

will. Are you—' it was hideously difficult, but I managed to get it
out, 'are you writing to Anna?'

He looked at me as if he was comparing my face with the one
he had seen on my pillow that morning. 'Why do you ask that?'

'Will you please remember me to her?'

He put down his pen. 'You ask to be remembered to her?'

'Yes,' I said, my eyes downcast. 'I've been a beast about Nora
and I've been a beast about Anna, too. I've been rotten to everybody. Sometimes I just don't seem able to help it.'

'I may then again speak of Anna to you?'

'Aren't you ever going to forget that, that I only said it because
I was in a bad temper?' I said, and in a moment all his resentment
was gone. His whole face lighted up.

'It was for you to speak first, Peter. Now you have spoken and
see, I have already forgotten it. Never, never will I remember it
again. Now you make not only me happy, but Anna too, for I have
had to tell her I was sad. So we are all friends again, *nicht wahr?*'

'I've been miserable too,' I said.

'It is past. All is forgotten. Would you like to hear what Anna
said only last week?' and he unlocked a drawer and fetched out her
letters.

And oh, how different it was hearing him talk about his Anna
now, so different that I did not realise at the time that with almost
every word he said the gulf that had opened between us yawned
wider and wider. I gathered that she had not yet promised to
make him the happiest man who walked the earth, but that was
the man's part, to be faithful and patient and gentle and understanding. It was sometimes a mistake to set even the woman you
loved too high above the world, he said. They must eat, and wear
clothes, and had their daily tasks to do, and perhaps sometimes
lost their tempers a little. We must not expect perfection. But even
so it was all very beautiful, he said, very beautiful and wonderful,
and seeing his face beautiful too I could only make my clumsy
little joke.

'But you aren't going to cry about things being beautiful, are
you?' for for a moment he looked almost like it, and it was not

in the least like my last rebuff, for he saw the joke and burst out laughing.

'Listen to him!' he said, laughing all over. 'I am talking a lot of nonsense, *ja*? You think that if she is as I say her place is up there?' and he pointed upwards, but a long, long way past Minna's garret. 'But you will see, Struwwelpeter! One day you will come to me and say "Heinrich, a wonderful thing has happened to me, a thing that I did not think possible," and you will tell me exactly what I am telling you now,' and he chuckled, as if clever as I thought myself there were things that even I did not know yet.

With Heinrich calling me Struwwelpeter again the tension of my life was eased a little, but it was not to any former life that within a week I had returned. Indeed I cannot think of that all too brief interval as anything but a pause and a marking time, as if my thoughts were an advancing regiment that must wait for the stragglers before moving forward again. Until this should happen I wanted distraction, and I wanted it away from the Herr Doktor's house.

For amusement young people to-day go to the pictures. They do not see their actors, but the shadows of actors on a screen, the same shadows doing the same things in half the cities of a hemisphere. The music they hear is not made in their presence, but has already been played to complicated instruments, that enlarge and multiply it a thousand times over. But the pictures of my day were the frigid canvases on the walls of the town's Municipal Art Gallery. They were the watercolours by local celebrities that the picture-framers displayed in their windows, or occasionally, if you were an adult and male and had a shilling, an oil-painting of a recumbent lady called Nana, shown without publicity in a specially half-lighted back room. And we saw our music besides hearing it, the busy fiddles, the grunting double-basses, the fellow at the drum. In the winter, when the great orchestras came and the famous singers, Albani and Patti, Foli and Reeves, the young men and women of the town formed the greater part of the chorus. But in the summer we sought out music in the public Park, and it cost you nothing unless you liked to throw a penny into the sheet. It was this lack of pence that now began to trouble me.

For in the Herr Doktor's house everything was found for me.
A tailor came from the town to measure me for my clothes, and
if I required anything for my studies Heinrich saw to it. A shilling
a week, indeed, I had for myself, but somehow or other I always
seemed to owe it to Heinrich for odds and ends he had got me,
and where was the amusement in walking a couple of miles into
the town, seeing everybody going about their business but myself,
looking in the shop windows at things I couldn't buy, and then
walking home again? And the town was a cheerful, brisk, sensible sort of place, where people had their normal faculties, not a
couple short and heaven knows what unguessable thing to make
up. The only pendulums there were the pendulums of the clocks
in the shops, and carriage-lamps belonged to carriages, not to the
spectacles on people's noses.

But, as I say, the town without money was a poor outing, and
money only the Herr Doktor could supply.

'But what would you do with it?' Heinrich asked, for he could
only think of one use for money, and her name was Anna.

'Vic Tenison goes to an office. He has four shillings a week for
himself, and Mr. Tenison isn't rich like the Herr Doktor. A bob a
week's rotten. Look at the size of me!'

'I am not the judge,' he replied. 'If I were perhaps you should
go to an office and have four shillings a week like your friend. But
I am not the judge.'

'I wouldn't mind going to an office. Anything's better than
being here all the time. Even the servants have their afternoon off.
How long's it going on?'

'The Herr Doktor does not tell me his plans. How much are
seats in the theatre?'

'Two shillings in the pit and a shilling in the gallery, and both
Vic and Wilf go every week.'

'It is true you had a holiday with your sister last summer, and in
the summer those who can do so like to take holidays. But if the
Herr Doktor were to give permission for you to go to Germany
would not that be a holiday, and one that would cost a great deal
of money?'

'Well, he's got lots, and if he won't let me go and earn some he ought to give me some himself.' (Besides, I thought, for after all I had begged the Herr Doktor to let him stay a little longer and already my treason was beginning to hurt me less, it wouldn't be much of a holiday to go to Germany and have him on one side of me all day and Anna on the other.)

'A shilling in the gallery, did you say? From the gallery does one see well?'

I could see what was in his mind. He was going to offer to take me, paying for me himself, but he thought it over again, and said nothing. Yet now that the subject was raised the opportunity was too good to be lost, and suddenly I appealed to him.

'But look, Heinrich. I can't go to him because—because I haven't to go till I'm sent for.' (I got this out rather hurriedly, without looking at him.) 'You said if I wanted anything you'd ask him for me. Well, I want to have pocket-money like everybody else. A bob a week! It isn't fair!'

And before you dismiss me as a callous young hound for deliberating making use of him like this, remember that the very roots of my being had recently been loosened, and that the town was the readiest way back to myself again. It was not that I had been mesmerised. It was not Minna. It was not even the pendulum, though that was getting a little nearer. It was that sense of the vast indifference of things descending on me for the first time as I had groped my way back along that moonlit roof. It was the thought that leaves its mark on all of us, that we are only one of millions such as ourselves, living on only one of the millions of worlds that fill the sky. I wanted the company of the town because of the feeling that then if one was annihilated all would be annihilated together. And after a while Heinrich spoke.

'I will go to him,' he said. 'It is not pleasant to me, but it is my duty, because I think you are right. He will not let you go to an office, but he should not make you different. I look at you and cannot believe you are only thirteen. It is a miracle, and I do not understand it, but it is not for me to judge. I will tell him what you say to-morrow.'

'In the morning?' I asked eagerly.

'I will go to him after the morning lesson.'

In brief, he did so. He returned with a face so scared that I feared for a moment the worst had happened and he had been sacked on the spot for his temerity, but he gave a dazed little nod. Five shillings perhaps a week had been the utmost that I had dared to hope for, but what had taken Heinrich's breath away was that I was to have, not five shillings, but a pound, and as he himself was paid monthly and his wages happened to be due I found myself with four golden sovereigns in the palm of my hand. It was a full minute before I could do anything but gape at them; then an 'Oh! Do tell me what he said!' broke from me.

'He not only agreed. He agreed readily. If you had not asked he was about to give it to you,' he said.

'But haven't I to buy something out of it, collars or handker-chiefs or something?' Even Vic had to do this.

'He did not say so. It's a month in advance. It is a great deal of money. Many thousands of poor people in this town must keep their families on less money than you will have each week. I do not know what to think.'

But I knew what I thought. Delirious with joy I thought of the cheerful crowded streets, the shops, the theatre, lights, laughter, life. So should my bruised thirteen-year-old roots make fast their hold again.

CHAPTER XI

OUR town was one that employed much young female labour. In those days the knocker-up rattled with his long stick on the bedroom windows at half-past five in the morning, and lying in my bed, if I happened to wake early enough, I could hear the distant whews and buzzers, urgent and uplifted and prolonged, as if the very stones of the factories called the operatives to their toil. In the daytime the girls wore shawls over their heads and clogs on their feet, but if they rose early they knocked off early too, changed their clothes, and came out at the end of the day like evening-blooming flowers.

And I told you that our summer music was the band in the large public Park.

From the main gates a broad path ran between shrubs and variously-shaped flowerbeds, with blackened statues of the town's benefactors at intervals, each with his name and achievements on its red granite base. This path ended on a sort of plateau-terrace, in the middle of which was the raised octagonal bandstand. This was the vortex. About its circumference the older people sat, and there circled slowly and unceasingly past them the youth of the town. The readiest way to count the revolutions of this human wheel was to make a note of one dressed-up damsel and to wait for her to come round again.

It was here, on a pleasant May evening, that Vic and I were walking, with Wilf and a fellow called Pat a few paces ahead of us. This Pat was a tall slack-mouthed fellow with a facetious tongue and a cheeky eye for everybody who passed. But I was not on the lookout for individual charms. The more people and the louder and gayer the music the better I liked it. But suddenly I saw Pat give Wilf's arm a shake and heard him say, 'Look, those are the two.'

'Where?' said Wilf.

'There. They've seen us. A bit of a racer I call her—no, you chump, not the one with the flowers in her hat, the other. Edge out a bit and wait till they come round again.'

But I had seen too, and didn't in the least want to wait till they came round again. The bit of a racer was Minna.

Somehow it seemed utterly unfair that she should be there. She belonged to the house, and in the house it had not been difficult to avoid her. I had always been busily doing something or other whenever she came into the room where Heinrich and I sat. I didn't come to the town to be reminded of the things I had left behind me, and by the time she and her companion came round again my face was turned the other way.

'Isn't there somewhere else we can go?' I said to Vic. 'I'm tired of this.'

'I've only got a tanner.'

'I've plenty. Let's go to the theatre.'

'It's half over by now.'

'Somewhere else then. I'll pay.'

'Perhaps Pat'll know somewhere.'

Pat did. I had only heard of the music-hall he mentioned, but I didn't care where we went as long as we got out of the Park. The way was all downhill and by walking quickly we could be there in less than a quarter of an hour. I grabbed Vic's arm, and we left the vortex and its music and stepped out. Wilf and Pat followed twenty yards behind.

The music-hall cost me four shillings for the four of us, but I didn't pay very much attention to the performance. I saw people laughing, and laughed too, but the more I laughed the more something inside me seemed to be asking what there was to laugh at. And slowly a frightful thought crept into my mind: suppose she should have discovered she was going to have a baby! Hand in hand with my abnormal growth lingered these vestiges of infantility. And though the thought died down the fringes of it remained with me. There kept tapping me as it were on the shoulder an invisible Minna, not dressed as a bit of a racer for the bandstand, nor in her print house-frock carrying a brush or a dustpan, but a Minna in bare feet and a cotton nightgown, who at the foot of the turret stairs had held me up from falling, and whispered to me not to make a sound, and promised me I should not be alone. I had paid four shillings to get away from these things, yet here she was.

I had not thought of it as a thing that would never happen again, or for that matter as a thing that might easily happen again. I had simply done my utmost not to think of it at all. But what was the good of pretending to myself that it hadn't happened? I remembered her words to Alice as they had pegged out the washing, that they would have to be calling me Mister Peter soon. I remembered her 'How many wells make a river?' and the way she had flattened herself in the doorway for me to brush past her. And Pat's roving eye had rested on her, and Pat was not the sort of fellow to let the grass grow under his feet in matters of that kind. She had seen me, and Wilf and Vic had been at my birthday party, and it was all mixed up together in the beastliest sort of way. She might say something to one of them. Pat might come nudging me in the ribs some time, leering, and saying, 'Hey, young Byles, you aren't a bit of a dark horse by any chance, are you?' Perhaps I had started her on the road to ruin. She might end up in the workhouse or drown herself in the canal. What was the good of pretending? There it was.

The interval came. Pat, it appeared, though he had let me pay for him, had a half-crown in his pocket, and the place had a bar. At meal times Heinrich sometimes allowed me a glass of beer, always with a 'Prosit' or 'Gesundheit ist besser wie Krankheit', and the look in his eyes that meant Anna. At the bar Pat paid for four glasses of beer, which was eightpence. Vic had only sixpence, Wilf had just bought an ounce of tobacco, so I paid for four more, and for a time we were quite lively. But the whole evening seemed stupid to me now, and as the bar began to empty and people to move back to their seats I said something about having a headache.

'Headaches? We don't have them till the morning,' said Pat.

'I'm getting along home anyway. I'm tired.'

'Why, the Comical Carlos haven't come on yet—they're a treat——'

But even the Comical Carlos weren't going to keep me, and I left them there and made my way to the square where the steam-tram started.

It was getting on for ten o'clock, and Heinrich had lent me his key, but I knew he wouldn't go to bed till I got in. The tram moreover only took me half-way home. While it continued on its way I had to get off at a point where largish houses set back in gardens began. These were succeeded by a half-country lane with dark trees that made overhead tunnels at intervals, black holes with the road appearing again beyond. After this all was open, with nothing but hedges and fields as far as the Herr Doktor's house.

I had walked perhaps half the distance and was entering the last tunnel of trees when it happened. A slight shape came suddenly forward out of the shadow of the hedge and stood before me on the grass. It was a transparent black night, with many stars, and I could distinguish the outline of her face. But why should she say 'Mr. Peter' in that frightened way? Had something happened? Had she seen some unnerving accident? Had somebody molested her, or was she merely afraid to go through the tunnel of trees alone?

'What's the matter?' I asked, for I could see her brows knotted together.

'What time is it?'

'Nearly twenty past ten.'

'Oh——'

Then I realised what the trouble was. Even fear is a matter of scale. She had to be in at ten o'clock, and she was shaking in her shoes at the thought of Mrs. Pitt.

'Do you mean you'll get into a row for being late?'

'She locks everything up at ten, and that parrot——'

'All right, don't take on like that. I've got a key. I can let you in by the front door and you can slip your things off and she won't know you haven't been in all the time. But——' I stopped. Heinrich would be waiting up, but I didn't want to say that this time it must be she who mustn't make a noise.

Without more words we fell into step side by side.

Mrs. Pitt as an object of dread seemed somehow to put fear into its place again, but as that became proportionate another disproportion took its place. Here was a girl who had taken me into her bed. As grimy as if I had come out of a smithy she had strained me close in her arms and had not let me go till I had slept out of sheer emotional exhaustion. And I did not know what on earth to say to her.

It was she who spoke first. 'I saw you in the Park,' she said awkwardly.

'I was with those fellows.'

'Yes.' Of course it made a difference when a fellow was with other fellows.

'What made you late?'

'Ada met somebody she knew. I walked about by myself after that.'

'I went with those chaps to the theatre.'

'Was it nice?'

'No, rotten,' I said shortly, and there was another silence.

'You won't have to be seen with me outside,' she presently said.

'Outside! What about inside?' I said, meaning Heinrich and the Herr Doktor.

'And—and *her*,' she said, and again the silence fell.

'Are your shoes hurting you?' I next asked, for she was walking slowly.

'You take such long strides.'

'He's waiting up for me—you won't have to make any noise——'

We were at the outskirts of the grounds. Her way led up the tradesmen's side path, mine towards the front gate, but as to-night I was letting her in they were both the same, and suddenly she stopped.

'What are you stopping for?' Already I had lowered my voice because of the nearness of the house.

She came a little closer to me, but instead of looking up looked down. And she was as pretty as a blackberry, rather reminded you of a blackberry in fact in her cheap Park finery and hedgefruit ripeness.

'Don't go so fast,' she said. 'If you're letting me in a minute or two won't matter,' and she drew closer still. 'I've been wanting ever so to ask you. What were you doing out on the roof?'

I stepped to the trees by the gate to see if Heinrich's light was burning. 'I wasn't doing anything. I was only having a look.'

'I thought it was robbers. And I thought you was never going to get up the next day, and I durstn't let Alice do your room. Did *he* say anything?'

'No.'

'Because—' and alone as we were she gave a quick look round before suddenly pressing herself against me and lifting her face, '—because—oh, I don't care if he did! I don't care if anybody did, because——' and she pulled my face down. A minute we stayed so, and then she tried to pull me back by the way we had come. 'I don't care for Mrs. Pitt either! For two pins I'd go and bang on the back door now, and then I should get the sack, only don't go in this minute—or else—if you like——'

From over by the house came the muffled sound of a blind going up. Through the leaves I could see the shape of Heinrich's head against the light. 'Quiet!' I said in a low voice, and after a few moments the blind went down again.

'Will you?' she whispered.

'Come upstairs? I daren't. He'd hear.'

'I looked everywhere for you in the Park after Ada'd gone——'

'I'm going in,' I said, and opened the gate and pushed her to the grass where we shouldn't be heard. Noiselessly I opened the front door.

In the chessboard hall we kissed again, but hurriedly as if the house had been full of ears. Then she disappeared through one of the doors and I was careful to make a noise as I ascended the stairs.

Heinrich was deep in his chair before the empty grate. He did not turn, and I was wondering about the distance to the gate and whether he had opened the window because he had heard anything. Then I noticed that a letter was lying on the floor at his feet.

'Is something the matter, Heinrich?' I asked.

'It is late, Peter,' he said in a dull voice.

'I missed the tram and had to walk all the way.'

He rose from his chair. He picked up the letter and read it through again as if there might have been something in it he had missed. Then he handed it to me.

It began: 'Dear Professor Opfer,' and it thanked him for his services during the past nine months. It congratulated him on the results of them, and told him that a suitable testimonial as to his ability and character would be at his disposal at any time. But it also told him that at the end of another month his services would no longer be required, and it was signed 'Kornelius Voyt'.

CHAPTER XII

'WHEN did it come, Heinrich?' I asked after I had got over the first shock of it.

'An hour after you went out.'

'But you were going before and you didn't go.'

'Before it was I who spoke of leaving. Now it is the Herr Doktor who dismisses me.'

'He says a month. Perhaps he'll change his mind.'

'He will not change his mind. So,' and blow as it was to him he tried to make a joke of it, 'we shall not have the fencing-lessons after all. But,' and the smile faded away again, 'there is one thing about the letter I do not understand.'

'What?'

'He speaks of the progress you have made. But until he has seen you how does he know what progress you have made?'

It was my last chance. Now or never must I tell him that the Herr Doktor *had* seen me, had tested me, had said that for a fool he had taught me well and might now go. And Heinrich had seen me as I had lain in my smirched bed the following midday. Now he seemed to me like a priest in the confessional waiting for me to speak. It was my last chance. And I did not take it.

'You said yourself he got to know things in funny ways,' I shuffled.

'So.'

'What will you do? Go back to Germany?'

'I have been thinking. I was thinking as I waited for you. I shall not go back to Germany just yet. I can live here very cheaply. The Herr Doktor says he will give me a testimonial. He has friends at the German club. Perhaps one of them will know of something. So I shall take lodgings in the town.'

'Then I shall be able to see you.'

'Should you like to see me sometimes, Peter?' he asked wistfully.

And as we all do when we make the refusal I tried to ease my conscience with a compromise. There would now be no holiday in Germany for either of us. His savings, instead of being set aside for his Anna, would be dribbled away on himself. Another place such as this would be hard to find, the Institutions were already staffed. Oh, yes, my compunction was genuine enough, and I broke out:

'You *aren't* going, Heinrich, there! I'm not going to wait till the Herr Doktor sends for me! I'm going to him! I'll go and talk rotten German to him, all full of mistakes, so he'll see for himself! If he says anything I'll pretend not to know what he means!'

Slowly he shook his head and looked at his watch. 'It is late, Peter. You have had a long evening and you had to walk all the way back. There is still a month. Go to bed.'

'Well, that's what I'm going to do,' I said, and full of my resolution went to my room.

My resolution held. The next morning, immediately after breakfast, I asked him what time the Herr Doktor got up.

'I do not think always at the same time. If he sits up late he wakes late. You mean what you were speaking of last night?'

'Yes. You wouldn't let me go to him on my birthday, but this time I'm going. I'm going as soon as he's had his breakfast.'

And I could see that he was torn two ways. He wanted to stay, but he had his pride and did not want to pass his difficulties on to me.

'It is kind of you, Peter, but it will not be any good. The Herr Doktor engaged me and the Herr Doktor has dismissed me. There is no more to say,' and he sat down to pour it all out in a letter to his Anna.

Only once, remember, had I seen the Herr Doktor in the daylight, and even that had been in the aquarium light of the billiard-room when he had done those magical things with his cue. The other times had been on winter nightfalls getting into his brougham and that single escapade of mine along the roof. But was he an owl or a bat that he should not have a daylight life too? Outside the birds were singing, the lilac and laburnum were in bloom. Along the yard wall the hollyhocks stood like tall ladies putting their flounces on from below. And surely he would have finished his breakfast by eleven o'clock. Heinrich was deep in his letter. But I intended that he should have other news for his Anna in an hour's time.

In the large drawing-room the clock supported by the two bronze horse-tamers was striking eleven as I passed through. A smaller room lay beyond it, and in a corner of it was a door that opened on a flight of steepish stairs. Closing the door behind me I mounted these. There was nothing on the walls but a bracket half-way up, with a porcelain phrenological bust on it, mapped out into counties called 'Alimentiveness' and 'Secretiveness' and 'Philoprogenitiveness' and 'Self-esteem'. At the top ran the passage that on my previous visit I had approached from the other end, with his closed door half-way along it. As for mesmerism, who thought of things like that at eleven o'clock in the morning? Boldly I advanced and out of force of habit knocked. I heard the faint clink of a cup being set down in a saucer. Then I turned the knob.

But could this be the same room I had stood in on that memorable night, half dressed, half stunned and dry-mouthed for a drink of water? Bright morning sunshine streamed into it through one of the two windows, both of which were open at the top. The air had blown away the smell of tobacco, and that of fresh coffee had taken its place. No compound pendulum filled the middle of the room, for it had been unhitched from its hook and set aside in a corner. It was just an ordinary, pleasant, lived-in first-floor room, with chairs and bookshelves and a writing-desk in the western window, and the Herr Doktor's pipe and tobacco-jar on the mantelpiece. In one respect only was it singular, and that was the number of the clocks that I now remembered to have confusedly heard. At least a dozen of them were ticking away as busily as the birds twittered outside. Either he or somebody else had evidently been a collector of clocks. They were on the walls, on brackets, on the mantelpiece, on the writing-desk, everywhere. They were of china, ormolu, gilt, Swiss fretwork, inlaid wood. After a minute or two you ceased to hear them unless one of them gave a 'ting'. And the Herr Doktor sat in his deep lug-chair, his smoking-cap

on his head, with a small table before him, having his breakfast
like everybody else, only perhaps a little later. He looked up as I
placed myself in front of him, and after a moment pointed to the
bell at the side of the fireplace. I rang it, and in so short a time that
he must have been close at hand, Fearnley appeared. I have told
you that Fearnley was big and bearded and taciturn, with a very
handsome pair of eyes, large and chocolate-brown and prominent.
The Herr Doktor made a sign that he was to bring another cup
and saucer. There must have been a butler's pantry close at hand,
for the cup and saucer seemed to be there almost in a moment.
The Herr Doktor pointed to a chair and poured out coffee for me.
Then his whole attitude became one mild, inquiring 'Well?'

'Please, Herr Doktor,' I said, rushing to the point all at once,
'Heinrich says he's got to go and I don't want him to go.'

He made no sign, only waited for me to go on.

'And I told him I should come straight to you, this was last night,
but you mustn't think he's sent me, because he didn't want me to
come. But I said I didn't care, I was coming, because my German's
simply awful.'

With an imperceptible movement, which none the less I understood as plainly as if it had been words, he told me to speak German, and I went on in that language.

'I'm always breaking off into English or having to get the dic-
tionary or something. I think it's a very difficult language. But if
I were to go to Germany and speak nothing else, well, I mean I
should be talking German all the time, and it would be a splendid
thing for me. . . .'

The morning light was behind him as he sat. There was a square
of sunlight on the carpet at his feet, and even where the room was
in shade it shimmered with reflections like a birch-wood in the
spring. There was no mesmerism about it, no trick of eyes or spectacles, he was simply watching my lips and not trying to muddle
me in any way. But the wording of the things I had been going to
say began to slip from me because he was leaving me to do all the
talking, and I presently found my tongue running away with me.

'And in Anna's family they don't speak a word of English, so I should have to talk German to them. That's her name, Anna. Her father's a Hofrath. He's writing to her now. I expect he's telling her he's leaving, but I want him to tear it up and tell her he isn't——'

Then it occurred to me that this was not in the least the way I had intended to plead Heinrich's cause, and I fancied I saw the tassel of the Herr Doktor's smoking-cap nod a little. But I went on, unable to get away from this stupid subject of my German, floundering, deliberately trying to make mistakes, arguing in excellent German how rottenly I spoke the language.

'At school I was rotten at it. I mean I got all the declensions wrong. Of course he wants to see her too, but what's that got to do with it? It wouldn't stop my learning German because he saw her. I've seen her photograph. She looks a bit like a sleepy fat wax doll to me, but that's nothing to do with my German, has it? Of course he thinks she's wonderful, even if she does lose her temper sometimes, but he's that way about her, and he says one day I shall be that way about somebody too. He says one day I shall go to him, and say a very wonderful thing's happened to me——'

The tassel of the smoking-cap quivered again. Could it be that he was silently laughing? I floundered on.

'Of course you'd be doing the paying. He's nothing but what he gets here, and he seemed scared out of his wits about my having a pound a week, and started on about lots of people having to keep their families on less than that. But he was going to pay for me into the theatre that time, I mean he did think of it, and he'll be just as cracked about Anna whether he gets the sack or not——'

Suddenly there could be no further doubt about it. Without moving a muscle the Herr Doktor was laughing silently in his beard.

And I had not fallen downstairs and half stunned myself this time. There was no pendulum to confuse me with its swinging, no mesmerism, not the shadow of an attempt at it. And I do not know how much you know about these things. The only explanation I can give is this: that when another will has been fastened on you *once*, when its power has been proved to you only *once*, you are more than ready to meet it half-way next time. And why should you *not* submit, collaborate, do your share and more? I can only speak for myself. I was not only doing my share, *I was doing all*. I, who had come to speak for Heinrich, was damning him out of his own mouth. I was telling the Herr Doktor that he was a lovesick fool who wanted to go to Germany and his Anna at somebody else's expense. It was time he learned that the world was not like that.

And it added to the absurd naturalness of it all that again the Herr Doktor made a movement. I was to get his pipe and tobacco-jar from the mantelpiece. After breakfast what more natural than the morning pipe?

I fetched them. He took the lid from the jar, shredded up the tobacco in his fingers and began to pack it into the bowl. The pipe had painted roses on it, Heinrich's cup and saucer had a motto about *Frauenlieb und Kindermund*. The Herr Doktor's eyes were watching me as encouragingly as a nurse watches an infant who is beginning to walk alone. And suddenly my whole errand seemed intensely funny to me. I broke into a boisterous laugh, and even the Herr Doktor's smile became almost perceptible.

'He doesn't ask you for much, does he?' I said, shaking with laughter.

I have to remember that you have probably not had my special training in talking to the deaf-and-dumb. Presently I shall have to write these conversations with the Herr Doktor as if they had taken place in the ordinary way of talk. But for the moment I will do as I did before, put the words I repeated after him in italics. When I said that Heinrich was pretty coolly modest in what he expected of the Herr Doktor, and laughed at his effrontery, the Herr Doktor I say smiled too.

'*Not bad, eh?*' I interpreted the smile to mean.

'Dashed cheek!' I said on my own account.

'*You think it cheek?*'

'Cheek! What's his girl got to do with you?'

'*What indeed?*'

'But when he goes, Herr Doktor? Am I to be sent away or to stop with you?' I heard myself saying this, with eagerness, anxiety.

'*Do you want to be sent away?*'

'Of course I don't. My German's good enough, and there are plenty of Germans here to practise it on.'

'*There is the Schillerverein.*' It was his German club opposite the Exchange.

'I can pick German up anywhere. I'm not a fool. I mean—' for I had checked myself; it suddenly seemed a matter of the utmost importance that in the Herr Doktor's eyes I should not be a fool, '—I mean I'm *not* a fool, am I?'

He gave a minute shake of his head.

'But why should you think Mr. Tenison is?'

'*Why should he not be? Should one not rather be surprised in this world when a man is not a fool than when he is?*'

'And Heinrich didn't want me to play chess, but if you'd let me play with you sometimes——' for I had seen the chessboard leaning against the wall by his desk and the mahogany box beside it.

'*He goes. In a month. I will give him a letter if he wishes to get another place. But this place—no.*'

But he was looking round the room, and my eyes followed him. There were papers and writing-materials on his desk and other evidences that he was a busy man. On his shelves were what I had at first taken to be books, but that I now saw were mostly files such as are used in offices, apparently records of some kind. He had his chessboard, his billiards, his pendulum, no doubt half a dozen other occupations. He would only be able to spare me certain portions of his time. Then he turned his lug-chair slightly, so that he could look out of the south window over the town, pale and airy that morning, with the smoke of its hundreds of thin chimneys more like incense to the sun than the grimy deposit that blackened roofs and the statues in the Park. And with that he began to talk.

I have said all I intend to say about the way in which I was able to jump at his meanings. There, a bare two miles away, his brows and eyes and the sensitive antennae of his fingers were saying, thousands of people were at that moment going about their daily tasks. He and I alone had no daily task. Others toiled that he might contemplate them at his leisure, I too had my wages without working for them. He paused to ask me whether I was following him.

'Yes, Herr Doktor.'

'And you needed money and had to ask me for it.'

'Yes, Herr Doktor.'

'I gave it to you. I did not do so in order that you might put it into a moneybox or a bank. It was not so that you might marry some stupid girl. It was not even to learn a trade. What did I say of these thousands over there who every day do the drudgery of the world?'

'You said—I think—that they thought they ought to manage it their own way.'

'I wish you to find out for yourself what makes them think that. If you think they are right you will tell me so. If you find that they love the truth better than lies you will tell me so. If you find they would rather be corrected and taught than flattered and amused you will tell me that too. I give you money to buy knowledge with, not the knowledge anybody may have who buys a book or goes to a lecture, but the knowledge you learn for yourself and that nobody can take from you. You will watch the faces of people as you are watching mine now, for perhaps their faces are saying one thing and their tongues another. You will hear what they say, remembering that what a man says is what is supposed to be in his mind. And you will report these things to me. At first you will judge wrongly, but that will not matter. It is what I give you money for. Have you understood?'

'I think so.'

'Repeat it. Tell me first what you are not to learn then what you are to learn.'

'I'm not to go to classes nor learn things from books. I'm to listen to people and watch them and try to find out what they're really thinking.'

'And if you make mistakes?'

'That's the way I shall learn.'

'Exactly, for how shall a man be anything but a fool if he knows nothing of folly or the base from the good unless he knows both? There is the town. Go and find out. And take off your jacket, for I wish to measure you.'

First the tailor had measured me, then Heinrich. Now it was the Herr Doktor's turn. He took my height, my chest-measurement, the girth of my biceps, calf, thigh, carefully noting each measurement and then putting the information into one of the files that he took from the shelf. Having done this he stood with his back to me, turning over other pages in the same file, till I had to attract his attention again.

'Is that all, Herr Doktor?' I asked, and he turned.

'In a month, when the other goes, I will send for you. It is useless to do so sooner,' and he turned to the file again.

So ended my begging-off of Heinrich.

And I told him—what? You can guess without my writing it. I told him how surprised and delighted the Herr Doktor was with my progress, and invented twenty compliments. I told him how no stone was going to be left unturned till another place was found for him. He had left his letter to Anna unsealed. Slowly he sealed it, and put his great hand on my shoulder.

'So,' he said. 'I said I did not want you to go to him, but you knew that in my heart I wished it, and you went. I think you can read the secrets of hearts, Struwwelpeter. You can read them by sympathy, which is better than reading them by the understanding. You did what you could for your friend. It means that you will be a good man.'

And he turned away murmuring to himself, 'A good man—yes, a good man.'

CHAPTER XIII

His preoccupation now was to find a place to live in, and as my secrets from him were already so many and so irrevocable that they were no longer a burden to me I several times accompanied him to the town on this errand. I had no idea how much money he had saved, but as we went from address to address it became plain that there would soon be little of it left if he proposed to live at this rate. Airy double-roomed lodgings, single rooms almost as commodious, lodgings where he could have a hot meal when he came home at night, lodgings with bed-and-breakfast only, rooms with this comfort or convenience, rooms with that—we saw them all, and still he seemed unable to make up his mind. It was then that I began to suspect that he was throwing dust in my eyes, for one day as we were coming out of a white-stepped double-fronted house with 'Rooms to let' in the window and underneath it in smaller letters 'No Theatricals' he stopped suddenly on the pavement.

'I have an idea,' he said. 'I wish to make myself comfortable, but not to have a room in a large house of which I should be paying the rent. I have heard of another place, a little smaller perhaps, but it is some distance, and why should I take you all that way? Tell me a café where I can meet you in an hour and I will go and look at this place myself,' so I gave him the name of a café, for the town had a dozen or more of them, and he left me.

In the domino-cafés you always heard the clicking and rattling on the tables before you entered, but the one I had chosen was in a basement at the back of the Exchange, not a stone's throw from the Herr Doktor's club, and the chess-silence lay over it as I entered. It was a place I had never been in before, and three or four games were in progress. I stood for some minutes watching one of them and then passed on to the next, and presently a player rose. His opponent sat on in front of the board, and presently, looking up and seeing me standing there, lifted his eyebrows? Would I care for a game? I had never played against a flesh-and-blood opponent before, and the only book on chess I knew was my father's Staunton, but I accepted, ordered coffee and sat down.

My antagonist was far from being a Master. No sooner had he left the first three book-moves than I was able to guess how much he knew and how much he did not know, and when I became sure of this I began to take things easy, making little bets with myself that his next move would be so-and-so, which it invariably was.

Then I began to take quite outrageous chances, such as I should not have dreamed of taking with even a moderately skilled player, and the time passed. I was still playing this double game, of chess and what my adversary supposed to be chess, when Heinrich entered. I called the girl, ordered coffee for him, and he sat watching us till after a long silence my opponent said, 'Hm! It looks as if I resign.'

'I don't think there's much else you can do. This is where you went wrong,' I told him, though there was no one point at which he could be said to have gone wrong, so little of the game was there in him. I gathered up the pieces and set up the mid-game position again, exactly as I had seen the Herr Doktor do under my father's lamp, and he pondered it.

'I see. I see. You have evidently played a great deal. I do not remember seeing you here before.'

'I've never been here before.'

'Where do you play?'

'At home, by myself. But I don't know that I'm really very fond of it,' and at that he gave a sage headshake and said exactly what I might have guessed he would say.

'Ah, you must not say that of chess. It is the King of Games, the King of Games. *Steinitz, Zukertort*—ah, it is the King of Games.'

I made a note of the expression, thanked him for the entertainment, rose, wished him good morning, and Heinrich and I came out into the street again.

'You beat him?' he said as we fell into step.

'No. He beat himself,' I said contemptuously.

'But he was not playing against himself, as you tell me you can.'

'He wasn't playing at all,' I retorted, and Heinrich pondered this for some moments and then gave it up.

'So. I do not understand. But you paid for my coffee. How much was that?'

'That's paid for. I asked you to have it.'

'No, no. I asked you how much it was.'

'It was threepence if you must know. Three whole pence.'

He fetched the pennies out of his pocket and forced them into

my hand. 'We had breakfast, and we shall be eating again presently. We did not need it,' he said.

'I did if you didn't. You can't go into a place and use their board
and men and not buy a cup of coffee. You mean I've made you
spend threepence you didn't want to spend, so why shouldn't I pay
for it?' I demanded.

'We will not quarrel about threepence,' he answered, and I
shrugged my shoulders. I had been about to suggest a meal at the
Station Hotel at my expense, but if he wouldn't accept a cup of
coffee he certainly wouldn't let me pay for a meal he could have at
the Herr Doktor's house for nothing, so we made our way to the
tram. And all the way I was so occupied with my own thoughts
that I clean forgot to ask him what luck he had about his lodgings.

But not all our last days together went as smoothly as this. Let
me whitewash my conscience as I could, there it waited, ready at
any moment to catch me off my guard. I had betrayed his most
secret and sacred things to the Herr Doktor, and I ought not to
have been able to bear it that he should have patted me on the
shoulder and praised my courage in going to him, and told me that
I had the understanding of sympathy, which was better than that
of knowledge, and that I was on the way to becoming a good man.
How far was I on that way at all? Was I not moving, at an ever-
increasing rate, in the very opposite direction? How readily and
naturally did not lies rise to my lips on the slightest occasion? Lies
to Heinrich, about having missed the last tram and being com-
pelled to walk all the way home? To Minna, that if she stole into
the house quietly Mrs. Pitt would suppose her to have been there
for the last half-hour? To Minna again, when I had told her that
Heinrich suspected nothing, though he had seen my blackened
face the very next morning as I had slept? Because I knew these
things I knew in my heart that I should be glad when he had gone.
He was a bore, a nuisance and my silent accuser all in one, and
again I sought to avoid him. If he was going into the town I wanted
a walk on the moors. If he proposed a walk I found something to
do in the town. I counted the days still left to him, and never had a
month seemed so long.

But the Saturday on which he left came at last. I did not see his leave-taking with the Herr Doktor, but I could imagine it, the click of his heels, his jerk of a bow, his formal speech of thanks, probably in German, the click again, the about-turn, his stiff back as he marched out. I could imagine the Herr Doktor, waiting till the performance was over, putting out a hand for him to take or leave, ringing the bell for Fearnley, and saying not a single one of the magnanimous things I had fathered on him. Midday came. The brougham was ready. Heinrich's single bag, a lumpy one with a large square check like a tartan, stood at the front door. In his comedian's pork-pie of a hat and belted brown jacket he waited for me.

I accompanied him, but the brougham did not take us to the door of his new abode. It stopped a couple of streets short of it, as if he did not want Fearnley to know his real destination, and he carried the bag himself the rest of the way—*not* to spacious apartments with a maid to open the door and a hot meal prepared for him in the evening. In a dreary street of small houses with outside closets and chalk-marks for children's games on the flags he had found a single small back room on the ground floor. His bed was behind a screen as you entered the door. A muslin curtain across the lower part of the window shut out the row of privies, there was a small table in addition to his yellow washstand, and the passage smelt of kippers. I sat on the edge of the bed and watched him unpack his bag. He put the photograph of Anna in the middle of the mantelpiece, there was room and to spare after his other belongings had been stowed into a couple of drawers, and he pushed the empty bag under the bed. I don't know whether he looked more brave or forlorn as, these things done, he stood before me.

'So,' he said, and again, 'So.'

I said nothing at all.

'It is *auf wiedersehen*, Peter.'

'But I shall be seeing lots of you.'

'You have the address written down?'

'Yes.'

'Then—*bitte*—', and he made the click and the rest. He didn't want me to stay any longer. He walked with me along an oil clothed passage to the front door, and from the pavement I watched the door close again. So that was over. I walked slowly away.

For one so suddenly and completely free to amuse myself as I liked there seemed singularly little that was amusing to do. The Station Hotel, where I went to get something to eat, was a bustling enough place in the evenings, but in the daytime it was far too big and three parts empty, and I got through my meal quickly. The bars and public-houses were open all day, but there were few people in them, and I felt as little like chess in a café as I did like the slabby oil-paintings and Roman coins of the Municipal Gallery. The best thing to do seemed to be to go home and to return later when the town awoke to its evening life. Perhaps I should find a message from the Herr Doktor.

To shorten the time I walked, and then arrived too soon, for things were no better there. The chessboard hall felt as chill as if it had a coffin in it, upstairs in my study was as if a heart had stopped beating. I thought I would sit down and write a letter to my sister, and got out pen and paper, but I could only sit there looking at the sheet. How *did* Heinrich always find so much to write to his Anna? And I was sitting there, feeling more miserable than I had ever felt in my life, when Minna came in with my tea.

That was another difference his departure made. What about Minna? No longer should I have to turn my back and be doing something else whenever she came into the room. There we should be, the two of us, with nobody to keep up appearances before. Up till then she had come in, put her tray down, attended to the fire perhaps, and gone out again, but it would be odd if she did so now. There was a shy but quick look in the eyes she lifted to me as she put the tray down. She fiddled with the things, moving them into their proper places. Then she glanced up again.

'It seems funny only bringing one cup up,' she said.

'You call it funny,' I said.

'Is anybody else coming instead of him?'

'No.'

'Sakes! You up here all by yourself! Whatever will you do all day?'

'I don't know yet,' and she pushed out her mouth.

'It's lucky to be some people! Aren't you going to pour your tea out?'

'I don't want any tea.'

'Oh, but you've got to have your tea,' she said, and peeped into the teapot. She filled my cup while I sat with my hands thrust into my pockets. She set the toast in front of me. 'There!' she said, and I wished it had been Alice instead of Minna, for that afternoon I just couldn't be bothered. But she went on.

'You'll have to show me where everything goes. Your cup and saucer always goes on the mantelpiece, and there's your collars and ties and pocket-hankerchers and everything'll be to tidy. Some people likes a cup of tea brought to bed. Is there anything you want now?'

'No.'

'Because if I'm out of the kitchen more than five minutes that old fick'll want to know where I am.'

'What old fick, and what's a fick?'

'You don't know what a fick is! I'll bet you do. They're these women that sits on doorsteps with their aprons wrapped round their hands, and when you get near 'em they've got long knives they stick in you. There's streets in this town *I* wouldn't go along by myself after it got dark, not for a hundred pounds,' she said, with a simple, serious look, and I thought she was getting at me.

'You mean to say you believe that?' I jeered, for I had never heard so many words come from her lips before.

'It's right. Alice once saw one,' she nodded.

So here was a half-wit for you, but she was standing with her shoulders against the edge of the open door, her hands behind her and her feet on their edges together, ever so much smarter-looking in her black frock and afternoon apron than in her Park finery.

'I've finished with teaching,' I said. 'He's going to teach me himself now,' and there was no affectation whatever about the startled look she gave me this time.

'Who? *Him?*'

'Yes. It's what I came for.'

Her hands were grasping her apron, pulling it tight about her. 'Goo! How's he going to teach you? On his fingers?'

'You've seen him, haven't you?'

'Seen him! I'd as soon see the Old Man himself as him! I'll see he doesn't teach *me*! I saw him getting into his carriage one night, just when it was getting dark, and he gave me a look that went right down my back! He's the sort that'ld smittle you as soon as look at you!'

'He'd what you?'

'Smittle you.'

'What's that?'

'What with having a man in the house that can't talk and a parrot that can! And mercy, I shall get into such a row if I stand talking here!' but she still stood against the open door, rubbing her shoulders gently up and down against it. 'What's smittled? You'll soon know what smittling is if anybody ever does it to you!'

But she suddenly stopped and listened, as if she heard sounds down below. She lowered her voice.

'I darstn't stop,' she said. 'It's her down in the hall. I'll come up again presently for your tray,' and drawing the door noiselessly to she was gone.

But so had I by the time she came up again. The offices would be closed and the places of amusement open presently, it might be my last free evening for some little time to come, and I had no wish to spend it by myself, thinking of Heinrich, anxiously counting his savings and gazing at Anna's photograph in his back room at the end of the passage that smelt of kippers.

CHAPTER XIV

QUITE early on, before I had begun to outgrow my clothes, I had been amusing myself one afternoon by giving myself a drawing-lesson. From the shrubbery I had brought in a holly-leaf, and with my chair drawn up to the window was trying to copy its glossy surface and curly edge of prickles. But presently I had lost myself in questions about it, questions that at first seemed simple and then turned out not to be simple at all. I wanted to know, for example, what colour it *really* was, how much of it was the light, and why if I moved it even a fraction it would be to draw all over again. And suddenly Heinrich had asked me what I was doing.

'Trying to draw this holly-leaf,' I said.

'But you have made a very good drawing of it.'

'I don't mean that. I mean for one thing, what colour is it?'

'Dark green,' Heinrich had replied promptly.

'But it's shiny, and where it shines it isn't green. It reflects things.'

'It is what they call a high-light. Where it is not a high-light it is green.'

'But it's shiny all over except at the back. It reflects what's near it, like the tiny window in the teapot. Look, I'll make it reflect this bit of paper,' whereupon I had approached the corner of the paper I had been drawing on. The faint reflection had of course appeared.

'But you can *see* it's green, Struwwelpeter!' he had laughed.

'And you can *prove* it isn't. I think everything's happening to it, like it happens to big things like the shadows of the clouds and the sun on the water,' and at that he had laughed again.

'That is too deep for me, Struwwelpeter. *I* call it a holly-leaf, and only a colour-blind person will tell you it is not green.'

But it still seemed to me that not one thing at a time, but everything at once was happening to that leaf, and that if a man could draw it he could as easily draw anything there was in the world.

My only reason for mentioning this trifle is that I do not know how better to approach these lessons of mine with the Herr Doktor that now began.

It was at half-past nine on the Monday morning after Heinrich had gone that Fearnley put his bearded head round the door of my room and told me that I was to go to the Herr Doktor in half an hour.

'He says you needn't bring anything,' he said, 'no books nor nowt. You know the way,' he said with a crafty look that suddenly made me wonder whether he knew anything about my escapade on the roof, and he withdrew his head again. At half-past ten precisely I presented myself at the Herr Doktor's door. He had finished his breakfast and lighted his pipe. He pointed to a chair in which he could see me most easily, and I placed myself in it. For some moments we sat looking at one another, and then his eyes rested on my lips. I was to talk.

And now I am going to omit altogether the movements of those fingers of his that sometimes seemed to have eyes in their tips like the horns of a snail, and sometimes were like the white walking-stick a blind man slopes before him, to find his way by an occasional tap. I will leave out the meanings in his eyes and the thoughts that passed like light over his face. I was to talk. I was to go on talking till something I said arrested him, when he would stop me. So to talk I began.

But as I was resolved that Heinrich's name should not again pass my lips I had not a very great deal to talk about, and presently I found myself telling him how I had played chess with the man in the café. Up at once went his finger. I was to stop. This man? What was he like to look at? How old? Tall? Fat? A moustache? A beard like himself? Had I asked him his name?

I think I must have been born with some gift for mimicry, and Heinrich's facial training had made me still more apt at this. And I had noticed one little trick of my friend of the chessboard. With my fingers I sketched a sort of make-up of a melancholy, studious sort of face. I bent forward in my chair, put two fingers like prongs to my brow as if I was poring over a board, and pulled at my chin so as to draw down the corners of my mouth. It was successful. Even the Herr Doktor gave an amused little nod. *Very* good. It was Mr. Hanson. He knew him, and I was to continue.

'I think I could play the game again,' I said, with a glance towards the chessboard that leaned against the end of his desk, but the Herr Doktor waved this aside. He didn't want to know anything about the game. *His* fingers too were like prongs under his smoking-cap, and there was a question on his brows. And then? While Mr. Hanson had played what he was in the habit of calling chess I had——?

'*I* was trying to find out about Mr. Hanson,' I said. 'It was rather funny. I said I wasn't very fond of chess, but he shook his head three or four times and said it was the King of Games, the King of Games. Like Scarborough or somewhere being the Queen of Watering-places. He talks like that, all little ready-made bits.'

'He is by trade a watchmaker, but he knows no more why men have watches than my pipe. You describe him very well. And what does one do when a man is like that?'

'Do?' I said, wondering what he meant. 'You can't do anything.'

'Can you not make him see that he is talking, perhaps talking a great deal, but saying nothing whatever?'

'Well, you could yawn in his face or tell him to shut up, but I couldn't do that. I don't think there *is* anything you can do about it. He was born like that and he'll go on being like that.'

'And is not this very sad?'

'Is it, as long as he's pleased? It would be a lot sadder if he suddenly *did* learn something and had to start all over again,' and the Herr Doktor gave me a long look and nodded.

'I see. And you are—how old?'

'Thirteen last November.'

'Good. It is very good. And now perhaps you remember Mr. Tenison?'

He spelt out the name, but I did better. I think I told you that to look at Mr. Tenison was a smiling, rather swaggering sort of man, always with his head well back as if he was pleased with himself about something, and just as I had sketched Mr. Hanson I was able to give a quizzing impression of Mr. Tenison too.

'But I haven't played chess with him,' I added more modestly.

'Never mind the chess. What of him?'

'Well, for one thing I should say he was a very touchy man. A bit conceited and very touchy. I went to his house one night. He says it was my father you came to see and not any of them, and when he died you didn't come any more. "We do not often see Dr. Voyt's carriage at our door nowadays," he said, and he tossed his head up like this. "We quite understand, we quite understand. We shall not trouble to ask him. And we still play chess, yes, even without him we still play a little chess——"'

'Yet he plays chess quite well, while Mr. Hanson——?'

'So he ought. He always had a little board in his pocket with a problem or a position on it. He takes it to the office with him. And he talks as if he'd invented the game.' (You will notice that while my father had been alive Mr. Tenison had always been my favourite 'uncle'. It was to his house I would have gone and on his sofa I would have slept when I had first been haunted by the chart of the talking hands.)

'So Mr. Hanson does not play chess well because he does nothing either well or badly. Mr. Tenison plays chess well because he neglects his other duties for it. So much for Mr. Tenison and Mr. Hanson. Go on talking,' and the Herr Doktor reached for his tobacco-jar.

But it is not easy to talk to order, and presently I began to run down. I was driven in fact to such a trifle as telling him that I had begun a letter to my sister but hadn't been able to think of anything to say. Up went his finger again.

'Stop. That is different. Mr. Hanson and Mr. Tenison are men. Tell me about this sister of yours,' and as talking about Nora really meant talking about Margaret I started on the pair of them. Again the finger went up.

'Stop. And this Margaret? She was the woman who used to open the door to me?'

'Yes. We'd only one, and she'd everything to do, but she always said the Lord gave her strength.'

'The Lord gave her strength?' the Herr Doktor repeated slowly with a thoughtful look.

'Yes. You see she was always talking about people's souls. That and singing hymns as she polished the fire-irons. She always said anybody'd need twenty souls to put up with a trial like me.'

'Do not stop. Go on.'

'About Margaret? Nobody wants to know about her.'

'Is she not in the world and therefore to be understood? You must not pick and choose. You do not know yet that she is not as wise as the others. Go on about Margaret.'

'Well, she was always at these hymns, and making Nora say her prayers, and she spent all her evenings off at the Gospel Hall.'

'Perhaps there was some young man who also spent his evenings at the Gospel Hall?' said the Herr Doktor, with such a look of serious inquiry that I burst out laughing.

'Margaret? A young man? Why, she was——'

But even as I spoke my tongue was suddenly checked. I felt myself going red. It was true. Mr. Hanson and Mr. Tenison were men, but Margaret—had he not himself stopped me and said that women were different? My confusion increased. Minna was a woman, and—women *were* different. Suppose he were to begin to ask me questions about the servants in *his* house? But his face was clear and not in the least stern.

'Yes?'

'She always called me a limb of Satan.'

'She called you a limb of Satan and did not go to the Gospel Hall to meet a young man. She talked about souls. Did she ever tell you what a soul was?'

'No, Herr Doktor.'

'But her soul must have been a valuable thing to her to occupy her so. Did she speak of its value?'

'I don't understand, Herr Doktor.'

'It may be that souls are not all of the same value. Everybody may have one; I do not know; but is the soul of a pawn the same as that of a knight or a bishop or a queen? Suppose you were to exchange? Might you not want two for one or some other odds?'

'I haven't thought about it.'

'Or the king? In what is he of a different nature? He is the centre of everything yet he has no value, since he cannot be taken. If he is in danger he can only get out of it, and if he cannot get out of it perhaps he does not even die? What then happens to him?'

'I—I don't know,' and this time the Herr Doktor relapsed so suddenly into thought that there was a long pause in our conversation.

But you no doubt see to what it was leading. It was simply this that I meant by my small illustration about the holly-leaf. Does a thing happen on the smallest scale? Then it happens neither more nor less on the largest. A great deal of this exceeded my grasp at the time, for I was only at the beginning of my education, but here, to-day, as I sit quietly writing in my place of peace with the sound of the chapel bell in my ears, I am able to see only too clearly that the small and the large are one. In Mr. Tenison, long since in his grave, there died a vain and touchy man inordinately proud of a gift, but he still lives as the type of *every* man who thinks that because he has a small trick at his finger-ends that trick is one of the important things of the world. And Mr. Hanson lies in the dust with him, but not the countless others who eke out their lives on the meagre and outworn sayings of others. But the Herr Doktor, I imagine, judged that to be 'lesson' enough for one morning. He had come out of his meditation and was looking at me again, at the size of my hands, the great bulk of my shoulders, at the first faint down on my upper lip. He was looking at me measuringly, appraisingly, as a farmer looks at a penned animal he thinks of buying, and when at last he spoke again it was to ask me the very question at the thought of which I had turned red.

'Are you well looked after here? Is there anything you have to complain of?'

'No, Herr Doktor.'

'There is nobody here to call you a limb of Satan?'

'No,' I said, hating myself for that colour in my cheeks.

'And when in a few minutes you leave me, what will you do?'

'I think I shall sit down for a bit,' I answered, and at that he looked at me quickly.

'Are you feeling tired? How are you feeling? Let me take your pulse.'

He did so, his eyes on my face. From his desk he took a small thermometer, and bidding me unfasten my jacket and waistcoat placed it under my armpit, where he left it. Then he reached for the file where he had placed my former records and made certain additions to them. He withdrew the thermometer again and its reading he also made a note of. Then he told me to fasten my coat and waistcoat again.

'Get yourself weighed,' he said. 'Get yourself weighed each week. At present the body is of more importance than the soul. Have you money in your pocket?'

'Only about two shillings,' I confessed. The rest had gone. 'I lent a fellow five shillings.'

'I do not ask you that. Here is more. And go and lie down on your bed for a little while. I do not wish to see you again till—' and he walked to his desk, where a little wooden panorama-calendar showed the day, Monday. He turned its knob, and the days rolled on to Tuesday, Wednesday, Thursday. At Friday he stopped.

'On Friday, at the same hour, I will see you. But this time I will come to your room,' and he turned the knob of the calendar back to the proper day again. My first 'lesson' was over.

But only when it was over did I realise what in some curious way it had taken out of me. I went and lay down on my bed, but my mind felt as your body feels after a hard and unaccustomed effort, all stretched and shaky with excitement, so that I couldn't fix my thoughts on any one thing. But I had been stiff in my body before, it soon wore off and left me stronger than ever, and it had been great fun. Where had it come from, all this knowledge I had not known I possessed? This taking to pieces of Mr. Hanson as he in turn pulled his watches to bits, all on the strength of a single game of chess and ten minutes' talk? This dissection of the excellent Mr. Tenison? Margaret and her soul? But no, I was wrong there. I had broken down on Margaret and her soul. Women were different, and I had had to confess that I didn't know about Margaret's soul. I felt a comfortable drowsiness creeping over me. Obviously women were different. Minna was different, when she stood rubbing her shoulders against the edge of a door, talking about her ficks and how I should soon know about it if the Herr Doktor ever tried to smittle me. He had said himself that the body came before the soul. Like a ripe hedge-blackberry Minna was, nobody's to steal, with not much more than a farthing soul perhaps, just the small change you don't bother about. But she was nice to kiss, and with her and the Herr Doktor in the house I should be able to get on very comfortably without Heinrich. My eyelids fluttered and dropped. Some people, she had said with a sly look at me, liked a cup of tea brought up to their beds. Of course I should have to be careful, but she was nice to kiss—she would be coming in to wake me soon——

But that day it was Alice who, at a little after one o'clock, banged loudly on my door.

CHAPTER XV

WHEN I told Minna that next time the Herr Doktor would be coming to my room instead of my going to his, and that she'd hear about it if everything wasn't up to the mark, she nearly dropped the breakfast-tray.

'Oh, lor! Do you mean we're going to have *him* all over the house now?'

'It's his house. Come here a minute——'

'Have done, Mr. Peter—stop it—I'm not tidied up yet——'

'When's your birthday?'

'What for?'

'What do you think? To give you a present, of course.'

'Have done, I tell you! A nice way this is to be starting the morning!' (for I had smittled her with a kiss). 'A present? I wish you meant it!'

'I do mean it. When is it?'

'Not of a long time yet.'

'When?'

'Not till January.'

'Then they'll do for the last one. Put your foot up on this chair—keep still! Now the other, and mind the old fick doesn't see them,' and I put them on for her.

'Lor!' she said, breaking away from my embrace. 'If anybody sees me up the steps cleaning the windows with *them* on!' and she slipped round the table and was off.

I, too, had been wondering why the Doktor should choose to
see me in my room when his own was so much more comfortable. It seemed to have become almost a rule of the house that he
kept to his own quarters and everybody else kept to theirs. Even
Fearnley did not sleep in the house itself, but had his own rooms
across the yard, over the stables, and it seemed right that the master should be the master and know his place as they knew theirs.
So at least both Minna and Alice declared, and if the Herr Doktor
began to question me about his servants as he had about Margaret
and Nora I thought I could tell him a few things about his own
kitchen.

But instead of that it was he who opened my eyes.

I caught sight of him from the landing that Friday morning,
shuffling across the hall with his pipe in one hand and his tobacco-
jar in the other. He mounted the stairs, but instead of walking
into the room Minna had made ready he went first into my late
schoolroom, and then wandered along the short passage both into
my bedroom and the one where Heinrich had slept, looking about
him rather like a tourist who sees some place of interest for the
first time. I was holding the door open for him, but he gave me a
questioning look and pointed to the ascending stairs. He wanted
to go upstairs too, and I led the way. Then he saw the turret stairs,
and those also we climbed. In the turret he stood looking about
him again.

And first he looked along the gutter, past the two chimney-
stacks to his own turret at the other end of the house. So that, he
seemed to be saying, was the way I had come that night. Then,
taking no notice of the other windows, he placed himself before
the one that looked towards the town.

And I can picture him yet as he stood that morning, the light
full on his face, his iron-grey beard very dignified-looking, not
unlike some Moses on his mountain, wondering what was to be
done about those rebellious children down in the plain. Yet he was
not in the least like Moses when you looked again, for Moses was
a passionate and angry man. He ground up their idols and made
them drink them in their drinking-water, and broke the tables of

the Law. But the Herr Doktor never had any tables to break, for his law was untabulated. Dispassionately he stood there, as if at the same time he was over-burdened with a responsibility and yet totally indifferent as to the result. He gave a sigh as he indicated it all to himself with a little gesture, and then turned his back to it. I followed him down the wooden stairs again.

But where the passage branched off towards the servants' bed-rooms he once more stopped. He sniffed for a moment, his head up like a stag. Then with his fingers he made a casual sign.

'*Bitte*, Herr Doktor?' I said, not understanding it.

He spelt it out on his fingers, letter by letter. There were four of them, and the word was 'musk'. We passed downstairs to my room, and I closed the door.

I am not going to take you at greater length than need be through all these 'lessons' of mine. Much of them were drudgery, which you do not wish to hear, so I will take this one up at a point where it had already progressed some little way.

'Very cleverly,' he said, from the chair that had been Heinrich's, 'you are able to show me this,' and he put his fingers to his fore-head in the abbreviation that now stood for Mr. Hanson. 'You find Mr. Tenison such-and-such a man, and this servant woman you spoke of a shrew who says her prayers. But all this is only "how". None of it tells me "why". *Why* is each so different from all the others yet never for a moment different from himself?'

And this, of course, being utterly beyond me he had to help me out. This he did by a slight horizontal movement of his palm, as if something passed over a card.

'Because the pendulum never makes two cards alike?' I ventured, and he gave a nod.

'It is an answer. But the pendulum is a senseless thing. It can only swing. Men and women are not supposed to be senseless things. They do not consider themselves senseless. They will tell you they are the lords of creation.'

'I'll bet Mr. Hanson would.'

'In the town we were just looking at there are more than a hundred and fifty thousand of them, all lords of creation. There are so many of them that they cannot herd themselves together at all without making a large number of rules, and they have agreed among themselves to call these rules they make the truth. Tell them any other truth and they will frown at you. Go on telling it to them and they will put you in prison. Each of them, who perhaps cannot govern himself, helps to govern all the others. What do you think of this?'

What could I say? I found nothing, and perhaps he realised that he was going ahead too quickly for me and that for the present the body was of more importance than the soul, for he broke abruptly off. He asked me whether I had had myself weighed, as he had told me.

'Yes. I'm eleven stone ten.'

'That suit of clothes, how long have you had it?'

'About four months.'

'It is tight under the arms and also worn. Have you no others?'

'Heinrich—' it was too late to recall the name '—he said I was growing and only ordered me one suit.'

'Get yourself some more clothes. When I go to the Schillerverein I do not do so in my old alpaca jacket and smoking-cap that I wear in this house. Get yourself some clothes. And now we will speak for a moment of something else. When we were upstairs you were going to ask me something.'

'When we were upstairs?'

'Before we came in here. Think. You were going to ask me something.'

'I don't remember.'

'This time I will not assist you. Try by yourself.' Then it came to me, for I had completely forgotten. 'Of course. I was going to ask why you spelt that word.'

He sniffed. 'Musk?'

'Yes. I didn't smell any musk.'

'You did not?'

'Everybody knows what musk smells like. I should have noticed it.'

'In a flower-pot, yes, but musk is not only a flower. It is also animal. There are musk-deer. There are musk-oxen. There are musk-rats and alligators,' and he spelt out each name in turn. 'It is a secretion, an excrement. It is to attract. It is why women use scent. Always, always it is a sex-call.'

I flushed crimson. I wanted to sink through the floor. But he might have been talking about the weather, he went on with such a complete absence of passion.

'Their first necessity is to multiply, these people each of whom may be an imbecile but all added together are so wise. It is by their numbers that they support one another when perhaps not one of them is able to stand alone. And if to multiply had been made a hard or an unpleasant thing they would not take the trouble, for they are lazy, and can only be flogged to a thing or tickled to it. Therefore it is made amusing and easy,' and as he said it he looked blandly round the room.

But I was still stunned. On the very spot where I had first flung myself all unnerved into Minna's arms he had stood and sniffed like a stag, and had spelt out the word musk. Here, in the very room where I had put the garters on her knees, he told me, as a thing not particularly interesting in itself, that it was a sex-call, and that without it people were too lethargic to beget their kind. For all his mildness he had snapped down on me like a trap, and was looking round the room, his eyes noting its contents.

'I see you have no clock here,' he suddenly said.

I think I muttered something about having my father's watch.

'You must have a clock. I must see if I can spare you one. I would not have you like Mr. Hanson, who makes watches and does not know what time is. And I noticed as I came through that the clock in the drawing-room had stopped. I shall have to see to the clocks of this house myself. I pay servants, but it is useless to leave things to these women. They are too busy smelling of musk. What is this?'

He had got up out of Heinrich's chair. He was standing by the mantelpiece. There in the middle of it, instead of a clock, was Heinrich's cup and saucer. He turned the saucer in his hands, reading the German motto.

'*Als Frauenlieb und Kindermund Nichts Schönres auf dem Erdenrund.*'

Twice he read it, and then, with an expression beyond me to describe, he turned the silver spectacles on me. What! This hireling he had dismissed had taught me that! With men so slothful that they would do nothing because it was right and their duty to do it . . . with women so cunningly scented by nature and art that they called for their mates even as the animals called, the rats, the deer, the crocodiles . . . I was told that the coming together of these two was the most beautiful thing in the world! I saw his nostrils twitch. At least there should be no more of that. Slowly he raised the cup and saucer at arm's length. He let them drop to the hearth, where they broke into fifty pieces. And again the lesson was at an end, for, with his eyes on me as he passed, he walked austerely out of the room.

My first bewildered thought as the door closed behind him and I sank into my chair again was simply that he was a nasty, diabolical old man. What other explanation could there be? Look (it came over me as it had never come over me before) at what *his* youth must have been, shut off by his infirmity from all the occupations and amusements proper to his years. *He* could not join in the sudden noisy mirth of those about him, for he could not know the occasion of it. *He* could not contribute his sally with the rest, for you cannot join in the general merrymaking with the tips of your fingers. What girl would whisper in *his* ear as he danced, what could *his* kissing have been? But now, in his latter years, he could do all these things through me. He was already beginning it by subtle suggestions. Perhaps Margaret went to the Gospel Hall because of a young man. Women were merely musk, but in a world full of them you had to take musk into the account too. He knew all about Minna and myself, and talked mildly about procreation at large and made me strip and measure myself. And my father had sent me to this! He couldn't, couldn't have known!

But he was giving me money. He had told me to get myself new clothes, and was turning me loose on the town, taking all the responsibility on himself. And one aspect of the town I was already beginning to know, that of its cheaper pleasures. I had acquaintances at the Station Bar and the Theatre Bar, and both these places were more amusing than chess in an underground café. He had spoken of his club, the Schillerverein, as if when I got my new clothes he might take me there too. Very well. If he wanted me to help him spend his money so that he might have this sort of experience of it that would suit me too. He had to all intents and purposes condoned my having a mistress under his own roof. 'Good! It was *very* good!' he had said when with my forehead and two fingers I had brought Mr. Hanson before his eyes, and 'Good, *very* good, Herr Doktor!' I said to myself now. He should be taken at his word.

But when had a lad of thirteen ever had such 'lessons' as these before?

CHAPTER XVI

MY last suit of clothes had been ordered by Heinrich. For cheapness's sake I fancy he had bought a remnant of cloth somewhere and had it made up by a jobbing tailor. But I went to Long's, in Market Street, that had 'Court Tailors' and 'Uniforms' on its wire blinds, and in a sort of horizontal library of cloth, cloth in racks up to the very ceiling, I was measured and fitted and told them where to send the bill. I also bought collars, ties, boots, a silver-mounted walking-stick and a pipe with an amber mouthpiece. My moustache was fair, like my hair, but by the time the barber had finished with me my hair was a shade darker, for I made him oil it and brush it down flat. Nobody was going to call me Shockheaded Peter now. Let the Herr Doktor lay out his money if he wanted value for it. I should presently be wanting a little more of it in my pocket too.

One evening, with a flower in my buttonhole and a new straw hat at the latest angle on my head, I had walked along Market Street as far as the Town Hall, for Market Street on a fine evening was something of a parade too, and at the Town Hall I had stopped. It was there, by the blue lamp of the police-station, that the notices were stuck on the walls, notices of rewards and men 'wanted', tenders for contracts, labour required for public works, I don't know what else. And it was there, standing reading them, that I saw a solidly-built figure in a belted brown jacket, trousers that stretched tightly over his calves, and a narrow-brimmed hat. I had had a couple of glasses of sherry at the Station Buffet with some fellow I had got into talk with, and I was feeling in great good humour.

'*Wie geht's*, Heinrich?' I said.

He swung round. For some moments he hardly seemed to recognise me. Then he jerked his back, clicked his heels and shot out his hand, but without speaking.

'What are you doing here?' I asked him.

He was still looking for the vanished Struwwelpeter, his eyes hoveringly about my moustache. 'I have been in the Public Library, looking at the papers,' he said. 'I go there every day. Still there is nothing. So I came on here.'

'What, do you mean the Herr Doktor hasn't done anything about that yet?'

'He gave me a letter, which I show. It is the summer and many people are away. Also trade is not good, and I am not the only one who goes to the reading-room to look at the advertisements. You are well?'

'What are you doing now, I mean this evening?'

'It is a fine evening. I was about to take a walk.'

'Well, I'm not doing anything much either,' I said. 'Come along.'

But I was just a little sorry I had said it. If deaf people are avoided because they are deaf so are poor people because they are poor, and when they see you in new clothes with a flower in your buttonhole it does not occur to them that you may have very little more money in your pocket than they have themselves. So we fell in together, and presently he asked me how the Herr Doktor was.

'Oh, just the same,' I answered lightly, and he would have been a wizard indeed who had guessed from my tone that this same Herr Doktor had picked up his cup and saucer, read its motto, and had smashed it into fifty pieces. 'I do nearly as much talking as he does now.'

'You go to him daily, as you were with me daily?'

'Not every day. Twice a week perhaps. It's just as he feels. Sometimes he comes to me. I say, Heinrich—' I said it a little awkwardly, '—I mean in a town like this there must be *some*thing, I mean some sort of a job——'

'And what do you do the rest of the time?'

'I've been coming into the town quite a lot. I say—' this I said more awkwardly still, '—I have been coming to see you. I've started off several times, but something's always happened——'

'And what,' he asked, 'is the Herr Doktor teaching you?'

This was rather difficult. What was the Herr Doktor teaching me? I had better be careful. The Herr Doktor seemed to be *un*teaching me most things that other people called knowledge. 'I hardly know yet,' I said. 'So far we just talk. We haven't properly started.'

'You have not yet discovered the end to which all is directed?'

'No. He says I have to watch people, and make up my mind about them, and try to find out what they're really thinking, and stuff like that,' I answered, for with Heinrich there it all seemed very vague, and we walked on in silence.

We were getting near the gates of the Park. Somewhere ahead of us there was music, and as we entered the gates and took the broad path between the ornamental flowerbeds and the town's blackened benefactors this grew louder. It seemed to cheer Heinrich up a bit, for he began to nod his head from time to time, and to say 'Ja, Gung'l', or 'Weber schön, schön'. We approached the vortex and the raised bandstand. I had no fear of seeing Minna this time, for I knew it was not her evening out, so cocking my straw hat anew I watched the passing couples instead, couples already linked up, couples coming together or coming apart again, young men on their mettle, young women who glanced at you for a moment and then looked away again, short, tall, dark, fair, plump, scraggy, all different yet all the same, and not one of them, according to the Herr Doktor, to be trusted with a simple thing like winding up the drawing-room clock. And it was not the couple of glasses of sherry I had had. That wasn't enough to have made any difference to anybody. But suddenly Heinrich stopped his nodding to the music and asked me what I was laughing at.

'Was I laughing?' I said. 'Well, *berser lachen als weinen, ja*? I expect it's all these chaps with their girls.'

'They are hardworking young fellows from the offices and the mills, enjoying themselves after their day's work. The girls too are from the mills, or the shops, or their homes, or perhaps some of them are domestic servants. I do not see anything to laugh at.'

But it was a pity he had mentioned domestic servants, whether he meant anything or not. I was not under his tuition now, and he was as stupid as ever. He and I would never laugh at the same things. He had stopped and was looking at me, and I heartily wished now that I hadn't proposed our walk.

'You look much older,' he said.

'I expect that's my moustache.'

'I was not thinking of your moustache. I was thinking of the Peter Byles I knew only a short time ago.'

'Did you expect me to go on being like that?'

'But in so short a time? It is strange to hear you talking as you talk.'

Well, as that was no longer any business of his, the smile remained on my face. 'Just because I laughed at all this? What else is it when you come to look at it? Shall I tell you? Then watch my fingers,' and just as the Herr Doktor had done to myself on my fingers I spelt out the word 'musk'.

'Musk?' he said. 'Musk, the flower?'

'They aren't even sure it is the flower. It might be an insect in the flower. I've been to the library too, and I looked it up in the encyclopaedia. It's a secretion, an excrement. What it really is is a sex-call. And so are all these here, and what I'm laughing at is that they don't know it.'

'It is a—what did you say?' he asked slowly.

'A sex-call. Like rats and deer and the rest of the animals.'

'And is he teaching you this? But no. It is not possible. It is something that some lout of your own age has told you. No man would say these things to a boy.'

'Well, he spelt it out for me, the same as I did to you. And you needn't bother yourself about my age any more.'

But he was standing erect in front of me. He was looking at me as if I'd offered him a mortal insult. Just as if I hadn't forgotten all about his saintly Anna! The scars on his cheeks showed like seams.

'You say that man told you these things?'

'Oh, I was a fool myself to tell you anything about it!'

'And you did not walk out of his house?'

'Walk out of his house? Why?'

'And you repeat this *Schmutz* to me?'

'Oh, if that's the way you take it——'

'You tell me that something I wish I had never mentioned to you is a secretion, an excrement? It is this that you run to the encyclopaedia to read? It is not of musk that you smell at this moment, and perhaps it is well I did not teach you to fence, or——' and he drew himself so rigidly up that a head or two turned to stare. 'Go! Go, I say, and tear up that address I gave you! I too will tear up that wicked man's letter! Do not dare to come and see me where I live—*nie, nie!* A good man! I said that of you! One can easily see already the kind of man you are rapidly becoming! You are—but I will not say it, for then I should be as *schmutzig* as you——!'

And through that musk-bed of girls who tittered and young men who grinned and called after him to know who his hatter was he stalked straight-backed away.

I was extremely angry with him. It was true that I ought to have asked him how his Anna was, but didn't my clean forgetting just show that I *hadn't* meant her? Should I run after him and explain? Not I. Damn his Anna and damn him. When he had had time to think it over perhaps I would write him a stiffish note if he wanted to be friends, but if he didn't—oh, be damned to him! That was the worst of talking to fools. You forgot they were fools for a moment, and said something sensible, and you were a fool too. I'd see it didn't happen again!

I gave him time to get away before leaving too, but my temper got no better with walking. He had as much as said I was drunk! On a glass or two of sherry! And because he was hard-up he had rubbed that in too, even if he hadn't put it into words. Well, I'd wasted one half of the evening on him and wasn't going to waste the other half. It wasn't far to the Theatre Bar. Out of the Park I strode. Damn Heinrich!

Five minutes later I was pushing at the double swing-doors.

It was called the Theatre Bar because it communicated by an inside way with the theatre without people having to go out into the street. But it was a street bar too, and there in the afternoons the actors could be met, and the ladies of the touring companies, as well as all the minor hangers-on of the profession. A small knot of nightly 'regulars' called itself 'the School', had its own prescriptive corner where a full-length oil-painting of a ballet-girl in muslin skirts and block toes hung flanked by rows of framed playbills, and I was by much its youngest scholar. That night a voice hailed me almost before I had got inside the doors.

'Come on, young Pete, you're just in time——'

And that happened to be one of the evenings when the School was a mixed one, for the group under the ballet-girl included two flouncy young ladies in smart jackets and saucy little veils. One of them was just saying, 'Oh, please, no more,' as I entered, but there was the fresh glass already beside the old one. At any rate they were not wet blankets, though the School was often just as hard up as anybody else.

'Now, young Peter, give it a name, and then come and give us one of your world-renowned imitations——'

The world-renowned imitations were a little line of my own, the bits left over from my exercises with the Herr Doktor. One or two people I 'did' so well that I had seen even professional actors exchange glances with one another. But I was still too full of my grievance to feel like imitating anybody just yet, so, though I gave it a name, the world-renowned imitations had to wait.

But presently I found myself listening to the talk, then joining in it. I'd be hanged if that fellow Heinrich was going to spoil my evening for me. And one of the School that night happened to be a fellow called Michelson. He had something to do with the theatre's printing, and it was plain that he looked on one of the two young women as his own private property. Presently he got up, said something about being back in a few minutes, and went out by the passage that led into the theatre. When he came back he found that I had taken his place at the girl's side. 'Here, none of that,' he said, and there was a playful scuffle between us. Then I remembered Minna, standing against the edge of my door, out of reach but allowing herself to be looked at instead. There are more ways than one of doing these things. So I returned to my stool at the counter and began operations at long range. I became animated, and the next time Michelson went out he told one of the other fellows to hold the fort, but gave me a look at the same time. So to show him that forts aren't always taken by storm, when he came back again I was calling his girl Rosie, because she looked like a rose, I said. Soon the Rose had become Musk-rose, and I heard the other girl whispering something about my being a young devil. Thereupon, though I was short of money, I ordered drinks for everybody. Be damned to Heinrich. . . .

After these drinks, and yet others, Musk-rose began to get very pretty indeed. Michelson pretended not to see my eyes, first on Musk-rose and then on the ballet-girl on the wall, then dropping from the ballet-girl back to Musk-rose again. But at something I said he suddenly turned.

'Look here, you, that's enough of the Musk-rose,' he said. 'Try something else for a change, will you?'

'Sorry, printer's error,' I said, and went on just as before.

She became more beautiful still, and when I looked at the other girl she was nearly as beautiful, both of them far more beautiful than the ballet-girl painted on the canvas. Then, remembering Anna's photograph, I began to chuckle. Women and their tricks— always up to 'em—smelling of musk as hard as they could—all except his Anna. Their toes under their flounces, their eyes under their lids, setting one fellow off against another, always seeing the next drink well on the way before they protested they didn't want any more—they were all alike, except his Anna. She must have come into the world in some different way. And at that point I noticed that they were talking among themselves, taking no notice of me grinning there on my stool. They were trying to shut me quietly out, and I wasn't going to be shut out. If only Michelson hadn't been there——

But suddenly he was very much there. I don't know what I had said; perhaps I had only looked it, but up he jumped, out his arm shot, and down I came toppling from my stool. There was a commotion, and when I picked myself up my jacket was already half-way off. He was ready too, but a couple of them were holding me, and you can't do very much when your jacket is pinning both your elbows down.

'Here's your handkerchief,' they were saying. 'Wipe your mouth. It serves you right, you know—you overstepped it a bit that time——'

'Let go my arms. . . .'

'Come and kiss and be friends to-morrow night. You asked for it. Come along—we'll see you to your tram. . . .'

But I wanted to fight Michelson, not to kiss him. Then I wanted to kiss Musk-rose—any Musk-rose—damn Heinrich. . . .

So between them two of the School saw me to the steam tram.

CHAPTER XVII

A T this point I lay down my pen to ask myself one of those plain questions that are sometimes so difficult to answer. What is it I am writing, and why? I said it was my personal story, but who to-day wants to hear what a lout of a lad did all those years ago, in a distant smoky town itself so changed that little of it but its name remains, which is why I do not give it one, since I might be thought to be speaking of some other place altogether? Nobody, and if that were all I should stop.

But it is all? I also said, if you remember, that in my spring-time years, my years of hope and promise, I was laid hands on, and vivisected, and crammed with a knowledge not my own, and forced in my growth till the very pores of my overstrained body sometimes seemed an inch apart. And as *this* is the story I have to tell, how much of it is mine and how much that of the man who did it all?

For paradoxically, even my own story does not belong to me. It belongs to the man who later made a mummer of me, a juggler with the personalities of others because I had none of my own. It belongs to the man in whose house I still was, with the arms of a servant-girl to fly to when women should have been still a mystery to me, and this with my 'lessons' hardly yet begun.

So, as I was only turned loose on the world that I might return with my spoils to him, I must tell my tale accordingly. Many turbulent things happened in that town of my birth, and I was present at them, but I was no more of them than he was. Overgrown and overdressed and noisy, I still remained an unknown quantity, flickering through it all like St. Elmo's fire or a corposant in the rigging of a storm-tossed ship, alight with a fire not my own. So though I may have to mention these things I shall do so no more than is necessary. He made my life, and was my life. Which, having made clear, I take up my pen again.

I think my first impression of his club, the Schillerverein, was a wonder that anybody as set apart from the world as he was should want a club at all. What had he to do with the town's trade and government, its politics Liberal and Tory, its partnerships and dissolutions, its impending bankruptcies, its social life? I remember it was early on a July evening that he first took me there, Fearnley driving us in the brougham, and I saw the heads that turned as he entered the smoking-room and then, seeing who it was, hastened to bury themselves behind their newspapers again. If that was all his welcome, why did he go? But at least his needs were known, for a waiter appeared with his whisky almost before he had sat down. As for me, I was given a copy of the *Illustrirte Zeitung* to look at. A serene July evening, the band playing in the Park, the School assembled in the Theatre Bar, the young couples parading back and forth along Market Street, and there I was, looking at the smoke-browned portrait of Schiller over the mantelpiece, the long gasoliers that hung from the high ceiling, the empty leather chairs, the half-dozen members behind their newspapers, in a faint odour of paint, for the decorators were in and half the rooms had 'Closed' on them. Had I exchanged Heinrich's slack discipline for this?

But I had been brought there for a purpose. Presently a secretary spoke behind me. I was to be so good as to follow him. Putting down the *Illustrirte Zeitung* I did so, and in his little office received a surprise indeed. Exactly what steps the Herr Doktor had taken I can only guess, but his name was one of the well-known names of the town and I was in a sense his adopted son. My German was fluent, not that that mattered much since everybody spoke English too, and it appeared that certain of the members had known my father. The club, the secretary explained with a covert glance at me, had no express rule about age. It was a question that had not hitherto arisen, and the Herr Doktor's own position was an exceptional one. So in the circumstances the Committee had seen their way, etcetera, and—well, there was the candidates' book and a copy of the rules.

So before I was yet fourteen I found myself a man of the world, an honorary member of one of the town's principal clubs, able to nod to the hall-porter on entering, to take a little towel from the top of the pile when I wanted to wash my hands, to listen to the talk of my bearded elders, glance at the European magazines and journals, and, when the fellows in the Theatre Bar showed me the latest in the *Pink 'Un*, to cap it with something from *Kladderadatsch* or *Le Rire*.

And having introduced me the Herr Doktor left me to myself, for except on one occasion which I shall come to, I never saw him in the club again.

By this time our talks together had taken a curious and sometimes comical turn. We had dropped the manual alphabet almost completely, and a pantomime of dumb show on both sides took its place. In this I was the leader, he the scholar, and to see him, profoundly serious and without a suspicion of the figure he was cutting, imitating my impish imitations, was sometimes as incongruous as if a street-lad had scribbled something facetious on a church wall. So I come to the next stage.

I presented myself in his room one morning after I had been a member of the Schillerverein for perhaps three weeks, and found him apparently cleaning or adjusting a small Swiss clock, for he had taken it down from the wall, removed its dial and pendulum, and was bending over it with a fine screwdriver and a little oil-can. But looking up and seeing me enter he carried it carefully to a window-sill and placed his tobacco-jar on the table instead. I sat down as usual in front of him and waited for him to begin. As he had not yet asked me a single question about the club it could hardly be much longer before he did so, and I was prepared. Again he was sitting with his back to the morning light, I facing it.

'How many times have you been to the Schillerverein?' he began without preface, just as I had expected.

'Seven or eight perhaps,' I told him.

'In the afternoon? In the evening?'

'Only three times in the evening.' In the evenings there were more amusing things to do elsewhere.

'And which of the members have you talked to?'

'Mr. Holtz came up to me and Dr. Müller. But they both knew my father.'

'Others?'

'Oh, yes. There was a gentleman over from Hamburg who only spoke German, so I talked to him. And I've played chess once or twice, and billiards with a man, but I don't know who he was.'

'And what do the members of the club think of you?'

This, you will notice, was an entirely new departure. He asked me, not what I thought of them, but what they thought of me, and as they naturally did not discuss me in my presence it was a thing I could only guess this time. I was to exercise my imagination not on what I knew, but on reasonable probabilities, and the new problem slowed me down considerably.

But it was not really difficult, for what *must* they be saying? 'Whose son did you say? The Byles who died a year or two ago?

I'd no idea he'd a son that age. . . . What does he do? Nothing? Just
lives out there with Voyt? He's a great hulking fellow anyway. Odd
though, his being a member here.' It could *only* have been this.

'You think that is what they are saying?'

'If they're bothering about me at all. And if Mr. Holtz and Dr.
Müller stop to think a minute they'll know how old I really am.'

'Describe some of these people to me.'

So there I was back at my first lesson again, except that now
I was promoted as it were to some Upper School, with men of
influence and leading as my subjects, for there were times when
the smoking-room of the Schillerverein rather resembled a senate,
with the painted Schiller over the mantelpiece as its President. But
when I tried to remember a few of the things I had heard the Herr
Doktor made an impatient movement, just as he had when I had
offered to play over Mr. Hanson's game of chess.

'Never mind their wisdom. What comes out of a man cannot
be more than the man himself. If it seems more he has stolen it
and I do not wish to hear about their thefts. You will please to
remember that, and speak only of the man himself.'

So, to begin somewhere, I began with Mr. Holtz. He was a bulg-
ing little man with an enormous jutting forehead, and because he
kept the large bookshop in the Arcade I supposed his eyes were
moist and peering because of the vast amount of reading he must
do. He talked importantly about 'my business', wrote letters on
education to the papers, and in the Grammar School there was a
tall wall-tablet with 'Holtz Gift' on it in gold letters and the names
and years of the prizewinners. To all this I added that he spoke
very good English.

'He is English.'

'What, with a name like Holtz?'

'Holtz was her first husband. He married the widow and took
her name. He even stepped into his shoes at the Schillerverein, for
she wished to have a husband who was a member. He sells the
schools its school-books but he knows nothing about books. It is
she who writes those letters to the papers. At the club he is—', and
the Herr Doktor struck a ludicrously portentous attitude, '—but

in his own house he goes about on tiptoe. Remember that the next time you see him and waste no further time on him.'

A little dashed, I tried again, but my next attempt, which was Dr. Müller, was not a success either. The Schillerverein seemed to me the dullest place on earth, its members the dullest people alive. But I have told you how we were sitting, I full in the light, he a shadow against it but lit by soft reflections. And again as I talked something seemed to break in me. Again I had that queer feeling that I was *being helped*, for suddenly I *saw* Dr. Müller. I saw him, not as a fresh-complexioned man of turned seventy, silver and pink like a newly-cut salmon, and continuously taking a gold repeater from his pocket and springing it open in the palm of his hand, but, as if he had turned himself inside out and showed me the workings of his mind. I was conscious of a curious sense of exhilaration, and again my lips were opened.

'Oh, I always know what *he's* going to say before he opens his mouth!' I said, full of this new sense, whatever it was. '"And how's your little sister?" It's always that to start with. I expect it's because he was there when she was born. Margaret always told me he brought her in his top hat. Then he shakes his head a few times—he means my mother when he does that—and pulls out his watch again. But—', and I paused, '—there's something else about him——'

'Yes?' said the Herr Doktor, watching me.

'I don't quite know what it is—wait a bit, I do though—he's very rich, and everybody says what a fine fellow he is, one of the old school—just a minute——'

And again it broke as the pod of a balsam explodes and scatters its seed. It was as if Dr. Müller himself had turned a light on in one of the rooms of his own house at night, with the curtain undrawn, and I, standing in the street outside, saw him in his own illumination. Already I had invented things said about me I had not heard. Now a Dr. Müller built himself up for me, for where had *I* heard about the bedside manner that women patients love, so that they will have this doctor and no other? Who had told *me* about family practitioners who had ceased to learn anything half a lifetime ago, whose only study was the whims of their patients, whose medicine for the poor was a benign smile and for the wealthy to send them from costly cure to costly cure? Yet so I now saw Dr. Müller, and at the revelation I could only whistle.

'Whew! So *that's* why everybody likes him——!'

And with that I had an inspiration.

I think it came from the distant skyline over at the other side of the town. There, solitary as a lighthouse, a landmark for miles round, a very king among chimneys, smoke-crowned on its height, rose the tallest chimney of all the chimneys in the town, the chimney of Rothmann's mill. And as far as the lesser though still considerable magnates of the town were concerned Mr. Rothmann himself was as invisible as his chimney was conspicuous, and perhaps because he kept himself invisible he was a legend, a name, a force, and the lives of two or three thousand people depended on the nod of his cloud-hidden head.

And, by a chance in a thousand, I had been permitted a moment's glimpse of this monarch among the princes of the town, for he was a member of the Schillerverein. One evening he had walked into the club accompanied by half a dozen strangers and had immediately been shown into a private room. Voices dropped to low comments of 'Rothmann! What brings him here?' but I should have guessed by instinct who he was. I had, I repeat, just been making conversations almost certain to have taken place. A Dr. Müller whose exterior only I had seen had just turned himself inside out for me. But here was a man of whom I had had no more than a glimpse in passing. I heard my own voice rise with a sudden jump.

'Don't tell me this time, Herr Doktor! Don't help me at all! I want to do it all by myself! Then you can tell me if I'm right. And I only saw him for a quarter of a second. . . .'

Whereupon, half closing my eyes, because it seemed to come easier that way, and at first half pretending but getting surer as I went on, I began to make a Mr. Rothmann up, all out of nothing, yet so true to its own outlines that if it was not true everything else about it was false too.

'First,' I said, my eyes tightly closed, 'you've got to think of one of those statues in the Park, not one of those in a row looking at one another across the flower-beds, but in a place all by itself, and you aren't to look at the name on it till I tell you. Have you got that?'

The Herr Doktor, his eyes steadily on mine, nodded. 'Yes.'

'Don't hurry me, please, Herr Doktor. This statue's in a place all by itself, and it isn't black like the others, because it's a new one, new white marble. Have you got that?'

Again he nodded.

'And now I come to see it,' I went on, my brow all knotted and my eyes screwed up so tightly that they hurt, 'it isn't in the Park. I thought it was, but it's in the cemetery, right in the middle. It has iron railings round it with new gilt spikes on them, and on a flat table there's a sort of urn, with two angels bending over it like this. Can you see it?'

'I see it,' nodded the Herr Doktor.

'And every day there are fresh flowers on it, because——'

He interrupted me for the first time: '*Every* day?'

'Yes, because this isn't just one day, but *all* the time —don't start worrying me. But you needn't think anybody else puts the flowers there, because he left a lot of money specially for it, and I think there's always to be a light burning that never goes out, but you bothered me so I'm not quite sure of that. I say, I'm not talking rot, am I?'

'I am not to interrupt.'

'And he was a big man at a chapel of some kind, and bought it halls and organs and things, and always put bank-notes in the plate, and so all the chapel people went to the funeral. But his work-people didn't go. The managers did, and the heads of the departments, but not the workpeople, because the mill was closed that day and they all went on a holiday. More than a thousand of them ordered a special train and went on a day trip.'

The Herr Doktor's gesture was so slight that it was hardly an interruption. 'Where did they go?'

'To Morecambe,' I answered. 'Have you guessed who it is yet?'

'Go on talking.'

But this I began to do with more difficulty. I put my hand on my forehead to keep the brightness in.

'Then—but no, it wasn't then but it was some time—you've mixed me up and I'm not quite sure when—but a very big thing happened. It wasn't just his workpeople. The whole town was very angry, and there's some red somewhere, and a tremendous row, shouting and throwing things and marching—wait a minute—it's all going funny. . . .'

But that minute I asked him to wait for never arrived, for with a jerk I came suddenly to myself. I opened my eyes and blinked in the morning light. What utter rubbish was this? I had set out to try to make up Mr. Rothmann, and here I was, burying him and giving him a statue before he was even dead! Why did I begin at the end, talking about him backwards before any of it happened? Indeed what did I know about him at all? And what was the Herr Doktor doing over at that cupboard?

For he had got up and was at the cupboard under the bookcase, where he always kept a large seltzogene and whisky and glasses. In the middle of the morning, and with a hand all a-shake, he was pouring himself out nearly half a tumbler of whisky. He gulped it down, breathing heavily. Though I had opened my eyes they were gradually closing again of themselves. I felt his approach. He put a glass to my lips too. He was feeling my pulse, listening anxiously to my breathing, and I spoke drowsily.

'Did you guess who it was?'

He gave me another sip.

'Did you guess——'

But he had laid his finger-tips lightly on my eyelids. A delicious feeling of peace stole over me. I was conscious of the ticking of the clocks, but they became confused with the shouting and marching I had just dreamed of, with the mingling of voices at the Schiller-verein. Confusedly ticking clocks, confusedly talking voices, some fast, some slow, some striking falsely, some not striking at all—all perhaps with their moves like the pawns and pieces of the chess-board, but the king couldn't be taken, so what happened to him when he died? . . .

Only the Herr Doktor, like his own pendulum, just swung,
weaving his patterns, never any two of them alike. . . .

It was late that afternoon that I awoke, in my own bed, fully
dressed except for my boots. But I did not know till afterwards that
the bearded Fearnley had carried me there.

CHAPTER XVIII

M Y body at that time needed an extravagant amount of food,
and my sleeps at night were abysmally deep. Our ordinary
sleep can be sounded. Its measure is the day's measure, as the
peaks of the mountains balance the depths of the ocean bed. But
mine were a deep within a deep, as if some sounding-line had run
out without finding bottom, to all intents and purposes the end of
all things. Those sleeps too, I can now only suppose, balanced and
restored to a level again the intensified experiences of my days.

But there were spells of lassitude too, when I avoided amusement rather than sought it, and, leaving the lights and street-
parades, wandered off into back streets, the dark business streets in
the middle of the town perhaps, of closed offices and warehouses,
depots and goods-yards and sidings with rows of horseless wag-
gons standing in them, meeting only an occasional night-watch-
man or policeman throwing his bullseye on fastenings, wondering
what all these activities were that seemed to die every night to
be born again the next morning. I did not know what this thing
was that men called 'their work'. My schoolfellows and contemporaries, Vic Tenison, Tommy, Wilf, had each taken his place in
some office or counting-house or shop or shed. In the evenings
they went to their technical classes or pursued their hobbies. Each
of them knew some small thing I did not, who was being educated
to comprehend it all, from afar and all at once. So though I dimly
understood that all this business of Town Hall and Exchange,
banks, schools, hospitals, shops and even places of amusement
were the town's very life-blood, I had only the faintest idea of the
social anatomy through which it circulated.

It was after one of these evenings that I returned home about eleven o'clock, went straight to bed, and fell into one of these sleeps I am speaking of. I was asleep without transition, as completely as if sleep had been severed from waking by the falling of an axe. But, at I did not know what hour, I awoke again as abruptly as I had dropped into the abyss. What was it? I lay awake listening, but heard nothing unusual. The tall clock on the landing half-way down to the hall was striking one, but so it did every night, striking the half-hours too, so that twice during the twenty-four hours a single stroke might have been half-past twelve, one o'clock, or half-past one, according as it was day or night.

Then as I listened I heard the clock strike again, and after a brief pause again, and then two strokes together, and then yet another single stroke. Either something had happened to the clock or somebody was doing something to it.

Only one person could be moving about the house at that hour of the night. The clock went on striking, three o'clock, half-past, four, but I had slipped out of bed. Noiselessly I opened my door, stole along the passage to the stair-head, and looked down over the rail.

He had placed his hand-lamp on the floor, where it shone on his bare ankles and Turkish slippers. In place of his smoking-cap a woollen nightcap was pulled down over his bald head, and a long grey dressing-gown enveloped him. The face of the clock stood open, and his fingers were pushing round the minute-hand, waiting at each half-hour—eight o'clock, half-past, nine, half-past——

But at ten he stopped, as if something perplexed and troubled him. I saw his hands feeling about his dressing-gown, for something that was not there, and it was some seconds before I realised what was the matter. Then it came to me. He had left his watch behind him in his room, and now that he had altered the clock could not set it right again, for except by guess he had nothing to set it by. He stood helplessly there, lost in a timeless world, with time going on all the time but *the* time lost to him for ever. For if he were to go on, all round the clock, and then to begin again, what help would that be to him?

A room full of ticking clocks in his portion of the house, and now he had lost the time in this. . . .

And he had called Mr. Hanson a watchmaker who did not know why men carried watches. . . .

He did not go on. He stood there for a moment sunk in thought, and then slowly closed the clock face. He opened its tall door instead. He stopped the broad disc of the pendulum, and there was a harsh whirring and rattling as he pulled at the mechanism that raised the leaden weights. He started the pendulum again, which resumed its measured tock-tock. The hands stood at ten. With a little click one of them moved a fraction forward. He gave a deep sigh, stooped, picked up the reflector-lamp from the floor, and slowly descended the stairs with it in his hand. The light died away across the chessboard hall, and tock-tock, tock-tock the clock mocked him, with the lie on its face.

But I heard a muffled sound on the landing above me. I was not the only one to have been brought out of his bed. A dim huddle on the upper floor showed where Mrs. Pitt was watching too, with the two girls cowering behind her. I turned away to my room.

No Minna brought me a cup of tea to my bedside the next morning, neither when I had dressed did either she or Alice bring in my breakfast. Mrs. Pitt brought it up herself, and being a downright woman she wasted no time.

'It's not that I mind for myself,' she said, 'but if things are going to be like that you can't expect girls to stop, and I don't blame 'em. Now don't you start asking me what I mean, Mr. Peter. You know well enough what I mean.'

'He was only walking in his sleep,' I said.

'No more than what I am now he wasn't,' she retorted. 'It isn't the first time, though I've kept it to myself because of them two. Not a fortnight ago down out of my bed I had to come, with a candle in my hand, thinking somebody'd got into the house, and there he was, at after twelve o'clock at night, doing the selfsame thing.'

'To that clock? I'm nearer to it than you are and I didn't hear him.'

'It wasn't that one. It was the one in the big drawing-room with them Arab men pulling at the horses. *I'm* not frightened of him, but the girls aren't educated up to my pitch, and as for Minna it's as much as I'll answer for if she can write her own name.'

She was dressed as always, in her blacks, with the jet brooch at her throat and her keys at her waist. Only a few hours before I had seen her on the landing above, in her nightgown, with a little white knitted woollen shawl round her shoulders and her hair dragged back for the night, and her face had been as white as those of the other two. She was only whistling to keep her courage up.

'She's the worst, Minna is. I won't tell you the hour I had with her last night. A good shaking's what she wants. She's saying now she's heard him lots of times. She says he goes down and plays billiards by himself, and one night she saw him in his nightgown in the kitchen passage with a razor in his hand, to cut the parrot's throat because it can talk and he can't. How long's *that* going to last, Mr. Peter?'

'But what can *I* do?' and at that she looked me up and down.

'Nobody'd say you weren't big enough! It beats all *I've* seen, the size you've got! If you aren't the master of this house I don't know what you're here for!'

'I can't stop a man winding up his own clocks.'

'The clocks were good enough for everybody else. If they weren't why didn't he send for Hanson? Nothing's gone right in this house since Mr. Opfer left. I said to myself when the brougham went down the drive, "Now we shall see what'll happen," I said, and as for you, Mr. Peter, you can always go out and stop out, but us three women has to be here whether we like it or not,' and with that she gave herself a shake, the keys at her waist jingled as if she had been a wardress about to lock the Herr Doktor up there and then, and she walked with dignity out.

So here, I thought with resentment, was a pretty state of things! *They* were only weak women, so *I* had to do something! But I wasn't going to. Mrs. Pitt was paid to keep the girls in order, so let her do her job. As for Minna, *I* knew the kind of shaking that would do her most good! For just look at all the things this silly

incident had interrupted. I was still tingling with excitement over
that last lesson of mine, when I had seen a Dr. Müller all lit up
inside like an uncurtained room at night. From that, unprompted
and all out of my own inspiration, I had gone on to 'build up' a
Mr. Rothmann I had only seen for a passing moment, and had
actually begun, not to-day, but at some unknown future date,
with his funeral and statue in the Park and a thousand people
taking a special train to make a holiday of it at Morecambe! What
had happened to me? I could not tell, but I knew already, almost
before I was into my teens, that these things are in the nature of
a curve, and what is a curve but itself a prophecy? Nobody has to
have the whole circumference before he can recognise the circle.
Start the parabola on its journey and it will not change its nature
throughout the realms of space. By the Herr Doktor, through
him, put it in any way you like, these things had begun to be the
ordinary plane of my thinking. I was bursting with an enhanced
and superabundant life. There were times, especially when I had
just left him, when I had the illusion of living for ever. So with all
this ahead of me what was youth that anybody should wish to
linger over it? The young themselves know better. All they want is
to be grown-up as quickly as they can. A lot of silly superstitious
servants? I ranged myself on the Herr Doktor's side. I wanted
more light, more, and only he could give it. And before I pass on,
let me mention just one small incident that happened somewhere
about that time.

I was walking to the tram one evening, and had got as far as
where the larger houses stood back among their trees, when I saw
a smallish figure ahead of me walking slowly in the same direction. I stepped out, caught him up in a dozen strides, and suddenly
said, 'Hallo, Vic!'

He turned quickly, looked up, and then said 'Hallo!'

'What brings you up this way?'

'Oh, nothing. I was just mooching about.'

But it came out a couple of minutes later, when he sighed and
said he wished he lived up at that end of the town.

'Why?' I asked.

'Oh, it's quiet up here,' he said evasively, and then, clearing his throat, 'Didn't you see?'

'See what?'

'Through the trees. The window to the left of the porch. Didn't you see anybody wave?'

'Oh!' I said, for when he had told me that he had told me all.

And talk about musk! (I am only trying to show you the sort of thing the Herr Doktor had delivered me from.) Her name, it seemed, was Beatrice, the same as Dante's, and that was where she lived. The window was her bedroom, and he walked up there whenever he could get off of an evening, and watched till her light went out, and then walked all the way back again. And I needn't think (this he said with a flush) that there was anything of *that* sort about it, he meant what the fellows at the office were always telling fresh stories about. He hadn't even kissed her yet, but sometimes, when she gave him a look—he knew it sounded rot—but it made him wish he'd never kissed anybody, so that she could have been the first.

'Then what do you do if you don't kiss her?' I asked.

'Twice I've come home in the tram with her, and one time she'd taken one of her gloves off, and—and—I mean she didn't seem to mind. But on Sundays her aunt's always with her. I wish she'd a sister.'

'Why do you wish she'd a sister?'

'Well, it's your way home, you see, and if there were four of us——'

And he was nearly seventeen, and his father, he said, had got married when he was twenty. He was getting a rise at Christmas, had saved eight pounds, and didn't go to the music-hall or theatre any more, but had started an account at the Penny Bank instead. And as he went endlessly on, all about an object in life, and hard work, and thrift, and unselfishness, and how you didn't know what happiness was till you tried to make somebody else happy, what was I to think except that there, but for the grace of God and the Herr Doktor, went I, Peter Byles? To think of it, that I too might have been standing under windows at night, thinking

myself happy if I saw even a shadow on a blind! That I too might
have written letters and then been afraid to post them, have been
plunged into despair by a pout or lifted up by a secret look or
a flower! That my breast too might have swelled with the wish
to do some gallant thing, even as I was adding up my figures at
a desk! But I had been rescued from these idiocies. I could treat
musk for exactly what it was worth, and as long as Minna didn't
have a baby she might talk as much as she liked about ficks and
deaf-and-dumb men who got out of their beds at night to cut parrots' throats.

And my greatest deliverance of all came at the end, for instead
of taking the tram we had been walking, and had come to the
Theatre Bar, and I asked Vic to come in and have a drink. He only
shook his love-bemused head.

'All her family's TT. She says the lips that touch liquor shall
never touch hers,' he said.

And as this time I could not restrain my 'Good God!' I left him
on the pavement, and Michelson had the drink instead, for our
other little difference had long since blown over.

And if I said all this before in two words when I said I had no
adolescence, then Vic was welcome to his as far as I was concerned.
I had only one aim in life. It was to learn as much as the Herr Doktor could teach me. The intervals between the lessons were now
as painful as a deprivation of breath to me.

I was crossing the chessboard hall one afternoon when I saw
Mrs. Pitt coming out of the big drawing-room. There was a look
on her face that made me stop and ask her whether anything was
the matter, and she snapped at me.

'What did I tell you? It's started!'

'What's started?'

'I told you they wouldn't stop.'

'What? You don't mean Minna?'

'No, I don't mean Minna, nor Alice either.'

'But you don't mean to say that *you*——?'

'Me? I'm only here to keep the house together, it seems. No, not
me either. Fearnley's the first. Yes, him. And so much for having

men about the place,' and she gave me a contemptuous look over
her shoulder as the baize door closed behind her.

But I was already after her. Fearnley! His own man! I hurried
along the passage, and the parrot gave a harsh 'Where's Peter?' as
I pushed at the door of her room.

'But—Mrs. Pitt—what's it about? What's happened? I want to
know,' and she turned.

'I know what *I'm* going to do. I'm going to make myself a strong
pot of tea,' and she bustled about, talking all the time. 'Where's
Peter indeed! But if he thinks *I'm* going to wait on him hand and
foot the same as Fearnley did—I wouldn't let them girls go as far as
the foot of his stairs! Where's Peter! Where's anybody if it wasn't
for me!'

'But what's happened?'

'Go and ask him, and you'd better go quick, because he's getting his things down from the loft now. He isn't waiting for any
wages, he says. Thank the Lord only me saw him, and him like
that!'

But I was on my way to the yard, to see what had happened for
myself.

A flat cart with a galloway between the shafts was drawn up by
the stable, and the lad who had driven it in was at the top of the
outside stairs of the loft, getting down a large round-topped trunk
a step at a time. Fearnley was standing with his hand on the cart,
swaying unsteadily on his feet, his head held stiffly back, his cap
pulled down like a bag over his eyes, so that he seemed all cap and
beard. And he was wet and dribbling about the mouth. Drunk! Of
course that accounted for it. He was almost too drunk to stand
upright. The lad had got the trunk as far as the bottom of the stairs
and was dragging it by the handle across the yard.

'Here, give me that,' I said, picking it up. 'Mind yourself, Fearnley. . . .'

But he tottered again, and I turned to the lad.

'Get his other things. I'll see to him.' I thought I might have to
lift him on to the cart too. But when I approached he pushed me
roughly away.

'You let be,' he growled menacingly. 'You let be, I tell you. I'll have nowt to do with either devil or dam——'

'Let me give you a hand up——'

'Will you let be?' he said in a raised voice. 'We'll see what the law has to say about this,' and I turned to the lad again.

'Do you know where to take him?'

'He says to the Infirmary.'

'Infirmary my eye. He's only drunk.'

But Fearnley heard me, and again raised his voice. He was still holding his head queerly, as if he had hurt his neck.

'Drunk, did you say? Did you say drunk?'

'Come on if you're coming. Your things are all here.'

But 'Drunk?' he cried again. 'You overblown young bastard, you say I'm drunk? Yes, I'm as drunk as what you were that morning, when his bell rang, and I went in, and there you was, half falling out of that chair and snoring your head off! Drunk? You? There's pretty tales going round about *you*, and not so far from this house if it comes to that! Folk can see into windows that's only a spit away across the yard! If this isn't off me by to-morrow—drunk, you say? Is *this* drunk?'

And he snatched the cap off his head. I told you he had fine, full eyes. Now they were like a cross-legged pen, leering together in the most fixed and atrocious squint I had ever seen.

'Don't tell *me* it's a stroke!' he cried. 'Strokes don't come on you just for looking back at a man when he looks at you! Out o' my way! Let me get my foot on that wheel! Straight to the Infirmary, you, and go easy, for I'm shaking wi' tic all over! This house hasn't seen the last of me! If this isn't off me by to-morrow——'

He crammed the cap down over his eyes again, but not before I had seen at the kitchen window, as horrified as my own, the faces of Minna and Alice. The lad swung himself to his seat on the shaft, and the cart moved forward with Fearnley lying on one elbow on it. As it passed the Herr Doktor's side door I saw him raise himself and shake his fist at the window above it. Then the cart passed at a walk down the lane.

CHAPTER XIX

FOR a minute I stood there thunderstruck; then as if of themselves my feet sought the outside stairs that led to the loft and Fearnley's quarters, and I stood looking in. There in the corner was his bed, in the middle of the room his deal table, his dressing-table against one wall, the empty hook where his cap and driving-coat had hung behind the door. But it was straight to the window that I strode, and stood looking out across the yard. Half opposite, only a little to the left, with its window wide open, was Minna's room. I could see the top of her yellow chest of drawers with her small square of looking-glass standing on it. True her bed was hidden, but I knew that beside it stood the chair on which she placed her candle, and Fearnley would have blown his own candle out before beginning to watch. How many times had he seen not one shadow, but two? Then my eyes dropped to the floor below. My own room was less nakedly exposed, being the next further along, but there too comings and goings on the landing outside it must have told their tale.

And Fearnley himself was at that moment on his way to the Infirmary, to find out whether the muscles of his eyeballs were set in that atrocious squint for the rest of his days. Slowly I turned away.

It was back in my own sitting-room that I tried to piece together what must have happened. Strokes of that kind, he had said, do not come over a man just because he returns another man's look, and then my thoughts flashed to that night when I had first visited him by way of the roof. I saw him again, leaning forward out of his lug-chair into the lamp-light, his empty porcelain pipe sunk in his beard, his pendulum slowly swinging, tracing its cold miracles on a card. And I knew now what had happened to Fearnley's eyes, because the same thing had happened to my own. The Herr Doktor had risen slowly from his chair, and his face had drawn nearer to mine, and like carriage-lamps far down a road at night two points of light had appeared, and drawn close, and had squinted together into one, and as they had blended as mildly as the rings of a spinning top I had known that I was squinting too. That was what had happened to Fearnley. He had tried the same thing on Heinrich too, and perhaps on the two tutors who had preceded him. Fearnley had done something to displease the Herr Doktor. Instead of accepting his rebuke he had had the temerity to withstand him. And a stiffened neck and a pair of distorted eyes was the result.

And strange as it may seem, I almost laughed. He had answered the Herr Doktor back! The fool! Had he been all that time in his service without knowing that it was not safe to answer the Herr Doktor back? Did not the Herr Doktor know what was going on in every part of the house? Was he not able to silence the chattering of a pack of boys at a birthday tea? Could he not fetch a stupid German tutor a whack over the knee as a reminder that his wishes had better be respected? It was right that fools should feel the weight of his anger, but what riches had he not reserved for myself if at his bidding I knew things I did not know, and by some strange glamour seem to see things that had not happened yet? So again, in this quiet place where I write these things, I lay down my pen. I have decided to cut the knot it took me so long to untie for myself. On the shelf over my pallet bed there are those few, those very few books, and I take one of them down. It is the Herr Doktor's own record of his education of me, and later, as you will see, he put it into my hands himself. But first a word about the appearance of this book.

Strictly speaking it is hardly a book at all, since it is in manuscript. But it is written with a fine mapping pen, in the same ink of a violet cast that he used for his pendulum, and its calligraphy is of such extreme beauty that in spite of its minuteness it is as easily read as a printed page. Each page, like a picture in its mount, consists of a smallish square of writing only, with ample margins for notes and annotations. But after the beauty of the writing the first thing you notice is its utter lack of idiosyncrasy. To copy a page of it would hardly be forgery, for forgery implies a personality, and this has none. It was in August that I first came to the Herr Doktor's house, but the book opens of itself some six months later, and this is what meets my eyes:

'*April 5th.*—Without resistance there is no strength. Perhaps it is no bad thing that he begins by being a little refractory and afraid of me. He is the first adolescent I have studied with any closeness, and what I learned last night encourages me to go on. I had perhaps been thinking of him with a little more concentration than I realised, but I certainly did not send for him, and in certain ways was not quite ready for him. He came of himself, out of what boys call adventure, which is curiosity stimulated by a healthy animal functioning. He came along the roof. He fell down the stairs, the pendulum recorded his fall, and since he was there I succumbed to a temptation. This question of the Sentient Image is deeply involved with the problem of bodily growth, and he was admirably dressed for observation. I noted the bone of his knees and the fine pubescent down on his big thighs. (N.B.: I must be on my guard against acromegaly.) What of his susceptibility? The experiment I tried was the simple "upward and inward", the fixation and slight lifting up of his eyes accompanied by a few passes. He is strongly "auto" and ought soon to be able to accomplish this upon himself. If he learns even reasonably quickly it will not be long before he is able to take his place among men and *women*. I underline this last word because the sooner that obstacle is out of the way the better. Where women are there can be no abstract thought. Their substitute for it, which they call emotion, is a sweet stickiness on the wings that clogs the flight. They have served their purpose when they have given a man possession of himself again. Some witty fool has spoken of "the eternal triangle". There is only one Eternal Triangle. It must be constructed on a known base-line, and its apex is the Source of Knowledge. It is what I am hoping one day to find.'

So if the 'simple upward and inward' had been enough for me, his protégé, what had he done to Fearnley, who had angered him? But a much more immediate matter was what Fearnley had done to me. It was useless to ask what he had seen, when and how often. Had he thought it his duty to tell the Herr Doktor what was going on under his roof? For all I knew that had been the cause of the Herr Doktor's anger. What did Mrs. Pitt know? But I quickly decided that she knew nothing. Her whole manner to me was against it. She would have had Minna out of the house instantly, or failing that would have walked out herself. And Fearnley had left, taking his secret with him. So on the whole things were not quite so bad as they might have been. I myself had not seen the Herr Doktor for some days, and very much wanted to see him. My reason for this was as ordinary a one as you could imagine. I had come to the end of my spending-money, and wanted more.

And I now wanted a good deal more. I still only had the pound a week, paid monthly in advance, that Heinrich had said was more than thousands of families in the town had to live on, but what was the good of my cutting a dash in Long's clothes when I had next to nothing to spend even in the cap-and-shawl places? I intended to ask him to double my pound, and it was immediately after breakfast on the morning following Fearnley's departure that I climbed the stairs where the phrenological bust stood on its bracket and paused for a moment outside his room. He was up, for the door of his bedroom stood open and I could see a corner of his bed, not yet made. He had finished his breakfast, for the things stood outside his other door on a tray. No sound came from behind it, and I tried its handle, but the door did not yield. He seemed to have locked himself in. I rattled loudly, not in order that he might hear me, but because percussive vibrations reach even the deaf. Still nothing happened. I tried again, again without reply. Then I turned away.

Without a single sixpence in my pocket I was to all intents and purposes tied to the house. Yes, I know there were the moors to walk on, and the Continental papers in his club to look at, or I could go to the Free Library for the day and watch the out-of-works scanning the trade journals, with Heinrich perhaps among them. But as long as I hung about the house there was always the chance that I might see him, shuffling across the hall perhaps to my room or sending somebody with a message that I was to go to his; so there I stuck, killing time at the billiard-table, kicking my heels in the shrubberies, passing under his window and wondering what he was up to in there, until finally, towards tea-time, I wandered into Mrs. Pitt's room.

But she was still in a bad temper and hardly to be spoken to. *She* knew no more than I did why Fearnley had left. She'd made his bed that morning, which wasn't a housekeeper's place, but if his sitting-room had been dusted and tidied up that day he'd done it himself. In short she wasn't going near him till things were put on a proper footing again.

'But perhaps he's ill,' I said.

'Ill? Well, he'd a good enough breakfast for an ill man, and his dinner the same, for I fetched the empty things away myself, licked clean as you like. But of course nothing's anything to do with *you*, Mr. Peter.'

'But I *want* to see him. I'm trying to see him. I've been up twice, once this morning and once this afternoon.'

'Well, Alice and Minna's taken your tea up, for since yesterday neither of 'em 'ill set foot outside the kitchen without the other, so you may as well go and lock *yourself* in too,' she retorted, and I remembered their faces at the kitchen window when Fearnley had called me an overblown young bastard and snatched his cap off. A look at them had been enough. Invisible in his room, the Herr Doktor filled the whole house with his presence far more than he had ever done when he had shambled about in his heelless slippers by night, waking everybody from sleep with the striking of a clock.

The next day was more oppressive still. No more did I feel that eager tingling of life coursing through my head and veins, and as the last of the virtue seemed to ebb out of me I knew myself again for just an overgrown, oafish lad, my education all to begin. At Christmas Vic Tenison would get his rise; the rest of them would be moving forward to their allotted places in the world; but I was—what? I remember I sat in my room that afternoon, asking myself, talking to myself as I had first talked to the Herr Doktor, taking both sides in turn. I was presenting myself before some imaginary employer and asking him for a job.

'*What was your last place?*'

'I haven't had a place yet.'

'*Well, what can you do?*'

'I'm pretty strong, and could carry things, or shovel snow off the streets in the winter.'

'*Do you speak any languages?*'

'I know the deaf-and-dumb alphabet.'

'*We had a fellow here the other day telling us that. Anything else.*'

'Yes, I can imitate people so you know who they are without mentioning their names.'

'*By why not use their names?*'

'I learned the other instead.'

'*Any references as to character?*'

'A man called Fearnley says I'm a young bastard, and he's heard tales about me, and he's seen me going in and out of a servant's bedroom.'

'*How old are you?*'

'Getting on for fourteen.'

'*WHAT?*'

So, as I could hardly expect anybody to swallow that, there it ended, and I kicked my chair away, and downstairs in the hall got my hat, and walked to the Schillerverein, where I needn't spend anything.

But there again all my confidence had left me. Even the short walk of a couple of miles had tired me, and I was as afraid of that solemn club as I had been when I had first arrived at the Herr Doktor's house, and had peeped into the great dust-sheeted rooms, ready to take to my heels if anybody caught me. Only one or two members were there, but I felt their eyes on my back, so I went upstairs to the writing-room, where hardly anybody ever went. And there I found occupation, for I made a discovery. The writing-room was the club's library too, and tucked away in a corner beyond shelves of directories and reports and dreary rows of Annual Proceedings I came upon a few stray volumes of the English and German classics. And remember that I had been expressly forbidden books. Of Shakespeare I knew nothing, of Milton nothing, of the Bible only such fragments as had fallen from Margaret's lips at home. I forget what the book was that I opened that afternoon, but I fell to reading it, and ended by slipping it into my pocket, and another one with it, for I wished to be at hand in case the Herr Doktor sent for me. Then, as tired as if the weight of my body was too much for the muscles that had to carry it, I plodded heavy-footed home again.

But on the evening of the fourth day all this stagnation came abruptly to an end. Again, with a pair of slippers on my feet, I had idled into Mrs. Pitt's room, just to talk to somebody. She had hung a towel over the parrot's cage to keep the creature quiet, and with her glasses on and a spiked file in front of her was busy with her household accounts. She asked me pointedly if I wanted anything and why I wasn't out somewhere instead of loafing about the house, and at that I blurted out the miserable truth, that I hadn't even my tramfare in my pocket. Up she went like fat in the fire.

'Then what about me and all these bills? What's going to happen on Monday if that door isn't opened by then? Every Monday Fearnley's always given me an envelope to take to the bank. I get the money and go round paying everything off. Regular as the clock the bills has always been seen to as long as I've been here, and you say *you're* short of money! What about all this? How many pairs of hands am I supposed to have? Who's even seen to the horse since Fearnley went? Horses has to be fed, and it isn't a woman's place. *You* haven't any money? . . . Now what's to do?' she cried, abruptly turning.

For the door that led into the kitchen had opened, and Alice's face showed there, with the corners of its mouth drawn down. She was a vacant, pudding-faced girl at best, and now she was shaking like a jelly.

'He's—he's on the move again,' she blubbered.

'Where?' Mrs. Pitt rapped out.

'Upstairs there,' said Alice, and again the housekeeper jumped down her throat.

'How do you know?'

'Me and Minna'd gone up with a candle, everything seeming quiet, and we was coming down again, but Minna took the candle and slipped back for something, and I wasn't going to stand there in the dark without a candle, and—and—she hasn't come down yet,' and the bird under the towel, hearing Alice's voice, croaked 'Wipe your boots, Alice!'

'Drat it if there's a minute's peace for anybody!' cried Mrs. Pitt. 'How long's this since?'

'Twenty minutes and more—I've been waiting and waiting——'

Mrs. Pitt was on her feet. 'You stop here. Somebody's got to go up.'

'Oh—I won't stop down here all by myself!' said the girl in a quaking voice.

'Mr. Peter'll stop with you then. Give me that stick.'

Whether she wanted the stick to lay across the Herr Doktor's shoulders I didn't know, but I wasn't going to be left there with the blubbering Alice, and I took the lamp and Mrs. Pitt took the stick and off we set.

There was no sign of anybody in the hall, nobody on the first floor. I was leading the way with the lamp, but at the foot of the upper stairs Mrs. Pitt rapped with the stick for me to stop, and called:

'Minna! Minna! Are you there, Minna?'

There was no reply, and again I went ahead.

It was in her bedroom that we found her, but she was not in bed. In her black afternoon frock and apron, with a lighted candle in a tin stick in her hand, rigid as a post and with eyes wide open that looked at nothing, she was standing a little way within the half-open door. I held forward the lamp, but she did not move. She was as marvellously smittled as I had been that afternoon in the hall, when I had seen just in front of me a chess-move of such perfection that I have never been able to remember it since. Mrs. Pitt pushed past me and shook her.

'Just look at that candle! She might have set herself on fire! You stop with her while I run down for my hartshorn,' and snatching the half-melted candle from Minna's stiff hand she was off. And on her yellow chest of drawers, the same I had seen from Fearnley's loft, I noticed a cheap wooden doll. I set down the lamp and put my arms round her and gave her a second shaking.

'Minna! Wake up! You can if you try! Wake up, I tell you——'

She gave a little turn in my arms, but did not wake, and with that I picked her up bodily and carried her to her bed. I laid her out on it, and as I did so her arms began to close on me of themselves.

'Stop that! Mrs. Pitt will be here in a minute! Stop it, I say——' for her mouth was seeking something as that of a sucking animal whose eyes are not yet opened seeks its nourishment. 'She's only gone for her salts—— God, don't be such a fool——'

Mrs. Pitt came bustling in again with a little bottle just as I managed to get myself out of her embrace.

'Sniff this,' she ordered, and at the smell of the pungent stuff Minna coughed and choked. Then her eyes opened and she looked blinkingly round.

'I couldn't find it,' she said.

'You couldn't find what?'

'The doll. I was dressing it for Mary. It was on the chest of drawers, and I'd finished its shimmy, and was just going to try it on——'

'Mary's her little sister—— Why, it's there, you silly goose, by the looking-glass. Have another sniff——'

'I'd just put my hand out for it, and I thought I heard somebody in the passage, and I thought it was Alice, and I was peeping round the door—then I came over I can't tell you how, all swimmy-like—and the next I knew somebody was shaking me——'

'That was me, you silly girl. You go down, Mr. Peter, and tell Alice to come up to bed. I'll come down and turn out in a few minutes. Minna'd better come into my bed to-night.'

'Don't you bother to come down. I'll turn out for you,' I said, and I left Mrs. Pitt unfastening Minna's clothes.

I turned out downstairs, and the light at the stair-head also. Then I went up again to see if there was anything else I could do, but Mrs.

Pitt, still fully dressed, said there wasn't anything, and it is my belief they all three slept in Mrs. Pitt's bed that night. Then I descended to my own sitting-room to turn out there too. But lying on the table were two objects that had not been there the last time I had been in the room. I picked up the smaller of them, and drew a deep breath of joy as I both felt and heard what it contained. It was an envelope, with four sovereigns inside it. Then I turned to the second object. It was the object that a little while ago, in this quiet cubicle where I sit writing, I took down from its shelf over my bed-head.

So, in my room in the Herr Doktor's house, with three women on the floor above me sleeping in one bed, I opened this thing which (you will remember) I then saw for the first time. I began to read it as I stood, but presently, with my eyes still on the page, felt behind me for a chair. I need not tell you who the 'O.' was. He was also the Cypher, or something else contemptuous. The entries were dated first at intervals of a week or a fortnight, but became more frequent as the record went on. It began with my first appearance in that smoke-blackened, Victorian-Gothic mansion that over-looked the town.

At any rate the Herr Doktor had come to life again.

CHAPTER XX

I READ:

'*April 20th.*—He arrived yesterday afternoon. I shall not see him till he has made the necessary progress with the elements, and O. has the most minute instructions about him. This young German will I think suit my purpose very well. Two before him seemed to think I wanted them for their perspicacity. Pushing and forceful young men both of them. One of them knew my requirements far better than I did, and the other also had to be told that I did not want anything of his services but the drudgery. But O. hardly has the wit to exceed his instructions. The rudiments, and German, and the rest I will see to myself when the time comes. So I leave him with O.'

'*April 27th.*—From O.'s reports he is pure Frederick, with little or nothing of his mother in him. At his home I used to look from one to the other, Frederick wasted on his wretched clerkship, the boy with his book by the fire. Frederick was a failure because he knew too much for a poor man; only the man whose means make him independent of the world, he or a hero, can afford to think independently. Frederick merely aroused the mistrust of those too stupid to understand him, and so the most serious man I have ever known was never taken seriously. A brilliant searcher *manqué*. Tenison played chess by the book and beat him. Tenison is a book-fool.'

'*April 30th*—So far eminently satisfactory. O. describes him as inclined to be reserved and secretive, and that has my entire approval, for nothing can be done without complete concealment of one's self. He will presently learn that the perfection of concealment is to appear to be somebody else altogether, since it is less easy for the world to practise on a man if it does not know which man he is. I am thinking now of this little incident of the billiard-table. He is utterly at a loss to imagine how I know anything about it, and thinks I was told by Fearnley or O.: but with my knowledge of Frederick and my observations of the boy in his home the place presently to be occupied by the Sentient Image already exists, *in the sense that nothing else occupies it.* It is excellent that he should not have confessed, but have allowed the accident to be discovered. That he lost his mother and so knows nothing of what is called mother-love is no loss to me. Apron-strings only lead to that little-bit-of-everybody that is called social morality. To conceal a fault is natural, and it is *not* moral that a boy should say he is penitent when he is only afraid. For this reason, finding the occasion an exceptional one, I advanced the date on which I had intended to see him first. In the billiard-room I gave him his first demonstration. I had meant to begin with chess, in which he is already deeply involved by association, but it is immaterial as long as social collusions and stupidities are not allowed to come between him and the phenomenon itself. That foolish theories and social stupidities are themselves phenomena will come later. So far I am well satisfied.'

At this point I felt myself a little out of breath. For what was this revelation, this other side of the picture, written in the same violet fluid he used for his pendulum and in characters so perfect that they did not seem to have come from a human hand at all? Frederick! My father! My early associations with chess, the Herr Doktor behind the lamp watching me all the time, and feeling nothing but satisfaction that my mother was dead! A place reserved for something he called a Sentient Image, reserved as if it had been a building-lot, the house itself to be erected later! *What* Image? Had an Image of some kind told him about that accident to the billiard-table? My head was already spinning, but my hand went to that perfectly-written page again, and I read on.

'*September 2nd.*—I foresee that this young German will have to be taught a little lesson. He is beginning to ask questions that are none of his business. He speaks of resigning. He will resign at my pleasure, not at his own. Already he is afraid of the boy, who naturally sees through him. I pay him for his stupidity, not his scruples, and there is the precious Force itself to be husbanded, for I do not know how much of it I possess. But someone must do these things if mankind is to be brought to knowledge. My physical disabilities began by being a handicap to me. To a large extent I have been able to overcome them, but it is still through the boy that I must work. Unknown to O. he is playing chess, but I did not find chess difficult to suggest to Frederick's son. And let no man think it is easy to lay out Force as I am laying it out. After the billiards demonstration I had to rest for over two hours. But I could see the impression on the boy was profound. So I make my mind a blank, wait for the *rapport*, and then concentrate on my chessboard. These foundations take time, but there is no hurry. If the boy knows when one man is stupid he also knows when another is not stupid. At present there is the friction of a third person between us. Wait till I take charge myself.'

And this was written in smaller but no less legible characters, down the right-hand margin:

'By the way, an odd little omission. I suppose its very smallness caused it to be overlooked, and I have no note of the date. But O. is so completely a Cypher that for the moment I disregarded him. I was thinking closely of the boy, and felt *en rapport*. I knew that he wished to come and see me and was actually making an effort to do so. Then I remembered the Cypher and that more than once he had attempted to assert himself. There is only one will in this house. If the boy wished to come to me, and the Cypher was interposing himself, it was necessary to make myself felt. It was only a few rooms away, and I did so. I do not think he will interpose himself again.—P.S.: I have remembered. It will be easy to ascertain the date. It was the boy's birthday, and he had asked whether he might have some *canaille* from his late school to tea.'

Then, in its proper place in the middle of the page again, a single line:

'The pendulum has arrived.'

Again I put down the book. Was I reading aright? 'Only a few rooms away!' He had 'made himself felt'! Something had happened to Heinrich's knee, and at first he had said it was an old fencing hurt, but later had admitted that it was a pang of pain! And this astounding thing was apparently such a trifle that he had forgotten it and had to set it down in a margin afterwards! I myself had been stricken as wooden as a pawn in the chessboard hall, and less than an hour ago I had seen Minna upstairs, frozen as stiff as an icicle, with a guttering candle in her hand! Well might they say that something to be feared was at large in that house! I continued to read, sometimes understanding what I read, sometimes not.

'*September 10th.*—I suppose that presently names will be given to these vital centres that not one man in a million knows he possesses. Then with the names more ignorance will be set loose on the world. Give a thing a name and it is already a prejudice and a falsity, capable of as many foolish interpretations as there are foolish men. These attract to themselves other prejudices and falsities, and presently we have the gigantic and inert mass that is called the Corpus of Knowledge. But truth itself can have no name. Only I, who can neither hear a name nor speak one, know that the phenomena is its own name. It is why Jesus Christ described himself as a Word. I alone therefore am emancipated in a world that does not know its own bondage. I would not have a tongue to distort meanings or ears to hear only echoes. Peter is all the tongue and ears I want, and to him I will teach their true function. Occasionally I see him from my window. This mysterious seat of growth I surmise to lie in the region of the kidneys, and that must be the basis of the Image, upon which all the rest is to be built up. But it must be kept in balance with the other components. I mentioned acromegaly. I must be prepared if necessary to check the processes as well as to stimulate them. He now has great longings to be alone and has discovered for himself the other turret. He will find it convenient for getting away from the Cypher and placing himself in relation to all that he sees from it. Height and distance, to seat him in a chair and approach close to him, all have their uses. I will be patient a little longer. Then, when he has become an Entity, the Nonentity may go.'

And of the entry that immediately followed this one I will only say that it was the one I quoted out of its place when I found that a knot that cannot be untied is best cut. It described my first nocturnal visit to him, his deliberate mesmerism of me, and his dismissal of women as an obstacle that must be got out of the way before anything else could begin.

The house was very still. The clock on the landing below struck a single humming note, but I no more knew which half-hour it was than the Herr Doktor had known when he had meddled with it and been unable to set it right again. And at the best of times it must be a strange thing to read your own day-by-day diary written by another person, but it is a hundred times stranger when that person is not only the recorder, but in some inexplicable way also the source and origin of it all. So, unable to put the book down, I read on to that morning when I had gone to him immediately after breakfast, to speak up for Heinrich and beg him off, but had found myself growing confused instead, and saying the very opposite of what I had intended to say, and then blurting out the bare and ugly truth. What had he to say about that? Merely this, which make the best you can of:

'I said he was strongly auto, and I now put this to the test. It did not surprise me that he should come to me about O.'s dismissal, but the question now was, Could he be induced to do *for himself* what I had hitherto done for him? And for this purpose the occasion was again favourable, even to the morning light of the room. He knew Opfer was a fool, but he was to say so, *unprompted by me.* Suppose I did simply nothing at all, but ordered him to talk on? Might he not arrive at it by a process no more complicated than he could see for himself every time he looked at the man? I therefore only spoke once. He was telling me with the utmost naïveté how bad his German was. I told him to speak in that language, speaking the truth to himself, to whom a man must speak the truth first of all and perhaps last of all. Whereupon it had to come out, that on any reckoning whatever Opfer was plainly a fool. Then why, or rather in what way, was he a fool? I am not often amused, but I had only to give the faintest of smiles and again the thing did itself. He poured it out so readily and copiously that only afterwards did I realise what an enormous stride ahead this was. Set him face to face with the truth and wait for his emancipation. I measured him, which I regret not having done sooner, but I had been misled by the apparent naturalness of his growth, and so have no true datum. In a month the Fool will be out of the way. Then we have finished with preparation and can begin.'

The clock downstairs struck three. Even the Herr Doktor would be asleep, if such a man did sleep like other men. My own lids were heavy, and I began to turn over the pages a number at a time. The last passage I remember reading that night was this:

'For long phrenology misled me, and I thought, as other men have thought, that the brain was the seat of the things I am in search of. Now I am persuaded I am at the true beginning. How these internal secretions are produced I do not know, but I know that they are there, and that unlike other secretions they do not pass out of the body. Remaining in the body they are therefore the reservoir of the elements with which to build. They produce sex and the phenomena of sex. They govern and control growth and strength, precocity and retardation, fear, energy in action and the desire to know. He who understands and can control them in another person should be able to build up out of them an invisible and quasiplastic Image of that person. Formerly the magician used wax. He stuck pins into his doll and melted it before the fire. But this is the living substance of the person himself, since the elements are found in him and do not leave him. Therefore I call them Sentient.

But *because* another person makes the Image the Image is therefore in the power of that other person.

So, somewhere between the two, the Image must stand. It stands as the medium of transmission. According as it approaches perfection so perfect will the transmission be. Suspend its animation and he is tranced through it. Give it my knowledge and he too will know. In short, know *one* other person as you know yourself, and measure the relation between you, and you are on the way to *all* knowledge. With the base and two angles the triangle is inevitable. Nay, with one angle only and the other assumed man has his range-finder. Convert your formula into human terms and where may you not end? Why should the final result not be a being who will be the Master of Mankind?'

But that beautiful writing was running together before my eyes. I felt myself sliding out of my chair as I had slipped from my seat in the chimney corner at home. I got heavily to my feet. In another hour or so the sky would be grey with day. The rest of the writing would have to wait.

CHAPTER XXI

T HE next morning there came a knock at my bedroom door, and Minna never knocked, but just slipped in. Alice stood there with my cup of tea and an awed expression on her foolish face.

'She's having her breakfast in bed!' she said almost in a whisper.

'Who is?' I asked drowsily.

'Minna! And she isn't getting up till middle-day!'

'Well, what about it?'

'Her!' But Minna, I gathered, was now a person of importance. She had strange experiences of an exalted nature and was taken into Mrs. Pitt's bed. I told Alice to be off, for I felt like sleeping till midday myself.

But bit by bit they came back to me, those neat squares of violet writing that had kept me up almost till cockcrow, and there was no more sleep for me. Phrases seemed to come and go before my eyes like the sparks at the back of the grate. Minna! Naturally if she had got in his way he had trodden her down as if she had been an insect under his foot. But myself? What was this he had set out to do and was doing to me? An Image of some kind, that was made out of something in me and therefore was me, but was made by him and was therefore him too! Not wax, to stick pins into or roast in front of a fire, but something he called Vital Centres, that were in people's bodies and didn't pass out of them! And presently somebody would be giving them names, and as soon as they got names they would become a prejudice and a lie! Slowly I struggled awake. I knew what name I'd give them! They were a lot of mumbo-jumbo, and the man who could think of them couldn't be right in his head.

For I revolted against it all. What was there in it that couldn't be explained in some perfectly ordinary way? The accident to the

billiard-table? Of course one of them had discovered it, and had
told him about it, and what good would turning me out of the
house have done? That queer silence that had descended on my
birthday tea? It was a thing that was always happening, so often
that people had catchwords about it, of angels passing over, and
twenty-past and twenty-to, and everybody'd forgotten all about
it five minutes afterwards. Heinrich's knee? He'd been sitting in a
cramped position, and jumped up too suddenly, and ricked himself or something, and as likely as not it was an old fencing-hurt
after all. Myself on the square in the hall? It had been just one of
those 'nothing-times', and there wasn't such a pawn-move, any
more than there was a moon at the bottom of the pond. Fearnley's eyes? Anybody can squint so hard that they strain their eye-
muscles, and as for mesmerism, it was all a trick to make your
eyes do something they weren't used to, making them look up
at something close and bright till they got tired and dizzy. And
Minna last night? Minna with her ficks and smittling! Minna'd
believe anything! Hugging me close like that and Mrs. Pitt half-
way back up the stairs! She'd have come round all right if just the
two of us had been left there! So I demolished it all, scattered it
piecemeal to the winds. In the next room were the four sovereigns the Herr Doktor had left for me. I would get dressed and
slip out of the house before he could send for me, and we would
see whether he could 'make himself felt' while I had a stroll in the
town.

But at that moment Alice came in again to fetch my cup away.
Again she spoke with an air of having something confidential to
impart.

'She's gone out,' she said.

'Minna?'

'No. Her.' She meant Mrs. Pitt. 'She's gone to the agency to get
somebody that can look after the horse.'

'Well?'

'And I shall be busy downstairs,' she said, but with such a world
of meaning that I felt a sudden longing to murder her. She and
Minna between them were making an opportunity for me, and

she was about six feet away, too far for me to reach. I wanted her nearer.

'Alice,' I said, 'come here just a minute,' and as she took a step nearer out my hand shot and I had her by the wrist. I gave it a twist, just to show her.

'Ooooow!' she howled.

'Now tell me what you mean, unless you want it worse!'

'*Oooooow!* Let me go!'

'Will you tell me?'

'Ooooow! She—she used to come into my bed—and sometimes I went into hers—and then she said I used to kick her, and she didn't come any more, but she wasn't in her own bed either——'

And that was enough. There was nothing of our murky affair that she didn't know. First Fearnley, and now this scullery wench! I flung her away and leaped out of bed. She was out of the door like a shot. There on a peg hung my Long's dressing-gown, and already my arms were inside its sleeves. I was on my way upstairs to Minna's room. I burst in. She was lying on her back, enjoying her unwonted comfort, gazing luxuriously up at the ceiling. I stood over her.

'What's all this about?'

She looked at me sleepily, making a little movement with her body.

'That Alice has just told me? How the hell does she come to know?'

'I didn't tell her—I didn't——' she lied, beginning to tremble.

'She says you did——'

'She—she——'

'Who else have you been blabbing to?'

'Mr. Opfer knew that next morning——'

Heinrich! Fearnley! Alice! And the Herr Doktor, only the Herr Doktor didn't care what I did as long as I got it over! Good God!

'What happened to you last night?'

'I was peeping round the door and I saw him there——'

'That's a lie, because I was moving about and I should have seen him, unless you mean he came along the roof too——'

'He came through that other door—it's open—and then I heard him going down to your room——'

'That's another lie, because you said you didn't remember anything till Mrs. Pitt came in——'

'I—I don't rightly know—I came over all funny, and if you don't go I shall scream for somebody because I'm going to get dressed——'

Her wretched moment of ecstasy was over. She was just Minna again, who blackleaded the grates and was careful how she cleaned the windows because of my garters. She put one not too clean foot out of bed, but I was no longer in the room. I was outside, looking along the servants' passage. I think I told you that I had once tried the first-floor door that led to the Herr Doktor's part of the house and had found it locked. But the topmost door now stood open, and I was looking along an unfamiliar corridor to the very spot where I had fallen down the turret stairs and had lain there till his reflector lamp had shone into my eyes above the level of the floor. And after all this I wanted no breakfast. I went down to my own room, hurried into my clothes, and made haste out of that dismal house. The streets of the town were by comparison warm and hospitable.

But even the streets seemed less cheerful than usual. I wandered from place to place, but the Herr Doktor might have been at my elbow, so did his presence weigh on me. Again that violet writing danced before my eyes, ringing fantastic changes in my head. Why, after four days of complete disappearance, had he shuffled into my room in my absence, coming by a new way and contemptuously flicking at Minna in passing? Obviously he had left the journal there for me to study, and would presently question me about it. Probably it was to be my next 'lesson'. I too was to be taught these incantations or whatever they were, and to be taught to manipulate the Centres of others, and to put into them a knowledge that was not theirs, and perhaps even to make their very bodies bigger. I was to be taught to do this, not to work wickedness with it, nor yet goodness, but because it was the truth and therefore so high and separate a thing that it must not even be given a name.

And in the middle of it all I suddenly found myself thinking of Vic Tenison and all those things I had been spared. While I was walking about the streets, looking into bars and finding nobody there and coming out again, he was sitting somewhere on a tall stool, with the smell of fents or woolwashing in his nostrils perhaps or the sounds of near machinery in his ears, drays rattling outside or the coming and going of busy commercial travellers, and the rest of the foolish theories and social stupidities that were themselves phenomena. And as he pushed his pen, he was daydreaming about his savings at the Penny Bank, and perhaps this was one of his sanctified evenings, when he would walk up to my part of the town and gaze at the window of a girl he hadn't kissed yet, and wait till her tiny hand waved, and that would be the perfect end of his day. But I knew better, so much better! A couple of sluts of servant-girls whispered and giggled together over me as they lay in the same bed, and one of them had given me her blackleaded kisses, and the whole house knew about it except the parrot and Mrs. Pitt. And then I remembered another little thing, at which I had to stop in the middle of the street and laugh. On Sunday mornings Mrs. Pitt always took either Minna or Alice with her to church. Vic went by himself to a chapel, and sat up in the gallery, and worked himself up into a goose-flesh of musk about his Beatrice, sitting with her aunt in the pew below. The unspotted Beatrice sitting there in the chapel, shyly taking her glove off to show him the little hand that had waved to him before she knelt down every night to say her prayers, the sinful Minna in the church, her lips over her prayer-book still tremulous from mine the night before! What else was there to do but to stop in the street and laugh?

Well, there was just one other thing to do, and I did it, for apparently it no longer mattered what I did. I was not going to set it down, but when I spoke of it to Brother John, he looked at me gravely for a long time, and then said, 'Why not?' 'What, a cold blooded thing like that, here, in this place?' I asked him. 'Where else if not here?' he said. But though Brother John and Herr Doktor both said, each in his different way, 'Why not?' I am not going into any details about it. It was the middle of the afternoon, and the town was at its most depressing. There were lots of people about, more than usual perhaps, but they were just standing in groups, none of them doing anything in particular. Many of the bars were empty, but some of them fuller than usual, and it was in one of these last that I met her. She was years older than I, but it passed the time. It also lightened my pocket, but was I not buying knowledge with my money? Enough. I wish I had not written it. But John says let it stand. So again, and within a very few hours, money had become the trouble, and when was I going to see the Herr Doktor again to ask him for some more? For four whole days, he had been completely hidden away. At the end of them, late at night, he had stolen out of his room again, not this time downstairs and through the hall, but furtively and by way of the top floor, unlocking a door that had been closed ever since I had been in his house. In my absence he had left a manuscript journal in my room, and in that journal I had read that 'this precious Force', whatever it was, had to be sparingly used, since he did not himself know how much of it he possessed. What then seemed to follow? According to my reckoning only this:

In striking at Fearnley he had drained something from himself. It had taken him four days to recuperate, during which he had devoured his food to the last scrap, and only then had he ventured out, hoping not to meet anybody *nor to be met by them*. He had furtively left the manuscript in my room and made all the haste to hide himself again that he could. There might be something even about his appearance that he did not wish others to see. The conclusion was irresistible. It might be days or even weeks before I saw him again.

CHAPTER XXII

THE summer was passing. Seen from my turret window the smoke-veiled town, its hundreds of thin chimneys each with its breathing of pale grey or its pouring out of curdled black, began

at sunset to have a wild and orange and angry look, and they had
started fires in my room. And though the Herr Doktor had left his
writing with me he had given me no definite instructions about
it, and I was in no state to wrestle with such problems as Sentient
Images alone. So, telling Mrs. Pitt that I didn't want to be dis-
turbed, I turned to the books I had borrowed from the Schillerverein library. I remember it was in German that I first read Hamlet.
When I had finished those I borrowed a couple more. To the notes
I pushed under the Herr Doktor's door I had no reply.

But I still had a few shillings, and one midday, having changed
my books at the club, I found myself sitting in a quiet bar, one that
I seldom entered, looking idly out of the window at the people
who passed. I have told you that while certain of the bars seemed
unusually full others were deserted, and in this one there was not
a soul but myself. But as I sat there came a multitudinous clatter-
ing on the stones outside. It was a procession of some kind, with
many shawled workgirls, and the pattering was the sound of their
wooden clogs. A few of them shook boxes, and I heard a coin or
two clink on the pavement. Then there entered a stranger, and I
asked him what the procession was about.

'Do you live hereabouts?' he said.

'Yes.'

'Have you been away?'

'No, but I live outside, and I haven't been here for a few days.'

'They tried to burn Rothmann's mill down last night and it was
as much as the police could do to turn 'em back. And it's time I
was getting along,' he said, and finished his drink at a gulp and
walked out.

Rothmann's mill! But it was not the moment for thinking. I too
sprang to my feet and made for the door and the streets, to see
what there was to be seen.

But there was little that I had not seen before, just the knots of
people at the street corners, some places full and others empty,
and the police who kept loiterers on the move. A man thrust a
leaflet into my hand, but I put it into my pocket without looking
at it, and I met no more processions. But outside a jeweller's in

Westgate the jeweller himself stood, watching a couple of work-men who were boarding up his windows, and when a shopkeeper does that it looks like the muttering before a storm of some kind. So from there I walked into the Theatre Bar.

And here I learned a little more, because, in the middle of the afternoon, I found the School at full strength. And it was a sub-dued school for once, for nobody knew yet whether the curtain was going up that evening or not. What was it? I asked. A strike? Well, I was told, they weren't calling it a strike yet, but it might break out any hour. A lot of damned mischief-making agitators, taking the bread out of honest hardworking artists' mouths, and I heard the name of Crawford bandied about. But somebody else jumped up, for there were others there besides the School, and for a minute or two there were hot words. If it wasn't for a few like Crawford, one man said, the bloody-minded sanctimonious Roth-manns would have it all their own way.

Then it was, at the sound of that name, that my nerves suddenly went all to pieces. *Rothmann!* A vapour seemed to rise from the floor. As the Genie was liberated from the Bottle in the tale it seemed to thin out till it spread through the whole bar. And it was as if the squint of a pair of carriage-lamps far away down a dark road undid itself again, and instead of concentrating itself became pervading and ten times life-size, for there seemed to appear somewhere up by the cornice two vast and faint and silvery lunettes, like a magnified pair of spectacles, and a shadowy smoking-cap above them, and a grizzled wisp of beard still faintly issuing from the Bottle on the floor. And as on that morning in the Herr Doktor's room the Spirit of Prophecy had descended upon me, so now I wanted to cry again to this Herr Doktor whose presence filled the place, '*Don't* tell me! *Don't* help me at all! I want to see if I can do it all by myself!'

And I had gone on to prophesy a big thing happening, and a marble tombstone in a graveyard with angels mourning over it, and a thousand employees taking a special train for a day's merry-making at Morecambe.

And here it was, close upon us, for they had tried to set fire to Rothmann's mill.

Then somebody shook me.

'Hi, young Byles, it isn't bed-time yet!'

I staggered out of the bar as if I was drunk, to revive myself in the cold air.

I forget where I went; I hardly knew where I was at the time; but by half-past six I was once more back in the Theatre Bar. Still nobody knew whether there would be a performance that night or not. Fresh people came in moment by moment, the newspaper lads pushed in and out. But I only wanted to watch, and as I did so—this was a little before seven—the inner door that led to the theatre opened, and Michelson appeared, carrying a newly-printed and still damp announcement. He sprang to a chair and then to a table and stuck it across the ballet-girl's knees:

THEATRE ROYAL

NO PERFORMANCE TO-NIGHT.

Then he jumped down again and mopped his brow.

'Hot work!' he said. 'Thirty-two minutes. The machine's running 'em off now. I've got a dozen lads—it'll be all over the town in half an hour. Florrie! A double one and another after that. Well, what about it, chaps?'

Strange wildfire that runs from man to man at these times, setting them all alight with the same flame! The actors, who only a few minutes before had been talking gloomily among themselves, were the first on their feet. They seized Michelson and hoisted him up as if he had been the bearer of good news. A 'Hooray!' broke out.

'Hooray! With a hip—hip—hip——'

The whole bar joined in. Up sprang the company's comic man. I forget what song he started, because he didn't get very far into it. The doors swung open again, and this time the news was that the tram service was suspended. Out broke the cheering afresh.

'Hooray! Now nobody's going home! Fall in, lads, and sing up——'

They fell in. Somebody held the doors back and out they marched, singing as they went. In three minutes the bar was empty again except for two or three of the School, who still stood looking thoughtfully at the notice across the ballet-girl's knees. I nodded a good night to them, and this time walked home, not only for lack of pence, but also because there were no trams.

I had got straight into bed that night, and was just dropping off to sleep, when I found myself awake again and listening. Perhaps the wind was in the south that night, for I heard, or fancied I heard, an uneasy, sighing sound that seemed to proceed from the town itself. The wind seemed to change, but presently it came again, and I got out of bed and crossed to the window. Over on the other side of the town there was a corona of light. It grew brighter as I watched it, and suddenly I was out of the room, on my way to the turret. As I opened the turret window the first tongues of flame appeared. The police had not been able to keep them back this time. It *was* Rothmann's mill.

Fascinated I watched. Slowly that portion of the skyline became the colour of a tritoma, flecked with tongues of yellow, and a tall chimney that looked like a white-hot knitting-needle standing up solitary in the middle of it. A rod of incandescence, it stood there against the red-bellied clouds that rolled away into the night, and if you want to know how a factory chimney falls when it is so disintegrated by heat that it can bear no more I can tell you. It buckles and breaks in two separate places, and as it rushes to its base there rises such a fountain of burning debris as lights up the land for miles around. I could see stray embers of it floating nearly half-way to the Herr Doktor's grounds. The turret glowed with a dull orange light, the turret along the roof was lighted like my own. And suddenly I stepped back from the window. No doubt the whole household was out of bed, watching from the windows below. But the Herr Doktor, like myself, had come up to the roof to see.

CHAPTER XXIII

WITH chimneys for pens and smoke-curds for ink that birth-place of mine has written its own story across the skies, but I have already said that I am the last of its sons to be its historian. As dispassionately as a stranger I looked on in those days at what my fellow-townsmen did with their grey lives, seldom livened by even a grudging mirth, on which beauty would have seemed a wasted thing and even the word hope one best unspoken. As for taking sides, to this day I have very little knowledge what it was all about.

But what I saw I saw, and I saw it with the summer over, and October in, and a nip in the air, and familiar streets suddenly unfamiliar, so that you wondered what was the matter till you looked up, and saw that the sky was swept as clean as creation again and not a chimney smoking. They stood up over roofs and lesser chimneys like spent matches, gaunt and useless at street-ends, as if the wind sweeping down from the moors was a sinister thing, that brought with it desolation and famine and cleanness of teeth. And without smoke even the wheels in the streets ceased to move. Not a loaded dray was to be seen, not a coal-cart, not a tram, only an occasional barrow with somebody's household belongings on it, and silent people everywhere. Strange unknown shapes crept out into the light of day, as parasites appear on the surface of a cooling carcase. They were the aged who had to be worked for, and the very young who had nobody to take them to school and fetch them away again, and those whose furniture stood on the pavements because they could not pay their rent. I have seen, but only as if it had been something in a picture or a play, not one shop-window boarded up, but whole streets, and public buildings with hardly a pane of glass left in them, for brawls and tumults broke out without a moment's warning. I was hardly out of earshot when the Black Maria itself was set on, and its door wrenched open with crowbars, and a prisoner taken out of it and carried shoulder-high. I have seen the redcoated soldiers advancing at a walk, with levelled bayonets, and my fellow-townsmen standing menacingly up to them, with showers of stones flying over their heads from behind, till they wavered and broke and ran. And none of it, I say, seemed any business of mine. It was merely something they did, these hundred and fifty thousand who ordered their worldly affairs that way, and on Sunday got together in their places of worship, and with the help of an organ and a choir sought to escape the consequences of their own acts, which they called their other-worldly life. And even now, as I sit writing about it, if I pretended to any particular emotion I know that I should be telling a lie.

But from these social stupidities that are merely so many phenomena themselves there separates itself an incident that brings me back to my own story again. It happened on the very day after the burning of Mr. Rothmann's mill, and in the Schillerverein. I had gone there that afternoon intending to change one of my borrowed books, but no sooner had I set foot inside its doors than I was seized by Mr. Holtz, the bookseller who had married a business and whose name was up in gilt letters on the Grammar School wall.

'The very man we want,' he said. 'We've done *our* best. Come on,' and he was pushing me towards the smoking-room door.

'Let my hang up my hat, Mr. Holtz——'

'Hang it next to his then, and then take him away,' he said, and there, hanging on one of the cloakroom pegs, I saw the large black wideawake the Herr Doktor always wore when he visited the town.

'We've all had a go at him. He just doesn't understand. What are you going to do with a man who's never heard of Hardcastle and Crawford?' and with that Mr. Holtz pushed me through the doors into the smoking-room.

I had last seen the Herr Doktor some fifteen or sixteen hours before, standing there in his turret, while the tritoma-glow across the town had died down to a sullen red. Now he stood on the hearthrug under the oil-painting of Schiller, dressed in his brown town suit, slowly turning his bald head, looking this way and that. The group of members about him had evidently given him up, for they were talking among themselves, half of them with their backs to him. As for lip-reading, the only idea Mr. Holtz seemed to have of it was to shout in the Herr Doktor's ear, and he shouted now, and shook him, and then pointed to me.

And something of his utter loneliness and helplessness touched me for the first time. Whatever he might write in that violet writing of his, now he could only stand there under Schiller, all his knowledge occulted, a lighthouse without a light, with the waves of life and its follies breaking threateningly about his base. The uproar of those angry breakers did not penetrate his astronomical silence. Give him a chessboard and the room would have gathered to watch him. But take it away——

'Tell him, and then take him home,' said Mr. Holtz. 'He can't do any good here, and it isn't everybody in the street knows he's deaf and dumb. He'll see burning mills best from his own house.'

So, as what was mystification to them was child's play to me, after a few rapid exchanges I turned to Mr. Holtz again.

'He wants to know about Voyt, Sons & Successors.'

'Yes, we guessed that. Tell him we don't know. We *don't* know. Nobody knows anything yet. Nobody'll lay a finger on him as long as he keeps out of the way. Tell him.'

I did so, and again turned to Mr. Holtz—'He wants to know where Mr. Rothmann is.'

'So do a good many other people. Tell him he's gone to France. Tell him anything you like. How did he get here?'

'His man left. We've got a new lad. He's coming for him at four o'clock.'

'See he doesn't come here again, and keep out of mischief yourself,' said a Mr. Holtz I didn't know, a short-spoken, practical Mr. Holtz, who might know nothing about the books he sold but knew that anything small and definite is good in an emergency, and at that moment the voices of lads in the street were heard, crying the latest edition. With his cap on his head and his bundle under his arm one of them appeared in the doorway, and there was a rush for him. In two minutes the smoking-room was a washing-day of fluttering, unfolding papers.

But the Herr Doktor neither bought a paper nor moved to go away. Voyt, Sons & Successors! A hundred times I had seen that furlong of serried roofs down by the canal, looking as if some monstrous sawfish had lifted itself out of the black water to bask along its bank. That too to me was one of these unknown activities that went to sleep every night just as the other half of the town was waking up to play. And he had never been even a sleeping-partner in the business. He had always been one of its liabilities, compassionately provided for out of its resources by a preceding generation. And now that I looked at him again he was not so much a lighthouse without a light, turning his blank spectacled head this way and that, as a lost child, that had strayed on to a battlefield, and might get hurt, and I was to get him back quickly to his Victorian house on the hill. Suppose his money went? Where was he? Where was I? What good would his Vital Centres do him then? But at that moment the door of the smoking-room opened again, and in walked Dr. Müller, and Dr. Müller, you may remember, had the bedside manner. He was far too practised in it to glance up from behind a newspaper and then to hide himself behind it again when he saw it was only poor old Voyt. Brisk and pink and smiling he came straight up to us, and held out his hand first to the Herr Doktor and then to me, as affably as if we had been just a party of three like any other.

'And how is the household Voyt? Playing chess I'll be bound! I'm afraid it's a game we poor practitioners can't spare the time for. Be anything you like, Peter, but don't be a doctor. You had a nice holiday this summer?'

I shook my head and told him I hadn't been away.

'No? Well, where you are the air's as good as you'll find anywhere. Straight off the moors.' And then, in a flattering aside to myself, 'And how's our friend keeping? He is sleeping well? Appetite good? He doesn't suffer from headaches at all or any trouble with his eyes? Excellent! Compensation's a wonderful thing. You'd really think sometimes nature gave more than she took away. Well, I just looked in to snatch a cup of tea——' and Dr. Müller rose and fell on his toes and looked at the gold half-hunter in his hand.

But the waiter who took the order for Dr. Müller's tea also announced the Herr Doktor's brougham, and I saw the looks that passed between member and member as, with a last uncomprehending stare that did not even include myself, he slowly turned his back and occulted himself away.

One more episode, and I leave it to you whether it concerned me or not. The Herr Doktor had left the club perhaps half an hour, and I was passing the front of the Exchange, when I heard from the arches beneath it the sounds of strident singing. I made my way towards them, and came upon a small but increasing crowd, with a man on a portable wooden platform in the middle of it. His hands were clasped above his head, his eyes were tight shut, and his face was all tortured as he cried to the cold sky that the Day of the Lord was at hand. Then somebody began to sing again, and at the first 'Oh——' he opened his eyes again and began to stamp his foot for them to sing faster, faster—

'Oh I'm so glad that Jesus loves me,
Jesus loves me, Jesus loves me——'

When it seemed about to flag another frenzied 'Oh I'm so glad' broke out, and it began all over again. Then there rose ejaculations and texts.

'Come unto Me——'
'Waiting at the gates——'
'Washed in the blood——'
'For there shall not be left one stone upon another——'

Suddenly the man was no longer on the platform, for a woman had jumped up and taken his place. It was Margaret, who had called me a limb of Satan, and her voice screamed shrilly out:

'Stand up for Jesus! Stand up, I say—you—you—you——' and at each 'you' out shot her finger at somebody. 'Oh my brethren, oh my sisters, I am speaking to each one of you—to you, Polly Binns, and to you, Jim Taylor, and to you, William Bottomley and him next you!' And then her eyes fell on me, for I had been pushed forward by those behind, and her voice cracked deliriously.

'Oh! It is the Lord's doing! Who shall say after this testimony that it is not the Lord's doing? And to *you*, Peter Byles, for it is written I will in no wise cast you out! He has taken your sister to his blessed arms, and is ready to take you though your sins be as scarlet! There she is at this moment, smiling down on you from up there, though she hadn't even a letter from her own flesh and blood! "Tell Peter I forgive him"—they were her own words—and now the Lord has sent him to me! Come unto me, Peter——,' and she threw out her arms as if to hug me as she had always hugged Nora.

But I was not there. The sound of her voice died away behind me.

It is no good telling me how I ought to have felt. I only knew how I did feel. I should have liked to take her by the throat and have throttled her. I hated her and her Saviour alike. Why hadn't she written? Why hadn't I been told? Nora, dead! Half a dozen times I had been going to see her. Now it was flung publicly in my face like this, and Margaret, having molly-coddled her through her life, must go and rant her out of it! Don't talk to me about natural affection. What in fact had my little sister been? Just a puling, tale-bearing, whimpering child, full of herself and her woes. And Margaret, as the Herr Doktor had said, was just a canting, prayer-meeting shrew. Liars and hypocrites! People couldn't even die decently for them and their righteousness! If Nora was in bliss what more did she want? Why did people want kids anyway? To keep them when they got old, and they called it honouring their father and their mother. Anyway Nora would never have been any good and it was a mouth fewer to feed. So this is what I did. I had no money, but I was known at the Theatre Bar, and the place had a slate. It was full of people, and every pair of eyes that met mine seemed to me to have the same thought in them. 'Look at him!' they seemed to say. 'He's just been told his little sister's dead. It was shouted at him in the street for everybody else to hear too. It doesn't seem to bother him much, does it?' It did not bother me, because I did not let it. I drowned it. As deep as they would supply me with liquor I drowned it, and would have drowned it deeper still if I could. Nobody saw my arrival at the Herr Doktor's house in the early hours of that morning. I didn't remember getting there myself. And how was I to guess, when I woke up at getting on for midday, that that was the last day I was to spend in that house for many days to come?

CHAPTER XXIV

IT was the lad Tim, who now made shift in Fearnley's place, who told me that they had brought my breakfast up but had taken it away again, untouched and stone-cold, a couple of hours ago. I opened my hot and heavy eyes. The lamp I had no recollection of having carried in stood totteringly near the edge of my dressing-table, and I had turned it up too high, for its chimney was blackened and broken and the splintered pieces of it were inside the globe. I had cut the laces of my boots, but was still wearing my shirt, with the collar unfastened in front but not at the back, so that it scratched my cheek. And Tim, who was an undersized lad of sixteen but as sharp as if he slept in the knife-box, was looking at me with an understanding grin on his face.

'Gor!' he said, and began to fish the pieces of the broken chimney from the globe of the lamp. But he broke off to pick up something from the floor, which he brought to me. It was a folded note.

'Didn't you see it last night?' he said. 'I put it there for you. He gave it to me hisself and said I was to give it to you. You must have been slewed and proper!'

I looked at the note he put in my hand. The writing was Heinrich's. The lad rattled on.

'He was helping 'em at the school. I was walking the horse about so the chill wouldn't strike through to him, and he knew the brougham he said. So he tore a page out of his pocketbook and wrote the note.'

'What school?'

'The board-school in Wellesley Lane. They're dishing the kids out soup there. They give 'em a ticket and they take it away in their jugs and millcans.'

I gave a groan and turned over on my pillow again.

But the stupor of sleep had passed, leaving only the nausea of waking. After a minute I unfolded the note. As if nothing had happened between us it began '*Mein lieber Peter*'. He had not yet found proper work, he said, but in times such as these, when all suffered alike, one did not think of one's self. He often thought of me, and would like to see me. Anna sent her love to me. Tim was still lingering, picking up my trousers from the floor, taking my cut bootlaces out of my boots. I lifted my head.

'What did you say he was doing?'

'Dishing out soup. He'd just come out to count how many more of 'em there were. He'd a big apron with a bib on. They're giving 'em half-loaves too. Him, mister—' and he jerked his head vaguely towards the other end of the house, '—is he the same Voyts as them down by the canal?'

'Yes.'

'Because I've heard 'em talking. The barracks is full of sodgers, and they'd better keep 'em there without they want the cobbles torn up. They're telling folk to keep to their houses. They fire over their heads first, but bullets has to go somewhere——'

'Get me some tea.'

I forced myself to dress. My body seemed to have no heat, it was a bitter day outside, and in my sitting-room I could only sit huddled over the fire, trying to remember last night, trying to forget, and wondering why I had been put into the world at all.

And it was that precise moment that the Herr Doktor must needs choose to push at my door and stand there in the doorway.

Dull, uncaring, with a head that throbbed and eyes I could hardly keep open, I looked at him without even getting up out of my chair. But I looked again. What was this? He hardly seemed the same man I had seen only yesterday in the club, uncomprehending, forlorn, a lost child strayed on to a battlefield, a blinded beacon that should have been a source of light. His bearing was upright, alert, authoritative. His face was the face of a man who was responsible for his own life whatever others chose to do with theirs, and he had a second book in his hand, from the look of it a continuation of the manuscript in my drawer. And he was looking at me searchingly, anxiously.

'You are not feeling well?'

I lifted myself slowly to my feet, and he repeated his question.

'You are not feeling well?'

'No. I've got a beastly headache.'

'Sit down in your chair again.'

But I did not obey him. Caring nothing what happened I remained standing, my eyes on the carpet.

'Why does your head ache?'

Well, nothing mattered that morning. 'Because I got beastly drunk last night,' I said.

Instead of frowning he gave me a quick, apprehensive look. 'You fell? You hurt yourself? There was some accident?'

'No.'

'Only that, that you got drunk?' I saw the look of relief on his face.

'It's enough if you've brought me something else to read,' I said with a glance at the book in his hand.

'And you got drunk because——?'

Well, he could have that too if he wanted it. 'I got drunk because my sister's dead, and they never told me, and the first I knew about it was that hell-cat bawling it at me in the street.'

'Some woman told you in the street? That your sister was dead?'

'Yes, and two or three hundred other people too.'

'You knew this woman?'

I made a sorry attempt to show him who it was.

'Ah, the scold who says her prayers. This time she was saying them in the street. There are such people as that. And you were very fond of your sister, and her death has troubled you so much that it has given you a headache. You wrote frequently to her perhaps?'

I was silent, for I cannot convey to you the irony of it. I

remembered Dr. Müller at the club, asking me how he was, whether he was sleeping well, had a good appetite, any trouble with his eyes. From the look of him now those days he had spent shut up in his room might have been days of recuperation and convalescence, himself a whole man again, master of all his faculties. He spoke peremptorily.

'Look at me. Do not look down at the floor. My time is not to be wasted on such frivolities as these. You have *no* headache,' and though I did not lift my eyes I could feel the passing of his fingers before my face. 'You have *no* headache, and my strength is not to be wasted any more than my time. Does your head ache?'

'No.'

'Is your brain clear? Can you think?'

'Yes.'

'Then remember that both my time and my strength are important things. Where is the book?'

I opened the drawer of the writing-table to get it, but as ill-fortune would have it I had slipped into the drawer also one of the books I had borrowed from the Schillerverein library. It was the tale of Peter Schlemihl, the man who sold his shadow to the devil, and his eyes fell on it. He strode forward and picked it up. The frown gathered on his brow. From the beginning he had strictly enjoined me that I was *not* to learn from books, *not* to listen to lectures, *not* to believe what I heard merely because a thousand people said it, and I feared he was about to break out. But if I must not waste his strength neither must he waste it himself, and he controlled himself. He threw the book where he had thrown Heinrich's cup and saucer—into the fender. Then he pointed to my chair.

'I prefer that you should not stand while I talk to you. Sit down.'

I did so, and his examination of me began.

My headache had gone, and with it that heavy stupor of indifference. Never had I seen him in a mood so little to be played with, and I was intimidated already. Already one of the covers of *Peter Schlemihl* was beginning to curl with the heat of the fire, but it might have been shrivelling under his gaze, so full of scorn was the glance he threw at it. Then he pointed abruptly to the drawer again. I was to get *his* book, *my* book, the book in the beautiful blank uncharacterised writing. I did so, and without being told sat down in my chair again.

'You know for what purpose you are here?'

'Yes, Herr Doktor.'

'That it is to study earnestly, not to go about the world believing whatever others put into your head?'

'Yes, Herr Doktor.'

'Enough.' He placed the book in my hands, open at a passage. 'You read this?'

'Yes.'

'Read it carefully now, and then close the book, and tell me in your own words what it means.'

It was the passage about phrenology. He had thought at one time that these Vital Centres of which he spoke had their seat in the brain. And he was waiting for my answer. I spoke sullenly.

'You mean that head on the bracket on your stairs, with the names of the bumps on it. It isn't bumps.'

'Go on.'

'It's something inside yourself, something soft, like wax.' (I had clutched at the idea that if I made myself stupid I might escape.)

'Go on.'

'And they don't come out of yourself, like tears when you cry, but stop inside.'

'And then?'

'They make you grow.'

'Only grow?'

I mumbled something about musk.

'What else?'

'Your mind grows in great jumps too.'

'In what way do these Centres affect the mind?'

'They make you angry and frightened and things like that.'

'They govern the passions. And then?'

'Then you begin saying things you never thought of before, but you know they're right, because they can't be any other way.'

'And these things are all in the body? But do not some people call them the soul?'

'That's only trying to explain something you don't know much about by something you don't know anything about at all,' I said, and he nodded, and paused for a moment before going on.

'So if you can find these things in another person's body, and can get control of them, you have control of that person, have you not?'

'Yes, if,' I said sulkily.

'And, if, instead of doing these things yourself, you can make that person do them for *himself*, is not that the same thing?'

'That's another if,' I answered, in so dogged a tone that he glanced sharply at me, a warning glance.

'Does your head ache now?'

'No.'

'Would you like it to begin to ache again, just a little, a very little?'

'No,' I said hurriedly.

'Then we will continue the lesson. So when you think of these things you have never thought of before, but know that they are so because they cannot be otherwise—what follows after that?'

'That perhaps the things themselves haven't happened, but they're going to, because all the things are happening that are going to make them happen.'

'But—think—is that not to make of the past and the future the same thing?'

'No—yes I mean—I don't know,' and he paused again, and I saw that he was a little out of breath. But after a moment he resumed.

'We will now see at what point we have arrived. There are then in every person certain elements that control his growth, his passions, his understanding of all that he sees about him, even his understanding of the things that are *not* about him yet but are about to be. These elements are the very essence of himself, and by close and patient study, much, much thought, and a measure of confidence and consent too, that person can be governed and directed. His inner self can be moulded with as much certainty and truth as a painter or a sculptor can depict his outward features. And if consent is given or otherwise obtained you and your subject are partners in the result. You have understood so far? Yes? Then I will rest for a moment while you think carefully of this.'

Again I must remind you of the fantastic form these interviews took. You are to remember that except for the occasional sound of my own voice, repeating something after him to show that I understood it, there was not a sound in the room except the purring of the fire in the grate. Now even the play of his eyes and features, variable as water with both the sun and the wind on it, came to rest. His fingers, so instinct with a thousand meanings, lay lifeless on the arms of his chair. He closed his eyes, and as if there had in truth been some physical interchange between us, I putting forth something to him and receiving something in return from him, he extending to me his support and then withdrawing it again, I felt the beginning of that dull headache again. But without warning he suddenly opened his eyes and resumed at the point where he had left off.

'So, a little at a time,' he said, slowly counting out the meanings, 'the Sentient Image comes gradually to birth. At first it is a delicate thing,' and I cannot express the delicacy he put into those now-awake-again fingers. 'It is a thing to be treated with the greatest gentleness till it finds its own strength. But presently it becomes what is known as Second Nature. And it is a compound of the elements of two people who have consented to one will. Would you not call that a very great secret to have discovered?'

'I'm too tired to think any more to-day, Herr Doktor,' I said, but he went on.

'Would it not be a secret to change the face of the world? To make its possessor master of the world if he wished to be master of so foolish a place? And in his hands, at his will, *need* the world be any more a foolish place? Could he not re-model it as he himself has been re-modelled? Would not then truth prevail over stupidity, and the passions and affections and all false thinking be seen for the misleading things they are? Has any other way yet been discovered?' His eyes were becoming carriage-lamps; I felt their approach. 'Would not that man be such a man as the world has never seen? Tell me——'

'I can't think of any more—I just can't——'

'One more little effort, in which I will help you. Then that will be sufficient for to-day. See, I place my hand lightly on your body——'

But as he placed his finger-tips just below my breastbone I was up out of my chair as if an adder had struck at me. Before he could bemuse me again I must summon every ounce of strength I possessed to resist. I shouted so that the sound of my own voice might wake me from the drowsiness that was beginning to cloud me over. I caught at the mantelpiece to steady myself.

'It's all a lot of balderdash!' I shouted. 'It's balderdash, and I won't, I won't, I won't! I will read *Peter Schlemihl* if I want! I'll do anything else I like! I don't belong to you! I belong to myself! I don't want to be made an Image and I don't want to be told how to make anybody else one! I don't care what you did to Heinrich——'

His brow contracted. 'Ah! The Fool again!'

'And I don't care what you did to Fearnley and Minna! It's you who're the fool, unless you're mad! Everybody isn't deaf and dumb like you! My father didn't know, he didn't know, he didn't know! He wouldn't have let me come if he had! I want to be like everybody else, and you've made me so that I can't be, and it's horrible, horrible——'

But even as I raved at him I was noticing his hands again. One of them was a little above the other, as if there was an invisible graduated glass between them such as chemists use when they measure out a dose of something. I even imagined the words to fit the gesture.

'Resistance—good—I expected it—without resistance there is no strength——'

'Yes, I am resisting!' I cried. 'I hate you—I hate you—I hate you——'

'Half strength, only half strength,' the hands seemed to be saying. 'Just this once—it will not be to do more than once——'

'Damn you!' I cried, and then, my voice rising to an agonised shriek, '*Stop! Oh, stop—let me alone——*'

For beginning at my throat, then shooting like an arrow to the back of my head and out beyond, only to re-enter and pass through my veins and begin its instantaneous circuit again, a pain such as I will not attempt to describe flooded me through. It blinded me, for I stood there in the darkness of a thousand years of night. And that Hand of Kornelius Voyt's might have been on the throttle of an engine, for the pain died down to the dullness of a sub-pain, that lasted another thousand years, and then leaped up again as if bellows blew on red coals. How many times he did this I do not know, nor can I tell you anything about that pain at full strength. The last thing I remember was its passing like a storm, away into some immensity of distance. His arms were about me, not this time to hurt, but with an astonishing gentleness, as if I had been a precious burden to be let so slowly and with such care down into the chair again. I did not hear him leave.

So who was going to stay any longer in a house where things like that could happen? Not Fearnley, not I. All my possessions would go into my father's gladstone-bag, and five, six, I do not know how many hours later I was packing it. I was doing so with numbed and bloodless hands, that did not feel what they touched, in a room without either heat or light, for my fire had gone out and the broken chimney of the lamp had not been replaced. My teeth were chattering, for the world outside had become more freezingly cold with every hour that had passed, and I had not eaten all that day. Eat I must, for I felt as if I had been gutted like a hare. Totteringly, like an old, old man, I left my packing half finished and groped my way downstairs to Mrs. Pitt's room.

And what a place of comfort and warmth that sitting-room next to the kitchen suddenly seemed to be! The towel hung over the parrot's cage, the fire was a great still glow of red that tinged the whole ceiling except the bright circles over the lamp, and there they were gathered, Mrs. Pitt with her glasses on, reading, Minna up against the fireguard with her petticoats drawn up and dropping them again as her shins got scorched, the placid Alice munching something, the lad Tim strutting about like the master of the house. Leave this house, they, with the town in the grip of a strike? Much they looked like leaving! But nothing was keeping me another day.

'Mrs. Pitt,' I said, steadying myself in the doorway, 'I want you please to cut me a packet of sandwiches for to-morrow morning. I'm going for a walk on the moors. Cut two packets so they'll go in my pockets.'

But before I had got half of it out she was on her feet, good soul, and hurrying towards me.

'Mercy on us! What's happened? What have you been doing with yourself?' Then, suddenly brisk, 'Alice, you go and make a bowl of hot beef tea at once and put some bread in it. Minna, shift and make a bit of room at the fire. As for you,' this was Tim, 'get out of the way, for you're under everybody's feet! Come here, Mr. Peter——'

And where should I be to-morrow night, sleeping in what bed, swallowing whose beef tea? The glow of the fire was all that mattered for the moment. Mrs. Pitt had put a shawl round my shoulders. Minna, close at my side, was cuddling and stroking herself as if she had been a cat. Slowly the blood returned to my body as I toasted myself and sipped the hot beef tea. Just to be free from that incredible pain was pure bliss. Now I had better set about making my plans.

I was still sitting there, making them, when Mrs. Pitt put down her book and ordered us all off to bed.

'You too, Mr. Peter, there's a good man,' she coaxed me. 'Don't stop down here watching the fire out—I'll see to your sand-wiches——'

But after they had gone I still stood there, with my back to the fireguard, the lamp out and my shadow spreading over the russet-lighted ceiling.

How much did I owe at the Theatre Bar? No matter; there was always something to eat there, if it was only the bits of cheese on the counter and the biscuits they gave away. And Heinrich was dishing out soup to the children at the board-school and I had his note in my pocket. He often thought of me, actually wanted to see me again! Why? The Herr Doktor had done nothing for him. I, a member of the Schillerverein myself and able to approach other members, had not lifted a finger to help him, and yet he wanted to see me again! And I was still warming my back thinking of it, when I saw the door move slightly, and then open, and there Minna stood, with her clothes slipped on over her nightgown and her bootlaces untied. They trailed behind her as she shuffled towards me.

'I thought I'd just pop down,' she whispered. 'What's the matter?'

'You pop back then. The matter? Nothing.'

'Yes there is,' she said, and anyway they'd all have seen the last of me before this time to-morrow.

'Will you promise not to tell anybody if I tell you?'

'Yes.'

'Well, I'm off. I've had a row with him and I'm going.'

She gave a shiver and an 'Oh!' of fear. 'Going away? From here? Not coming back?'

'And nobody knows, you understand, nobody.'

And she might as well have wrapped her arms about the frozen pump outside as about me. Musk? A stickiness that clogged the wings? Not now. My wings were for flight.

But suddenly a dire thought came to me. Her arm still held me, and I had heard somewhere, from Heinrich perhaps, that when women loved it was with a passion so headstrong that they would follow their man through fire and flood to the ends of the earth. She was blubbering that she didn't want me to go, didn't want me to go. I took her by the shoulders and shook her, shook her till her head nodded, shook her till she gulped and choked.

'Listen. You aren't going to have a baby, are you?'

'N–no——'

'Are you sure? How do you know?'

'I went—Alice knows somebody, and I went——'

'Very well. Are you listening? Remember, if I catch you following me——' and the rest was a menace.

But—I could hardly believe it—hadn't she heard me? Hadn't she understood? At the word 'follow' she gave another 'Oh!' of fright.

'Oh, I darstn't, I darstn't, sir! My father'd take the stick to me! I have to send all my wages home now—he'd break every bone in my body——'

'Shut up, you little fool! Who's asking you to come? You're *not* to come! Do you hear me? You're to stop here——'

But she either didn't or wouldn't hear. All she wanted was to hear her own voice, sobbing that she darstn't, she darstn't—her father'd kill her, and there were grand fires here and lots to eat, and she darstn't——'

This their famous musk! It was as much as I could do not to laugh outright with bitterness and relief.

'Get to bed,' I said, and she gave a hitch to some string or other and shuffled slipshod away. I called to her again as she reached the door. 'Mind—if you say a word to anybody——'

'Yes, sir,' she said, and closed the door.

By half-past nine the next morning, with the great shawl Mrs. Pitt had given me crossed over my chest and tied again round my waist, a packet of sandwiches in each pocket and my father's bag hidden by Tim in the bushes near the gate, I was out of that house and making as if for the plantation and the moors. Then, out of sight of its windows, I doubled back to where my bag waited. I was free.

CHAPTER XXV

FREE to do what? That was part of my planning of the night before, and the first thing I had to do was to ascertain how much I owed at the Theatre Bar. I pushed at its doors as Florrie was polishing up the glasses in readiness for her midday customers and flung my bag on the counter. I asked her how much she had against me on the slate. She looked at it and said fourteen shillings.

'All right, take care of that bag for me. I'll be back in about an hour,' I said, and walked out.

False pretences? Fraud? Theft? What else was there to do? The devil I had left had long since made away with all the differences between what other men call right and wrong. I had it in his own writing, that when one was afraid the natural thing to do was to conceal and lie. He told me himself that it was not in the least important that I should get drunk, but exceedingly important that I should not fall and hurt myself. As for musk—pah! So what had he to complain about if, having nothing of my own, I robbed him? There were plenty of valuables in his house I could have laid my hands on before coming away, but my bag was full already, they would quickly have been missed, and I had thought of something better. But before I come to these days of my freedom, when I haunted the town of my birth like a visitant from another world, flickering and dancing through it like St. Elmo's fire, let me tell you my reason for speaking of them at all.

If I have learned anything whatever in my misdirected life it is that there is nothing in the world so irrelevant as a logical conclusion pushed so far that it ceases to have any bearing on anything but itself. And whose training had been logical if mine had not? Playing abstruse games of chess without either men or board while I was still in the beginning of my 'teens? Striking my billiard-ball and reckoning the results in terms of planetary space? Who had been taught that men were symbols, tokens, pawns to be arranged in a pattern, and that the only real thing about them was that each of them had inside him the makings of an Image the existence of which was the last thing he himself suspected? Who had been told that if women had not been a secretion and an excrement even their own kind would have had nothing to do with them? Who had been cut out from his own stock and grafted on another, so that even the loss of a mother was a step to emancipation? If these things were the realities of life I knew them all. But of its unrealities, such unrealities as cold and need and hunger and sickness and the thousand daily miseries of a smokeless and workless town I knew nothing.

But already my lack of pence had told me that the bridge between such realities and such unrealities is money, and to begin with I had no overcoat. I did not go to Long's to be measured for one this time. A ready-made one would do, and I was known at the shop I went to and received with smiles and greetings. While I was about it I bought a warm dogskin waistcoat too, and a couple of pairs of thick gloves, and an enormous pigskin holdall, with so many straps and buckles and snaps and fastenings of one sort and another that it took several minutes to get it open. These things I ordered to be delivered at the Schillerverein that afternoon, in the Herr Doktor's name.

But the Schillerverein saw nothing of my next purchase, which was a splendid one indeed. For some weeks past I had seen, in the window of his own tobacconist, a magnificent smoker's cabinet, surmounted by an octagonal temple which, when you turned the knob at the top, opened simultaneously eight doors, each of them with an elastic band inside it for cigars. To this I added the largest and most expensive gold-mounted meerschaum pipe I could see, and these I brought away with me. I then walked into a café, looked round as if in search of somebody, and picked up what I had really come for—a discarded newspaper lying on a chair. From the café I walked to the third-class waiting-room at the station. There I undid my purchases from their tell-tale shop-wrappings and folded them in the newspaper instead. Because of my size and bearing I did these things boldly, throwing the Herr Doktor's name about right and left. I was asked no questions. The pawnbroker asked me none either, and I returned to the Theatre Bar and tossed down a couple of sovereigns on the counter.

'Clean the slate, Florrie, and change me the other,' I said, and turned to three theatrical acquaintances who were watching me from their seats under the ballet-girl.

Their news was not good. The company was in fact on the rocks, and somebody or other had gone to London to see what could be done about it. In short, foolish fellows, all three of them had neglected to provide themselves with that bridge between unreality and reality that is called money. But Mrs. Pitt's sandwiches were substantial and there were plenty of them, and two or three of the pawnbroker's shillings went on hot rum. I produced the meerschaum pipe, and the four of us discussed profitable ways of disposing of it.

Little did I imagine as we did so that I was on the threshold of whatever mockery of a career I have had. Even to-day I only see, like some faint double-image, a great overgrown fellow with a mime's face and a flow of ready patter, sitting in the Theatre Bar with framed theatrical playbills on the wall behind him and a ballet-girl over his head, discussing the pawning-value of meerschaums. Already in the course of an hour or two I had qualified myself for gaol half a dozen times over, but what was gaol after the miasma of the house I had escaped from? The problem now was what a man's Vital Centres were going to eat and whose sofa his Sentient Image was going to sleep on at night. And that morning I made what other people call a friend. I put it in that way because the friendship was all on one side. To the day of his death, only a year or two ago, this man could never do enough for me. I was a sort of god to him. Any sacrifice he could ever make for me he made, anything he could stint himself of that I might have it he did without, and how did I requite him? What did I think, what do I still think of him? That he was a sentimental, weak-willed, irritating buffoon. Hundreds of times I have said things to his face that I knew would hurt him, just to see how far I could go. So I am not going to give him his real name, but will call him Slapstick. It was Slapstick who accompanied me to the Schillerverein that afternoon to collect my stolen goods. It was Slapstick who made a further raid on the shops with me, and took me to his theatrical lodgings that night, and put me on his sofa, with half my clothes on and the reach-me-down overcoat for a covering. It was he who made my breakfast the next morning, of bread and butter and tea and condensed milk. All this he did for the gift of a new pair of gloves that had cost me nothing, and I thought the less of him for the thanks he gave me. Then, with half his breakfast inside me and leaving him to do the washing-up, I set out in quest of Heinrich.

Again I should not be dwelling on all this, but Brother John, who I sometimes think is what is nowadays called a bit of a psycho-analyst, tells me that having started I had better go on. A straggle

of children began to show me the way while I was still a quarter
of a mile from the place. Every score yards or so I overtook one of
them with a millcan or a basket or a jug, all trailing to the board-
school. The cold had turned their hands and cheeks and noses
to all shades of blue and pink and purple, and past a single iron
gate that led to a large gravel playground a second stream filed
out from another door at the farther end of the building. And as I
waited at the gate, for a man stood there regulating the numbers
to be admitted, one of them began to pucker at the mouth and to
wrinkle up his brows under the scrap of shawl wrapped round his
head, out of sheer cold and misery. Seeing his example a couple of
others behind him looked like doing the same. In another minute
they would all have been doing it, and I was about to turn my
eyes away from the shivering little wretches, but instead I suddenly
puckered up my face too in mimicry, and made as if I too had a
shawl round my head and was going to cry, and at that a couple
of the others burst out laughing. Well, it was better than making
them cry, which I could have done as easily. So they wiped their
purple noses on their purple hands, and I crossed the playground
in search of Heinrich.

I found him too doing exactly what he would be doing, what he
couldn't help doing, what he would be doing to all eternity if the
same emergency arose. The only difference in him was that he was
not upright now, with his back stiff and heels clicking together, but
stooping down to the youngsters. He wore a bibbed apron instead
of a fencing-jacket, and looked like an army-cook with his ladle in
his hand and a steaming boiler of soup behind him. The awkward-
squad that straggled past him held its cans and mugs at all angles,
with one hand or with both, as he filled them with the steaming
stuff. They sipped it as they shuffled away, and a fresh lot took their
places, and even when he saw me, and his blond face broadened
with gladness, duty must still come first. So I waited till a bell rang
as a sign that no more would be admitted till the evening opening.
The door was closed and the last hungry child filed out. Already
the women were at work on the floor.

'So! It is our Peter!' Heinrich beamed.

'Yes,' I said.

'*Gut, gut!* But I must talk as I work. Look, twice a day it is all to do and to make clean again,' and he laid about him with hot water and mops and rags, wiping down the boilers and utensils and refilling the breadbaskets and talking all the time.

'*Kindermund, Kindermund!*' he said, shaking his cropped head. 'It is a very calamitous thing, this strike, and it is not their doing. But wait. I am not doing it for nothing. Do not think I am a fool, Peter, I am not doing it for nothing. Mr. Burgoyne is the headmaster of the school. He has organised all this, and when you make friends with headmasters they remember you afterwards, *nicht wahr?* It is a good thing to make friends with headmasters, for one day there is a vacancy, *ja?* A German master is wanted, and they look round and say, "Where is that fellow Opfer?" Do not think your Heinrich is not cunning sometimes, Peter! But tell me what you are doing here.'

'I got your note.'

'And you have come to help? But what will Mr. Burgoyne say when he hears you speak German to me? "Aha," he will say, "here is somebody younger, somebody better looking," and so when the school opens again you will read "German Master, Peter Byles", not "German Master, Heinrich Opfer",' and he chuckled at his own astuteness as he scoured a pan, and that was my reunion with Heinrich.

So from the board-school I flicker to the *Nottingham Arms* and my comings and goings there. It was the headquarters of a football club, and it had a large room on the first floor that was let off for dancing and entertainments and I fancy for Masonic gatherings too, for over the platform there was a large buffalo's head, together with other emblems. And put Slapstick at a piano and you had to trap the lid down on his fingers to get him away again. The theatrical company was in the ditch, and there seem to have been certain iron regulations about not taking money at the doors, but nothing was said about not passing round a cap. So again I see that ghost that was myself, doing the only thing left to it if it was ever going to get a penny out of the world. For there came a night when I stood on the platform, by Slapstick at the piano, and he was playing at a furious rate, but out of the corner of his mouth he was muttering desperately to me, 'For God's sake stamp or clap or something and see if *you* can't get 'em going!' and it was then that I remembered Musical Jack.

He used to go about the town with a big drum strapped to his shoulders and a pair of cymbals and a triangle on it. Tucked into a muffler round his throat was a mouth-organ, and his hands were free to swing a concertina about. The drum and cymbals he worked with a strap that ran down to a hook in his heel, and he could ring a chime of bells by nodding his head.

And in some quiet corner or other I had once come upon Jack getting into his harness of instruments, and here was Slap, at his wits' end what to do with a stone-cold house. And if they laughed they laughed and if they didn't they didn't, and it didn't much matter either way, so I made a sign to Slap and dragged forward a chair. Placing myself on the chair I swelled myself out and went though the pantomime of Jack putting his orchestra on. I turned up my coat collar, stuck an imaginary mouth-organ into it, took an imaginary concertina between my hands, hooked an imaginary strap to my heel. Jack furthermore had a long nose, that always gave him a lot of trouble in the cold weather, and as I attended to it with my handkerchief the silence was suddenly broken by a short laugh. Slap knew what to do with a laugh when he got one. When I got on my feet, and started my 'Boom! Boom!' of a march, whining into my mouth-organ and swinging my concertina this way and that, in he joined with the best the piano could give.

And it was new. Nobody had expected it, and get an audience to do a thing for itself and your troubles are over. In they joined. They banged on the tables to the jerking of my heel, catcalled to the concertina. I forget what antics I invented next, but when I wiped my nose for the last time down came the roof of the *Nottingham Arms*. Anyway, anything was better than saying 'Yes, Herr Doktor' or 'No, Herr Doktor' and then being struck by his lightning.

'That got 'em,' said Slapstick that night as he mixed my cocoa for me, for by that time I was quartered on him. 'Can you do any more like that?' and the earnestness with which he asked the question was twenty times funnier than anything he ever did at the piano.

I could, if perhaps never again anything quite so spontaneous, and from that moment he took me in hand. He taught me my tinsel trade, which was to make people laugh at themselves without knowing what they were laughing at.

But there came another night when they didn't laugh, for the lower the funds ran the more embittered that cruel strike became, and already it was spreading to other towns, and strangers began to struggle into our own, while many of our own men straggled out, if only to see which was worse, the place they came to or the place they had left. The landlady of the place warned us that evening as we were setting foot on the stairs.

'I'd take a night off if I were you,' she advised. 'They don't look much like music to me.'

'Then a bit of cheering up's what they want,' quoth Slapstick, and in he marched and took his seat at the piano.

But he had hardly played half a dozen bars when a head was turned and a gruff voice spoke. 'Stop that damned row over there, will you?'

He didn't take the hint. With a grin on his face he lifted up his voice, and had got out about three notes when a thick glass missed his head by an inch and smashed itself against the piano top.

'I told you,' said the landlady as we came hurriedly down again. 'Hardcastle's in the lock-up, and nobody knows where Crawford is.' These were their organising leaders, wanted by the other side with or without warrant, dead or alive, and as it happened the landlady was wrong. Hardcastle was not in the lockup. The Black Maria hadn't got so far. I told you how they waylaid it, and wrenched it open with crowbars, and took their man out of it and carried him away shoulder high. It took more than a song from Slapstick to deal with a temper like that.

And what were you going to do with the women, who met the strike-breakers with shrill cries, and thrust out their babies at them, and taunted them that at least their own should grow up to be men and not rats and blacklegs? Hapless, hapless town, if all its collective wisdom could bring it to was this!

So picture follows picture, each melting into the next, as they do to-day on the screens, a phantasmagoria of crowds at the factory gates, and pickets stopping all who tried to go in or out, and the redcoats under orders, and the leaflets that began 'Soldiers! Brothers!' and the advance at a walk with bayonets levelled. And lastly there starts up that morning when I was lying on Slapstick's sofa with my overcoat on to keep me warm, and he came in, his braces hanging down behind him and his chin covered with shaving-soap.

'Voyt's?' he said without preface. 'Isn't that the lot you were telling me about?'

I pulled my feet up under me, for he had left the door open and his sofa was not my length by a head. 'Eh? What about them?'

'Mrs. Preston's just told me. There's a shindy of some sort on down there.'

'What sort of a shindy?'

'About these outsiders they're getting in. The train's coming into the station and they're getting them along the sidings to the mill.'

'Voyt, Sons and Successors?'

'Yes, laddie. They're getting picks now and digging up the setts from the streets.'

I was off his sofa at a bound and looking for my collar. The kettle was just boiling, he said, but I wasn't waiting for any breakfast. In three minutes I was making for the railway station and that mill that lay like a huge sawfish along the canal bank.

Soon I could hear confused and angry sounds ahead of me. Police guarded the station gates, but I dodged round by side streets to the regions at the back. The main approach to Voyt, Sons & Successors was by way of a bridge over the canal, but so many idle barges were moored there that you could have stepped across them from bank to bank. The attacking men had pushed past the bridge and the gates marked 'Workpeople Only' and had mounted the long lines of trucks that stretched back to the station. They were coal trucks, and they were stripping the tarpaulins from them and throwing down the coal. There was a fierce roar the very moment I arrived.

'Here they come! Let 'em have it!' and I was rushed off my feet into the affray.

For black as coal could make it was the blacklegs' reception. The splitting and smashing of blocks of coal filled the air. The men on the trucks threw down the ammunition to those in front, and who would be a policeman at such times? For I dodged under the couplings of a truck just in time to see the tall uniformed fellow who was usually to be seen at the Arcade corner receive a heavy cob behind his ear. He dropped with his ankle between the points and lay there still, his leg in an unnatural position. I pushed forward. Volleys of coal were following the retreating men, and angry cries broke out.

'Tear the tracks up!'

'Fire their bloody trucks!'

'Smash their machinery——'

'Let's get hold of Voyt——'

'There isn't a Voyt——'

'Then let's ha' them Sons and Successors——'

'There is a Voyt—he lives out there past the trams——'

'Half stop here—t'other half fall in——', and back over the trucks and barges they swarmed, a full two hundred of them. It was eleven o'clock in the morning. Much good it would do the Herr Doktor that he had probably never set foot in that zigzag of shedding that lay like a sawfish along the canal bank. They were about to march on his house.

But they would go through the town, and I knew a shorter way. Already I was cutting up a breakneck back street, saving the best part of a mile that the tram could only take on the level.

CHAPTER XXVI

For there was one tiny thought that had begun to nag at the back of my mind, and this was the extraordinary gentleness with which the Herr Doktor, having first wrung me with that indescribable pain, had let me down into my chair again. Now I suddenly knew that this outweighed every other consideration. It was not a question of what I could do. If they wanted a Voyt for a Hardcastle I should not be able to stop them, and as I panted up that steep lane I could see it all in my imagination, first one blow struck, then another, then his silver spectacles gone, then a coat sleeve torn off, till down he went and the clogged feet did the rest. And still it fretted me, that one little thought—that he *had* his part in me, that he *had* built something in me that was both his and mine, him and me, and that whatever befell we were henceforth linked together. At least I could be there before them, warn him, get him into some place of safety. Out of breath, I crossed the road along which the trams ran.

And one more phantom, the ghost of a ghost this time, before the Herr Doktor and I are reunited, united to remain. It materialised itself apparently from nowhere just where the overarching trees began to make tunnels of the road. On the same spot where Minna had appeared before me one night, late from her evening-off and without key, the bushes parted, and two quite unremarkable men stood there, with this spectre between them. He stood before me, or rather towered over me, for he was as tall as if he stood on stilts, emaciated to such a degree that I at once thought of Mr. Rothmann's chimney, a white-hot knitting-needle against the sullen red, tottering to its fall. He wore the clothes of at least three men. The ear-flaps of a stalker's hat were tied under his chin, disappearing into the mufflers that swathed him about. He had two overcoats, the upper one a heavy ulster that reached nearly to his heels. The nose under the peak of the stalker was more like an eagle's than a man's, and the deep-set eyes on either side of it could hardly hold themselves open for sleep. Out of one of his pockets stuck the horn handle of a riding-crop. The other two men kept station a little behind him, and I knew in a flash who he was, could only be. He was the legendary Crawford, their ubiquitous leader, who never slept two nights together in the same place, and was 'wanted', with or without warrant, dead or alive, that they might put him into the prison they reserved for those who had another truth than their own. And swaying there above me he spoke in a husky voice.

'Where are you from?'

'The canal.'

'Where are you going?'

'To the house just up there.'

'What are they doing down there?'

'Stoning blacklegs with coal from the trucks.'

'The canal? That's Voyt's?'

'Yes. And they're coming on here. Listen, you can hear them.'

'Who are you?'

'Byles. Peter.'

'What do you want up at the house?'

'I live there.'

'Then I've heard of you. Is it true he can neither hear nor speak?'

'Yes.'

'Has he been interfering?'

'He doesn't even know what's happening.'

'Yes or no, has he interfered?'

'No.'

His sunken eyes were almost shut. He muttered to himself. 'Damn their worthless souls! Are they worth it? Put them in the right and in an hour they've put themselves in the wrong again. Why was I born! Why don't I end it! You say he isn't in the business?'

'He never was. How could he be?'

'Then you be off. Leave them to me. Oh for a night's sleep, oh for one night's sleep!' and he turned to his bodyguard.

But I lingered. Turning again he saw me, and took so formidable a stride towards me that I fell back.

'Didn't you hear me? Isn't one rich man enough to have on your hands? Am I to be saddled with you too? I hate 'em, but they're only flesh and blood——'

'I thought perhaps I could help—it's only because of him I've come back.'

He looked at me quickly, and a little of the fierceness went out of his voice. 'You get along. You'll help best by keeping out of the way. If I can't hold 'em it's the end. Oh, God, sleep, sleep, sleep!' and he turned unsteadily down the lane, a man supporting him on either side.

The ghost of a ghost, he still sometimes visits me in my dreams. Sometimes, lower down the lane there, he is appealing to their reason. Sometimes he is damning their souls to the Pit, sometimes driving them back with his whip. But all that I actually heard, getting on for a quarter of a mile away, was his voice lifted up, half carried away by the wind, a voice in the wilderness if ever there was one. Then came silence, and the sound of the distant Town Hall clock, striking midday. I turned up to the house.

It was by way of the yard that I entered, not by the front, and what was this that almost brought the tears to my eyes as I pushed at the kitchen door? After board-school soup and Slapstick's bread-and-butter and the bits of cheese from public-house counters? At the table Minna was singing contentedly to herself as she beat up batter in a bowl. Alice was just closing the oven door. Roast beef!

If those fellows down the lane had smelt what I smelt and felt as I felt twenty Crawfords would not have kept them back.

But roast beef on a Tuesday? It was always Sunday's dinner. And suddenly Minna, pouring the batter into a square tin, saw me and stopped her singing. Alice dropped the cloth from her hand. Even the parrot in the next room seemed to know of my arrival for he rapped out a short 'Where's Peter?'

'Where's Mrs. Pitt?' I demanded.

Minna was trying to look as if she hadn't been singing. Alice answered for her.

'Upstairs with him.'

'Him? The Herr Doktor? Is something the matter with him?' I asked quickly.

'You can ask her yourself,' Alice replied, and, turning, I saw Mrs. Pitt in the doorway.

Mrs. Pitt never showed surprise. She handed a milk bottle to Minna.

'Scald that out, and put a spoon in it so you don't crack it,' she said. Then, without even a good morning, she turned to me. 'I expect you'll be having dinner in your own room,' she said, as if I had just come in from a walk.

'I'd like a word with you first,' I said, and she turned towards her own room, leaving me to follow.

She had her dignity to consider, and I the suddenness of my return, so I began by telling her of the visitors she might have been entertaining at that moment, which took some little time. Her only comment was that if I told Tim that I'd seen Crawford in the flesh there'd be no getting a hand's turn of work out of him for a week.

'So,' I ended lamely, 'I thought I'd better look in.'

'I thought a few sandwiches in your pocket wouldn't take you very far,' was all she had to say about that, and we were quickly on terms again.

'It's like this,' she said at last. 'I had to tell him once for all that I wasn't going on living anywhere where doors were kept locked. It's neither fair nor right. He might go off in a faint or something and you could knock and knock and go on knocking. It's what they do in hospitals, bedroom doors or any other doors. You might be taken in your bath or sitting on the seat. So I made him open his door for a start.'

'Do you mean he's ill and you're looking after him?'

'If I didn't look after him who would? Not them two! Filling their bellies and burning coal by the truckload's what *they've* come to!'

'But what's the matter with him? Is he in bed?'

'Not he, without he likes an extra hour sometimes like other people. Had you words with him that you walked out like that, Mr. Peter?'

'No, not to call words.'

'Well, perhaps you'd better come up and see for yourself,' she said, and rose.

As she led the way through the large drawing-room she pointed to the white marble mantelpiece. Where the clock with the bronze horsetamers had been was a gaping space.

'That was the first one to go,' she said. 'As for the one on the stairs—but you'll see for yourself when you go up to your room. Anyway it keeps him quiet,' and she led the way along the upper passage.

The doors, both of his bedroom and sitting-room, stood open, but it was into the sitting-room that I stood gazing, while Mrs. Pitt watched me with an expectant look on her face. He was not there, but what had he been doing to the place? To begin with all was deathly silent. The furniture was as usual, the pendulum looped back in its corner, but the ticking and the tocking of the clocks had stopped. Neither on wall nor bracket nor shelf was there a clock to be seen. Their cases, porcelain, gilt, ormolu, wood, were heaped together about the pendulum, and the works of which they had been gutted occupied the table, the seats of chairs, his writing-table, the window-ledges. Everywhere were spread brass wheels, pinions, escapements, spirals of springs, bits and pieces of every sort. Carefully set apart on one corner of the mantelpiece was a piece of paper with a double handful of screws on it. Mrs. Pitt, at my elbow, spoke bitterly.

'He's in his bedroom. He'll be in in a minute. But lay a finger on one of them wheels and see what'll happen to you!' she said, in a tone that for the moment made me wonder whether indeed anything *had* happened to her, as it happened to Fearnley and myself. 'Hours and days he spends, trying to put 'em together again, but he'll never put that lot together again in *this* world! It's my belief he reads his books upside down too,' and even as she spoke there was a shuffling sound, and the Herr Doktor's spectacled and alpaca-jacketed figure filled the doorway.

Ill? No, he bore none of the noticeable marks of illness, but on his face was a look that I can hardly describe but by the word *else-where*. For that matter I might not have been there either, or only partly there, for if it was my face he meant to look at he was look-ing for it inches lower than where it actually was. Then, slowly lifting, his eyes found it. Just as when he had first seen me in the billiard-room, he put out his hand for me to take, and for one dazed moment I seemed to see that hand all freshly and anew, as I had

seen it over my father's chessboard, as I had mimicked it to Nora
in our moonlit garret, as its four white fingers had stolen round the
edge of the door when Heinrich had haled me downstairs to see
the damage I had done to the cloth. Then his eyes left me. They
fell irresolutely on one of those heaps of scrap and brasswork. I
felt the wavering of his mind. He wanted me, but he wanted the
clockwork too, and wanted it more. He looked at me almost shyly,
and Mrs. Pitt turned away.

'You can come downstairs. Nothing's going to drag him away
from those. Look——'

He had turned his back on me. He had picked up a small pendulum, and was gravely watching it swing as he held it by the flexible
bit at the end.

'You can come up again a bit later,' said Mrs. Pitt, and led the
way.

In the hall I smelt again that agonising smell of roast beef. A
sniff like a stag, that was musk, but the tears that I swear were in
my eyes were for mere roast beef, and the one need is as elementary as the other. At least Mrs. Pitt understood, for she held the
door open and gave me a push. The Herr Doktor must not leave
his doors unfastened, but that flap of red baize closed behind me
of itself.

CHAPTER XXVII

WHEN a man begins to take his clocks to pieces to find out
what time is made of there is no longer anything to be
afraid of in him. When at the same time, at getting on for sixty, it is
on his mind that his body has been neglected and that the neglect
must be made good, he is surely well out of harm's way. I returned
to find both these traits now well developed in the Herr Doktor.

Up to then I had taken his general stability for granted. It was
I who had varied, who had been weighed and measured, had had
my pulse taken, and had occasionally been told that it would be
well if I were to lie down and rest for a bit. He had kept a faithful

record of every one of my fluctuations, my abnormal need of food and sleep, my sudden and violent desires, the exhilaration of my quickened perceptions, my collapses afterwards. But now *I* read, in *his* writing, such a passage as the following, from the same manuscript I have told you of:

'I see that in certain things I have been rash and unwise. The proper preparation of *my own* body should have come first of all, and this I am afraid I have a little neglected. *Note urgently for future use:* No unexercised man must attempt the things I am attempting. My wrists, for example, are frail to look at, but at one time they were of exceptional strength. Now I have just tried to raise an ordinary cane chair. By my wrists alone I can hardly get it an inch off the floor. Several times already I have miscalculated, and a sudden occasion might catch me totally unprepared. I have not been out of doors enough. I must walk more, watch my breathing, etc.'

So I returned to find him stretching himself at odd moments in mild exercises, standing before open windows, and counting the breaths he took as he walked, so many steps to the breath. He smoked no more than two pipes a day, and I remembered Dr. Müller and his questions. It was obvious that he would have to be watched.

But that was precisely where the difficulties began, for it was equally plain that he did not want to be watched. He would not have accepted Mrs. Pitt's injunction about the doors with such docility if he had not known that something was wrong, and he wanted to keep that knowledge to himself. Mrs. Pitt had had a large fire made in my sitting-room, and that afternoon he shuffled in, looking as he had looked at the Schillerverein, a lighthouse without a light, desiring my company, but in a nervous sort of way, as if he wished to keep himself to himself too. He sat over the fire chafing his dry hands, glancing frequently at me, but asking only an occasional question about what I had been doing. And as it was only a matter of time before he discovered that for himself I took the opportunity to kill two birds with one stone, that is to say to make my confession while carefully watching him in return.

'I'm afraid I've been doing a lot of things you won't like, Herr Doktor,' I told him.

'What are these things?'

'One of them's a rather expensive smoker's cabinet. Another's a pigskin portmanteau. And there's an overcoat, and a pipe and some gloves, and a lot more. They asked me whose account, and I said yours.'

'But naturally I buy your clothes,' he gave me to understand.

'You do for me to wear them, not to take them straight to the pawnshop.'

'You took them straight to the pawnshop. You wanted money. And then?'

'You don't understand. I wasn't coming back. I wasn't ever coming back. I was just telling them you'd pay, and when they caught me I was going to prison.'

'Prison? It is always the wrong people they put in prison. And you have come back. Tell me, did anything in particular, any special thing, bring you?'

But his interest was only momentary. It had flickered out again almost before he had finished asking the question, and it was useless to try to tell him (which I now know beyond any doubt whatever) that I had come back because he had wrung me with excruciating pain but immediately afterwards had used me with a wonderful gentleness; and why should he know that there had been a disturbance down by the canal, and that a horde of angry men had been marching on his house? So I avoided his question, and told him instead how they had been feeding the children at the board-school. And in the middle of my narrative I saw his eyes straying round the room. They rested on the mantelpiece, for the middle of which he had at one time promised to spare me a clock. He had evidently not been in the room during my absence, for there the clock was, a cheap thing of painted wood with a little window behind which its pendulum wagged. He was watching the pendulum, and his eyes came shyly to mine. He made a little movement with his forefinger and thumb: would I go up to his room and get him a screwdriver? I went for it, looking into Mrs.

Pitt's room on my way and telling her we should be having tea together.

But when she came in with it she had to wait till he had carefully picked up the brass wheels and spindles that littered the table. There was only one conclusion to draw. First he had struck at Fearnley, then at myself. Now, with his exercises and his breathing he was beginning to pick his own faculties to pieces as he dismantled his clocks, and until he should recover there was only one way to treat him. It was as an invalid and a child.

'You can manage him better than what I can,' Mrs. Pitt said to me that evening. 'Don't meddle with his bits of wheels, that's all. And see he's well wrapped up if he goes out. Just lonely, that's what he is, just a lonely soul. Fearnley never dared to touch a book on his shelf, but I take them down and dust them and he just sits there watching me, glad of anybody's company I think. Have you told him about Crawford and that lot?'

'No.'

'Then don't. Just tell him anything that pleases him. And dear me, the bills there is to pay! I think I'd better bring them to you now, Mr. Peter.'

She brought them up to the Herr Doktor's room the next morning. He was smoking the first of his two pipes a day and striking match after match in his efforts to keep it alight. I showed him the bills, and he nodded towards his desk. I got out his chequebook and placed pen and ink before him. But he looked at them for a moment and then made a sign I was to write for him. I had never filled in a cheque before, but I wrote all but the signature and placed it in front of him. He signed with hardly a glance at it. He would have been a thief indeed who had robbed the Herr Doktor now.

So I, who only fifteen months before had come to his house a shockheaded, rather undersized schoolboy in cap and knickers, now ruled it as its virtual master, to do in it as I pleased.

Yet even then it took me some days to discover *what* I now wanted to do more than anything else on earth, what I had come back specially to do, what I alone of all men living could do for him and for myself. He knew, and had written, my story. What had his own been? Was that to die when he died, locked up in his mute breast?

He had gone out for one of his short walks that morning, helped by Mrs. Pitt into his muffler and gloves and heavy coat. I was sitting in his room, frowning under the weight of my new responsibilities. And suddenly I found myself gazing up at his shelf, at the long row of brown files that even Fearnley had never been allowed to touch. It was then that all this came to me. It did not come in any sense as a pious duty. It came to me first as something that it would be a pity to omit, then as something that cried urgently that it must be done, and finally as a thing that, if I did not do it, would in some unimaginable way do itself. The doctor does not ask his patient's permission to make his diagnosis, and I got up out of his lug-chair. I took down a couple of the quarto volumes and began to read. I read for an hour, and at the end of it he came in from his walk and saw what was in my hand. He did not frown or shake his head. On his face was nothing but mild acquiescence. He went straight to his clockwork, as if his walk had given him some new inspiration about it, and I continued to read.

And I read, not with the mere interest with which one reads a thing for the first time, but as if that first reading had really been a second, flooding all that had gone before it with a thousand new meanings and lights. As I turned page after page there took form and feature a Herr Doktor, not in the flat, as a painter might have painted him in his smoking-cap with his porcelain pipe hanging down his grizzled beard, but a Herr Doktor in the round, complete, his hidden parts revealed, his very background alive with his own unique life. So he had *not* always lived in that house on its ridge overlooking the town! He was *not* indifferent to money because he had always possessed it nor to men because he too had not had to struggle amongst them! True he had been settled there for more than twenty years, but I read, in faded German *schrift* and in inks of a dozen different kinds, how prior to that he had been penniless, alone, living a hand-to-mouth life in this part of Germany or that, getting his meagre sustenance as he could. He had been a hack, a ghost, a hireling, a familiar of libraries and reference-rooms, a digger-out of facts for others, now devilling for some Herr Professor almost as poor as himself, now passed on somewhere else, and always with that leaden weight of his deafness and dumbness upon him, a shunned man because it was too much trouble to talk to him. From town to town he had trudged, often begging his lodging for the night, shaking his head when he was spoken to and pointing to his ears and his mouth. People had given him letters of introduction to be rid of him, odds and ends of employment because nowhere else could they get anybody so cheap. And I read too more, far more than his personal story. Those pages were also his commonplace-book, his everyday-book, the record of a great part of his reading. Among scraps of paper of all sizes and sorts, written with all manner of pens or cut out from newspapers and pasted down, leaves torn out of notebooks, the backs of envelopes, the backs of hand bills, were whole chapters he had laboriously copied out from the tomes he must read and could not afford to buy. I read of philosophers I had never heard of, each with his page-reference and edition and the date and place of publication. Oh, he had not thrown books to the winds without first having had his fill of whatever was inside them! And from time to time I glanced up with wonder at him where he sat, playing with his bits of clockwork as a boy plays with a puzzle. Could this indeed be the same man? What had he been like to look at then? Had his grey beard been a student's straggle or had he gone clean-shaven? How had he dressed those thirty or forty years ago? Had he really been 'exceptionally strong in the wrists'? And what instinct had led him to keep all those scraps of paper together all those years?

Then Mrs. Pitt came in, and started a fierce attack on the fire with the poker, scolding meanwhile as if he had been a naughty child.

'If he isn't laid up in bed to-morrow it'll be his luck and not his wits!' she cried. 'Not a dozen times out of the house has he been all this summer, but as soon as this weather comes out he goes! You saw me put his muffler and gloves on for him. He feels a bit warm, and off they come, his topcoat unbuttoned too, and it'll be a miracle if it isn't on his lungs! *I* shall do the locking-in if there's any more of this!' and she flung what was left in the scuttle on the fire and went downstairs for more.

She was only too right. There was no need to lock the Herr Doktor in his room the next morning. He lay in his bed with a great fire burning in the room and did not sweat for all the blankets that were heaped on him. His dry hands whistled like silk as he rubbed them together, his cough brought the veins out on his temples but ended nowhere, and the lad Tim had been sent into the town to fetch Dr. Müller.

CHAPTER XXVIII

FOR some reason Dr. Müller seemed far more interested in me than he did in his patient. After a short examination of him, at which I was not present, he rejoined me in the sitting-room across the passage. I put down the *Peter Schlemihl* I had taken up.

'Keep him where he is for a day or two. Rest and warmth and nothing to worry about are the best doctors,' he said briskly. 'Who's looking after him?'

'The housekeeper has been. Now that I'm back I suppose I am.'

'Now that you're back? Do you mean you've been away?' he asked.

I covered my slip as best I could. 'I mean I've been in the town a lot and haven't seen much of him,' and he looked at me with his pink and silver head a little on one side.

'Let me see. How long's your father been dead?'

'Just over a year and a half.'

'But as I seem to remember you——,' and he looked at me again.

'If you mean I've grown quickly that's what everybody says,' I replied.

'Yes, yes, it's the time for growth. And I see you read German for amusement.' He had picked up *Peter Schlemihl* and was looking at the oval imprint of a rubber stamp on its title-page. It was the stamp of the Schillerverein library.

'I borrowed it and haven't quite finished it,' I said, and he rose and fell on his toes.

'Do you go to the club often?'

'I haven't been since the last time I saw you there.'

'I remember. You had to do his talking for him. Well, poor fellow, a blind man needs a dog—ha ha, not that I'm suggesting that you're a dog. All the same it's remarkable. According to my reckoning you're about fourteen years old and a member of the Schillerverein. What's the meaning of all this clockwork lying about?'

I was a little flustered, because all this seemed just a little pointed for the bedside manner. I said that clocks had always been a hobby of the Herr Doktor's.

'Well,' he said looking at his watch, 'he can do that in the house. You must keep him indoors and see he doesn't take further cold. You are feeling well yourself?'

'Quite, thank you,' I replied, and he looked at his watch again as if he hadn't just done so a moment ago.

'Then I'll look in again in the morning. A little black-currant tea will ease his throat—the simple remedies are often as good as the expensive ones—and then we'll see about getting him away. Don't come down——'

But I accompanied Dr. Müller to his carriage. Whatever his manner was to his patients it seemed to me that he had a pertinacious way of getting at little tell-tale facts, and I was glad that for once he had quite forgotten to ask me how my little sister was. His carriage rolled away down the drive.

That afternoon, to make things easier for Mrs. Pitt, I changed my quarters. The room next to the Herr Doktor's, that corresponded with the one that had formerly been my schoolroom, became my bedroom, in case he required attention during the night. I installed myself in his sitting-room, surrounded by his belongings, and resumed my inquisition into his past life.

So, in the middle of those *Wanderjahre* of which I spoke, I came upon the passage that had so strangely made a single thing of our

so different lives. For he had written that should a miracle ever
happen, and should he ever find himself in a position to do so, he
would one day adopt a youngster of parts, some youth *not* disabled
by the lack of a couple of senses, and bring him up on lines of his
own. And the miracle *had* happened. One day these relatives in
England had remembered him, and he had found his subject, his
victim to be crowned, in his friend Frederick's son.

And it was to be a royal road for me. Here, in this cumbrous
miscellany, were all the stages through which I should *not* have
to pass, all the knowledge I should *not* have to learn and then to
unlearn again. We were to be as continuous as two ropes spliced
together, his years unstranded at one end to receive my first begin-
nings at the other, and where and in what was it going to end?

But already it was beginning to disturb me that he gave so little
trouble. He had admitted that he had over-estimated his strength;
but was this docility yet another attempt at concealment? And I
now had many, many questions to ask him the moment he was
well enough to answer them. They were questions that fascinated
me as they had formerly fascinated him, about closely-reasoned
passages that suddenly broke off into etceteras, why he used an
equation when the context demanded a name, the meaning of
a Greek letter, why, having spoken of creeds perhaps, he all at
once lumped them together as 'the formula'. And one afternoon
I carried the volume I was reading in to him. He was lying there,
apparently looking at nothing, but for all I knew it was just such
a nothing as I too had looked at when, with Heinrich at the other
side of the table, writing one of his letters to Anna, I had played
exciting chess without men, board or antagonist. I put the page
in front of him and my finger on the passage. What, I asked, did
he mean by that? and he knitted his brows over the page. Then he
looked mildly up.

'Yes? What do you wish to know? Is it not plainly expressed?'

'No. I mean it is up to a point, and then you seem to leave something out. Why do you suddenly call things something else?'

But he only shook his head. If I wanted any further light I must
find it for myself. '*Wissenschaft, ja,*' he said gravely. 'But much must

be destroyed before a beginning can be made. Perhaps all must be destroyed. I have heard of these things. I once knew a man—no, not a man, *einer Junge*—fourteen years old but six-foot-four in height and extremely responsive—*ach, ach*—wait——,' and up went his hand in sign of an approaching fit of coughing. He got it over, but it left him exhausted, and I brought the book away again.

But that feeling that he was holding something back only grew stronger in me, and as I now felt completely responsible for him I was not above setting something like a trap to catch him. For a man may convey his meaning by glances and little fleeting face-waves and these things are their own language, no matter whatever other language they may be translated into afterwards. But talk with the fingers is already translation, since it is something necessary to use the name of a person or a place, which may not be the same in all languages. And I had been reading of his days in Vienna, which place he naturally called 'Wien', and suddenly it occurred to me that for some little time past our conversations of this sort had been based on the German language and on no other. I lost no time in putting this to the test. Again I went to him. I asked him, as if I didn't know, where this *Wien* was, and he told me to go and get the atlas. I did so, and he showed me.

'But that's Vienna,' I said, and spelt it out in the English form on my fingers.

'*Ja. Wien,*' he nodded.

'Spell it, Herr Doktor.'

'*W,i,e,n,*' he spelt out, and I turned my face away so that he should not see the blank look on it.

Another little incident, the very next day, put the matter beyond any doubt whatever. He had a favourite egg-cup, which Alice had broken, and when Mrs. Pitt brought in his tea there was a different one in its place. He noticed this, and his eyes appealed to me.

'You mean your egg-cup. Alice has broken it,' I spelt out in English.

He didn't understand, and I put it into German for him. '*Eier-becher,*' I said, and he made a little impatient movement, as much as to say, If I had meant *Eierbecher* why hadn't I said so?

He had forgotten or was forgetting his English. He knew it, and was deliberately keeping the knowledge to himself. So was that none of Dr. Müller's business?

It seemed to me that it was, and the next time he came I told him about it. He seemed even more startled than I was myself, and completely dropped his usual manner.

'How long have you known this?' he asked sharply.

'Only the last two days to be quite sure,' I told him, and he began to walk about.

'What's your position here?' he suddenly turned to ask. 'Are you formally adopted? Is there any deed? Have you anything to show?'

'I don't know anything about it. I just came here. He never spoke about it.'

'Who are his lawyers? Who attends to his business? How does he receive his money?'

'He hasn't any business.'

'Tush! Every man has his business. He may not go daily to an office, but he has his rates and taxes to pay like everybody else. He's on the Register. He can't get out of being a member of society just by being deaf and dumb. You aren't old enough to know these things. They're part of the price you pay for living in the world.'

'He doesn't live in the world. He thinks it's full of fools.'

'He may be right, but I hope he doesn't say so.'

'But he does say so!' and Dr. Müller began to walk about the room again, looking at the clockwork, then at me, then at the pattern of the carpet.

'But you must be mistaken,' he said at last. 'A man doesn't live all these years in a country and forget its language. Does his mind seem clear when you speak to him in German?'

'It's difficult to explain, Dr. Müller. He only speaks, as *you* call speaking, when there isn't any other way. We can talk for hours without using a single word.'

'But you say he reads your lips, and when you speak in German he understands, but when you speak in English he doesn't?'

'It isn't all lip-reading either. There isn't really very much of that. We just understand without anything at all. I was specially taught it. You could do it yourself if only——' but I stopped. I didn't know how to explain to Dr. Müller that there had to be something between you, something that the Herr Doktor called a Sentient Image, that made talking to a deaf-and-dumb man or to any other man as easy as talking to yourself.

'In that case,' said Dr. Müller, with a look at me that made me wonder whether I knew anything about him at all, 'in that case, and he *is* deliberately concealing something from you, and you talk to one another as you say you do, it might have been going on for weeks and months, and you would not be the first, but the very *last* person to notice it?'

And my mind flashed back to see whether Dr. Müller was right. Like a panorama the Herr Doktor's recent history unrolled itself before me, his midnight tampering with the clocks, his shutting me out of his room, that visit to the Schillerverein, the fatal day when he had spent himself in demonstrating what he could do to me, his fluctuations since. Dr. Müller was right. There was no saying how long it had been going on. It had all taken place under my nose and I *had* been the last person to notice it. I could only look at Dr. Müller's pink serious face.

'What shall I do?' I asked.

'Make quite sure he's forgotten English first. Drop that fantastic way of talking and *make* him look at your lips. Then see whether he understands. And if you can't do it in English find out in German who his lawyers are, and whether he's made a will, and what documents there are lying at his bank. What do you do about that by the way? This house costs money to run.'

'Mrs. Pitt brings the bills to me, and I write out the cheque and he signs it.'

'His signature's always accepted?'

'I suppose so.'

'Well, find out what you can. And do it at once, this afternoon. I'll look in again to-morrow. His cough's nothing, but this other——' and Dr. Müller became himself again and snapped the gold half-hunter open in his hand.

I did as he said before he had left the house an hour. I began to talk to the Herr Doktor in our habitual way. Then I broke off into German, while he watched my lips. And suddenly I changed to English and watched him instead.

And you cannot make a man watch your lips if he doesn't want to. All he has to do is to shut his eyes or look somewhere else. He did *not* understand a word, and it was too late now for him to try to make me think that he did. He looked at me reproachfully, turned his night-capped head on his pillow, and sulked.

When on the following morning Dr. Müller came again he had a second doctor with him.

CHAPTER XXIX

A MAN is master of his own house and can shut its door against anybody he wishes to keep out of it, but he cannot prevent things happening elsewhere. On the day when the Herr Doktor frowned on Dr. Müller and told me not to admit him again he set a machine in motion that to this day I know very little about. It is the way with life. Nothing seems to be happening, any more than anything had seemed to be happening all the time the Herr Doktor's English had been slowly ebbing away from him, but one day some small thing happens, showing what has been going on underneath, and with the Herr Doktor the small thing was a letter from his bank that he neglected to answer.

About that time I myself received that rare thing for me, a letter. It was from Dr. Müller of all people, and it said that he would be extremely glad if I could make it convenient to meet him at the Schillerverein on a certain Wednesday afternoon. I went, setting foot in the town for the first time since I had hurried away from the coal-battle on the railway-sidings.

I found Dr. Müller at his most affable and accomplished. The two men he had with him did not look like doctors, and one of them, though he did not say so, had every appearance of being a lawyer. Dr. Müller ordered tea for us, not in the smoking-room but in the small room Mr. Rothmann had used on the single occasion when I had seen him at the club, and at once the lawyer took charge.

And at first I thought he was some personal friend of the Herr Doktor's, so great was his solicitude about him and so sympathetically did he ask his questions. To myself his manner was kind and encouraging. It was common ground, he said—that was to say it was common knowledge—that I was in constant and intimate touch with the Herr Doktor. I might rest assured that anything that was said was in the strictest confidence and would not pass beyond those four walls. But this unhappy strike had placed Messrs. Voyt, Sons & Successors in such a position that they had to reconsider certain matters and examine them solely on their merits. For this reason they had been in communication with the Herr Doktor's bank, with the result that the bank had written to the Herr Doktor. To this letter they had up to the present received no reply. So—well, in short, it had occurred to them that I might be in a position to help.

'You see, Mr. Byles,' said the lawyer, and his glance at me was a hundred times swifter and sharper than any glance Dr. Müller had ever given me, 'a bank, as you know, is a great corporation. It is its duty to scrutinise even the most innocent appearances. They have themselves to protect while at the same time safeguarding the public. That they are acting in Dr. Voyt's own best interests goes without saying. So may I ask you a few questions?'

'Yes,' I said.

'You are familiar with Dr. Voyt's handwriting?'

'Yes,' I said, while violet-written pages rose before my eyes.

'How would you describe it?'

'It's small and beautifully shaped and you can read it as easily as if it was print.'

'Exactly. That agrees perfectly with the bank's account. Lately I believe you have been in the habit of writing out his cheques for him to sign?'

'Only because he was ill,' I said shortly, because I had seen the lawyer glance at Dr. Müller in a way I didn't understand.

'Quite so. And any cheque is good provided its signature is in order. But when a highly important letter from a bank remains unanswered?'

'Why are you asking me? I didn't know the bank had written to him,' I said.

'As well as other letters? There are other letters too to which no reply has been received. Who takes Dr. Voyt's letters to him?'

'They go up with his breakfast. I don't think he gets many.'

'We will come to that in a moment. I may take it that there is nobody in his house who would—er—intercept his letters?'

Intercept his letters! Mrs. Pitt! Alice! Minna! 'Of course there isn't,' I answered scornfully.

'But say they were pressing letters? Letters asking for the payment of accounts? There is nobody who would have an interest in his not receiving them?'

'No—at least——'

But that 'at least' was my undoing. He now had me in his hand any moment he liked to close it.

'One other question. But no. Dr. Müller will deal with that better than I can. Perhaps, Müller——'

'What Mr. Vernon means is this,' said Dr. Müller. 'Our poor friend's English had been leaving him for a long time before you made the discovery. Presumably most of the letters he received would be in English. If one faculty can go another can. He has been exceedingly careful to conceal this failing. Suppose he is now concealing from you, not that he cannot read his letters because they are in English, but that he can no longer read *at all*?'

I was thunderstruck. Of course it was perfectly possible. But the lawyer took up the running again even more suavely than before.

'So far, Mr. Byles, the bank has been satisfied. But place yourself in the position of the manager of an important bank. Suddenly cheques begin to be presented in another hand. The signature, shall we say, begins to show a marked deterioration. Dr. Müller or another medical man is able to certify that this is the after-effect of a severe chill. But Dr. Voyt is now up and about again. It is undesirable that signatures subject to remarkable variations should be appended to documents written in another hand. Think how easy it would be for some person with an ulterior motive, some person in difficulties, some person in a position to exercise undue influence——'

But I heard no further. It all broke on me like a flash of lurid light. In the third man, who had not opened his mouth, I tardily recognised Mr. Bannister, one of the magistrates of the town. The ulterior motive the lawyer meant was my frauds on the tradesmen. These were pressing for their money and received no reply to their letters. How were these people to know that I had confessed everything to the Herr Doktor and that his reply had been that the prisons were full of the wrong people? For the threat was not against myself but against him. Let the tradespeople have their money and no further questions would be asked. Nobody would know that one Peter Byles, a minor, had pledged the credit of a man who in law was not even his guardian. *That*, I say, was the threat—not the punishing of Peter Byles, but that if Peter Byles would only do what was required of him the Herr Doktor would be placed under supervision as no longer capable of managing his own affairs. I was on my feet, boiling over with rage at the way I had been tricked.

'You wouldn't have done this three months ago!' I was shouting. 'You wouldn't have dared, not one of you! *You* don't know what he could have done to you three months ago! Why, he could have shrivelled you! Go to the infirmary and ask them there what he did to a man called Fearnley! Or *I* can tell you if you want to know! You think he's mad because he knows something about you you don't even know yourselves! You want me to spy on his letters, and if I don't you'll call the police and put me in prison! Do your own dirty work! I won't help you! And look out for yourselves if ever *I* learn to do what he's able to do!' and I kicked over my chair and marched out.

But I was not too beside myself to notice, as I passed the board in the hall, that a new announcement had been stuck up. It was headed 'To Members,' and it said certain books, the property of the club, had been improperly removed from the club premises and that whoever had taken them should return them without delay.

Peter Schlemihl and a volume of Goethe were returned the next day, and with them went my resignation from the Schillerverein.

Now that I knew what to look for I was able to watch the Herr Doktor, not for the benefit of Voyt, Sons & Successors and their lawyers, but on my own account. This I proceeded to do. And I had not at that time seen that sombre design of Dürer's that is called 'Melancholia', with its wrecked symbols of dusty globes and cogs and compasses and the cobwebs of accidie lying thick over all, but when I came to see it later I asked myself what manner of man this Dürer could have been, to have seen the end of all knowledge so crumbled away as that. Had he too known somebody who forgot first his acquired language, then his native one, then words and how to read and write them, then the very alphabet, as if in the end the alphabet itself might prove to be nothing but a stumbling-block to mankind? I discuss these things with Brother John, and somewhere or other Brother John has picked up a certain amount of medical knowledge. Such things, he tells me, are only interesting as being symptomatic of the disintegration of a mind in the last stages of what he calls GPI, and this seems strange to me, coming from him. For unless a man becomes a little child again how is he going to enter the kingdom of heaven? And when he tells me that the Herr Doktor did not believe in heaven that again shows me that he does not understand, for after his own peculiar fashion who sought heaven longer or more earnestly than the Herr Doktor did? But I find John a good deal like other men. Having said all he has to say, and as he thinks confounded me, he always ends by reminding me that his vows do not permit him to discuss these things. So we agree to differ. I have seen what I have seen. But Dürer saw it with me.

I was now never away from the Herr Doktor for more than an hour or two at a time, and if for any reason I had to go out Mrs. Pitt saw to his needs in my absence. The day-by-day jottings that I made of his state could be quite safely left in his room, for very soon he was unable to read a word of them. I had added my

pound a week to Mrs. Pitt's bills, but I had little need of it. If I
went into the town it was usually to get some little comfort for
him. That dreadful strike was slowly dragging to its red conclusion, and when I say red I mean the red of military tunics. Crawford, I heard, was in gaol in another town. A snow-covered heap
showed where Mr. Rothmann's proud chimney had once stood. I
no longer wished to get drunk, only to know from time to time
how Slapstick was getting on at the *Nottingham Arms*. The Herr
Doktor had only to beckon with his finger and I remained by his
side.

As he no longer had a clock he had to guess at the time, and
I had made him comfortable one evening and was preparing to
leave him for a couple of hours when he put his hand, which was
now extremely white and frail, on my sleeve. He wanted me to
take away the handful of clockwork I had placed on his bed-table
for him to amuse himself with. I smiled at him. But what would he
do while I was gone? I asked him. I didn't want to leave him there
just doing nothing.

'Take them away,' said the hand, 'take them away.'

'I'll stay with you.'

'No, you go, you go.'

'Then will you have your chessboard?' He was far, far past chess,
but the pieces were smooth to the touch and slid about prettily on
the polished board.

'Yes,' he said, but when I came back with the board he was
gazing at a corner of the fireplace, as if he saw a shockheaded lad
in knickerbockers sitting there, reading his book when he ought to
have been in bed. Then his eyes went to somebody who was not
there, but I think the somebody was my father. He signed to me to
set the board, admiring with childish pleasure the skill with which
I did so. Then a look of humour crossed his face. Hesitatingly, as if
he was not quite sure whether he was right, he put up two fingers
to his dome of a brow. I did the same, and our eyes met in a long,
friendly look.

'You'll play chess with Mr. Hanson till I come back?'

He nodded with pleasure. Yes, chess with Mr. Hanson, the

watchmaker who did not know what Time was made of. I slipped
out, telling Mrs. Pitt that I was going.

'Slap,' I said in the Theatre Bar an hour later, 'I want you to do
something for me.'

'Anything up to a thousand, laddie,' he replied.

'You know Wellesley Road board-school?'

'I think I could ask the way, sonnie.'

'There's a fellow called Opfer there, a big German. He's helping
with the soup. He's wondering what's become of me, and I want
you to tell him I can't get away just yet. Say it's the old man. He'll
know who you mean.'

'It is already done, professor,' said Slap, and I bought him a
couple of drinks and lent him five bob. A pound a week was now
more money than I knew what to do with.

So that fatal visit happened in my absence. I was nearing home
again when a closed carriage passed me on the road, but I paid no
attention to it, and made my way round by the back so that Mrs.
Pitt should know I had returned. But as I entered the side path I saw
a light disappear from the window of the big drawing-room. Somebody inside was carrying a lamp. In the yard I met the lad Tim.

'Where's Mrs. Pitt?'

'Locking up again.'

'Again? Do you mean somebody's been?'

'Ay. A carriageful of 'em.'

'Where is she now?'

'Upstairs I expect,' and upstairs I hurried. She was just coming
out of the Herr Doktor's bedroom, again flushed with temper.

'Months'll go by and not a ring at the bell, Mr. Peter, but the
minute you turn your back in they come.'

'Who?' I asked, but my voice faltered.

'Dr. Müller we're used to. I don't know who the others were.
There were three of them, and one of them had a lot of papers.
First they asked for you, then they talked among themselves for a
bit, and said they'd better go up.'

'To his room?'

'There he was, just as you'd left him. I'd just been in to see if he was all right. He was playing with the chessmen. He was popping one of them little ones in and out of his mouth and I had to take it away from him and wipe it.'

I didn't wait for any more, but walked into his room. The upper part of the turned-down sheet lay smoothly across his chest, with his grizzled beard outside it. Mrs. Pitt had taken off his spectacles, and I could see the veining of his eyelids, and he was as tidy as if he had just been tucked in by a hospital nurse. The only movement he made was with his feet, which played with the hot-water bottle. Then his eyes rested on mine, and there was a queer look of complicity in them, as if now that his visitors had been and gone he had some very great secret to tell me presently but I wasn't to ask him yet what it was, because it was a *very* great secret. Mrs. Pitt put her head in at the door again.

'Will you be wanting anything else to-night, Mr. Peter?'

'Don't go for a moment.' Whatever language we had been speaking in the Herr Doktor would have known nothing from our lips now. 'How long did these people stay?'

'They'd be here the best part of an hour. I showed them up and told them to ring if they wanted me.'

'And did they ring?'

'After a bit they did. They couldn't make head of him and they couldn't make tail.'

'What was he doing when you came in that time?'

'He'd some papers in his hand, but he knew no more than a babe what was in them if you ask me. Dr. Müller said were you likely to be here to-morrow night, so I told him straight you'd hardly left his side for a week and you needed a mouthful of fresh air like other people.'

The Herr Doktor's feet were still playing with the hot-water bottle. Mrs. Pitt's eyes met mine.

'You know what they came for?' I said.

'I can guess,' she answered grimly.

'They don't think he's fit to look after himself.'

'Well—is he?' said Mrs. Pitt without much expression in her voice. 'Will that be all for to-night?'

'Yes. Good night,' and as she went out the Herr Doktor again looked at me, as if I should know that very great secret of his presently.

But I think that something in me was half aware of that secret already. Just as I had not seen Dürer then, so I had not read *Hamlet*, but when I came to do so, and my eyes saw the words 'Oh my prophetic soul!' might they not have meant at least as much to me, who knew beforehand when mills were going to be set alight, as to most men? He was still making no movement but that of his feet. I had an impulse to feel for his hand, but he lay there so peacefully, so old yet so suddenly young, that I did not disturb him. Then I remembered my own young days, that vast distance of only a few years away, and left him for a moment. I returned with a nightlight. I lighted it that he could see what I was doing, and his face had a look of profound understanding and rest and thanks. I turned out his lamp, and left him there, gazing at the nightlight.

But I was careful not to go to sleep at once. I had finally cast in my lot with him when I had defied them at the Schillerverein, and anything in me was his, and he knew it and trusted me. Twice I got out of bed to peep round the edge of his door. The nightlight still burned, a little blue head by his bedside, but he was lying on his back with his eyes closed. The Town Hall clock had long since struck two. It had struck three when weariness overcame me, and I dropped off to sleep.

An unimaginable sound awoke me. It seemed to come, not from his bedroom, but from his sitting-room. Possibly it was still mixed up with some fragment of a dream, for it did not at once strike me as an extraordinary thing that a deaf-and-dumb man should be talking to himself.

But the sounds continued. He was not only talking, he was expostulating with himself, impatiently arguing, scolding himself that he had never spoken before, had never uttered that secret of his aloud, however harshly and throatily. And then, as with a last effort he got it all out of himself, I was suddenly awake and running to his room.

The curtains of his sitting-room had been closely drawn

overnight, and because behind locked doors men might drown in their baths or faint away as they sat no doors were now closed. All was dark in the sitting-room except for the bead of the nightlight, still upright on the floor and expiring in its last few drops of wax. But on its back beside it lay an overturned chair.

And now that he had told his secret he was still too. It was to the pendulum rope about his neck that he had told it, and that talking I had heard had been his final struggles. The nightlight glimmered upwards on the bare feet that had chafed themselves against the hot-water bottle. Above that was the dim greyness of a nightgown, that ran off into shadows, as that enlarged Genie of himself had run off into shadows that afternoon in the Theatre Bar. Any doctor, any lawyer might manage his affairs for him now. Somewhere, in some place he had sought, his frozen words were thawed into universal speech, and with his clocks in pieces about him he knew what Time was in the light—or in a deeper darkness as the case might be.

TO-DAY

TO-DAY

I KNOW what I know, and believe what I may, but not very much of it comes from that short row of books on my cubicle shelf. As long as I have the writing out of which I have told this tale of the Herr Doktor and myself anybody may have the rest. But nobody shows much interest in me except perhaps Brother John, and what after all can Brother John have to say to a broken-down old actor, a comedian, a busker, a mask, a man who has spent the greater part of his life on earth in fit-ups and Number Three companies? I could mimic the Brothers themselves if I had a mind, and were it not that by their hospitality I am fed. So he asks me what I am going to do with this writing now that I have finished it, writing ever more slowly as I drew near the end, for the best of my physical strength was spent before I was eighteen, and but for the attention of a well-meaning, loud-voiced, tiresome fellow called Slapstick I should have ceased to trouble the world years ago. Why, John asks, should I do anything at all with it? Is it not enough to have written it? Do I not feel easier in myself now that I have written it, and is it not off my mind? Which is why I sometimes suspect him of being one of these newfangled persons they call psychoanalysts. For even John's company can become tiresome. He will not even play a game of chess with me in the refectory, and there is no billiard-table here.

But that ready-made Faith of his seems somehow to be a strong thing, and I sometimes wish he could force it on me, if only because it seems to fit him so well. I have wished that something stubborn in me would break down, so that perhaps I could shed a simple tear, for now that I look back I cannot recall that I have shed a tear in the whole course of my life. If I had I should remember it, for I have an idea that a tear might be a very precious thing.

But no tears come, and now that I have nothing to do I miss the

Herr Doktor a thousand times more than I have ever done. The trains come in from the North, and the Brothers look up from their breviaries or their barrows to see them pass, but I no longer look up. A glow-worm in the grass can be a nightlight on the floor to me now, and I know what I should see if I lifted my eyes above that. I have nothing to do. The time hangs heavy. I wish it would pass. I will go and feed my chickens.

ALSO AVAILABLE FROM VALANCOURT BOOKS

CPSIA information can be obtained at www.ICGtesting.com
Printed in the USA
BVOW04s1757280914

368332BV00001B/9/P